NO(L

MAGIC

DEMONS OF FIRE AND NIGHT

BOOK 2

BY C. N. CRAWFORD

Nocturnal Magic

Demons of Fire and Night Book 2

Copyright © 2016 C. N. Crawford

All rights reserved. No part of this book may be reproduced in
any form or by any electronic or mechanical means, including
information storage and retrieval systems, without written permission from the author, except for the use of brief quotations
in a book review.

ISBN-13: 978-1540377111
ISBN-10: 1540377113

Edited by
Cover art by Rebecca Frank
Interior design by C.N. Crawford

www.cncrawford.com

Contact the Authors:
cn@cncrawford.com

Twitter: @CN_Crawford
Facebook: cncrawfordauthor

First Edition

Printed in the U.S.A

Also by

C. N. CRAWFORD

The Vampire's Mage Series
Book 1: *Magic Hunter*
Book 1.1: *Shadow Mage*
Book 2*: Witch Hunter*

Demons of Fire and Night
Book 1: *Infernal Magic*
Book 2: *Nocturnal Magic*

The Memento Mori Trilogy
Book 1: *The Witching Elm*
Book 2: *A Witch's Feast*
Book 2.1: *The Abysmal Sea*
Book 3: *Witches of the Deep*

For Audra

Chapter 1

Through the wide bay window, a summer breeze blew in, bringing with it the earthy smell of Central Park. Ursula paced over the hardwood floor, catching a glimpse of her reflection in the glass—her skin ten shades whiter than normal, her curls framing her face in a wild auburn halo. She was on edge tonight, tension tightening each of her muscles, holding her stomach in a vise-like grip.

Zee sat on a nearby sofa, a laptop propped on her knees. "Ursula, you need to relax."

From outside, a car horn blared, and Ursula jumped.

"See?" Zee let her shoe dangle from her foot. "You're all tense."

With a shiver, Ursula glanced through the window at the pearly moon. "What time is it now?"

"Time for you to calm down. No matter what comes next, getting worked up isn't going to help." She turned her laptop to Ursula, showcasing a catwalk model dressed in nothing but lilac ribbons, strategically covering her nipples and crotch. "Come look at Francesco Sforza's fall line. It sort of puts things in perspective, you know? Like, maybe you're going to be forced to stay in the

Shadow Realm with some psychotic demons, but at least no one has made you to wear ribbons over your tits." Ursula forced a smile, turning to stalk across the room again. "Thanks for trying to make me feel better. I'm having a hard time putting aside my impending damnation, though."

Zee plucked a glass of chardonnay from the table. "Well, there's nothing you can do to change it. When you made the deal with him, it sealed your fate."

Ursula folded her arms. "Emerazel made the deal after I stole Bael's soul for her." A twinge of guilt pierced her chest. *He got his soul back, but Nyxobas had probably killed him for his failure.* "If it hadn't been the only way to get your soul back, I'd never have agreed to it. Nyxobas literally shows up in all my worst nightmares." A shiver crawled up her spine. "He always has, in fact. Even before I knew who he was."

"Well, he didn't show up tonight."

Ursula turned to scrutinize the elevator once again, but its bronze doors remained tightly shut—just as they had been all day. Did gods arrive in elevators?

Nyxobas was supposed to summon her to the Shadow Realm today. For six months, she'd have to live with him, work for him, do whatever he wanted. Fear snaked up her spine. *And I have no idea what he wants from me.*

She glanced at the bags she'd packed. Honjo rested on top of a black duffel. At least she'd have her trusty katana with her, in case that psychopath Abrax tried anything. The incubus had attempted to drain her soul more than once.

But she wasn't going into this unprepared. In the bag beneath Honjo, she'd packed a collection of daggers and her finest ass-kicking boots. Plus, she had the reaping pen tucked in her pocket.

"Ursula," said Zee, her glass now empty.

"The bottle's in the kitchen," Ursula said absent-mindedly. "If it's empty, you can open a new one."

"Ursula!" Zee snapped, her eyes wide. "There's someone behind you. At the window."

The hair rose on the back of Ursula's neck. Now, the wind on her skin felt positively frigid.

Ursula grabbed Honjo from the duffel and spun, ready to defend herself. A dark form hovered in the window, cloaked in shadow. Dread crawled up her throat. Nyxobas had definitely *not* forgotten about her.

"Ursula?" said the figure, its voice light.

She jumped, her fingers tightening on Honjo's hilt. She'd been expecting Nyxobas's deep voice, but this shadowy form was definitely female.

"That's me," she said, trying to see into the darkness. *Who the hell is this?*

"Wonderful," said the woman as she stepped through the window, hopping onto the rug—not a human, but a small, sharp-toothed demon. The kind with an affinity for human flesh—an oneiroi.

Ursula raised the blade defensively. With her cherubic face, the oneiroi looked harmless enough. Her long, silvery hair hung over a simple dark gown, and something like kindness glimmered in her pale eyes. She was almost matronly. But Ursula had encountered oneiroi in the fae realm. And they'd tried to rip her face off. Matronly or not, if this demon was going to leap for her throat, she'd be ready.

"You're not Nyxobas," she said, gripping her sword. *Way to state the obvious.*

"No, Ursula." The demon's pale brow furrowed. "I was sent to collect you. I am Cera."

"Oh. All right, then." Ursula couldn't think of anything better to say.

Cera's gaze landed on the laptop. "You do have such interesting fashion here. Who is it?"

Zee muttered something that sounded like *Francesco Sforza*.

"Fascinating," said the demon, before turning to Ursula, all business again. "Are you ready to go?"

So this was it—tonight she was leaving for the Kingdom of Shadows.

"I guess I don't have much choice." She shot a panicked look at Zee, who simply shrugged, before she faced Cera again. "How are we getting there? And where do I put my bags?"

"You won't need the suitcases." Cera flashed a lethal smile of razor-sharp teeth. "You'll have anything you could possibly want when we arrive. The lord is very generous, milady. Besides, Sotz won't be able to carry it."

Before she could ask who Sotz was, she caught a glimpse of movement through the window—enormous leathery wings beating the air and shining dark eyes. A chill crawled over her skin. As the creature moved closer, she made out a pair of long diaphanous ears. *Is that a giant bat?* "What the fuck?"

The bat's eyes widened. Did it understand what she was saying?

"Shhh..." said Cera. "Don't upset Sotz. He has very sensitive hearing. The creature squeezed its body onto the windowsill, gripping the stone with fleshy feet. It was enormous—the size of a small horse.

"Don't worry, little buddy," Cera said, scratching the bat's head. "I don't think she's ever met a lunar bat before." Sotz nuzzled the demon and a low rumble filled the room. The creature was *purring*.

Ursula crossed her arms, staring at them. "I'm confused. I thought Nyxobas was coming to get me."

"The god?" Cera laughed. "He's far too busy to come himself. Sotz and I will be taking you to his kingdom." She glanced at the bat. "Sotz, can you turn around?"

The massive bat inched out of the window, flapping his wings twice before backing up into the window. A leather harness and saddle were strapped to his back.

Lifting her skirts, Cera hopped onto Sotz's shoulders, twisting her fingers into his fur. She looked back at Ursula expectantly. "Whenever you're ready, dear."

Ursula turned to Zee who now stood, her empty wine glass forgotten on the coffee table. The fae girl had been keeping her company for the past six months. While Ursula had helped Zee recover from her soul-sucking trauma, Zee had tried to distract Ursula from her terrifying fate in the Shadow Realm. Their tools: champagne, loud music, and trips to Madison Ave—at least, in between all the hellhound work. "Zee, I'm really going to miss you."

Zee's eyes glistened, and she wrapped Ursula in a hug so tight it threatened to crack her ribs. Despite being only a size two, she was surprisingly strong. When she finally released Ursula, a tear was streaking down her cheek.

"Go." Zee gestured at the oneiroi woman. "I'll see you in six months."

Ursula flashed Zee her most stern look. "Make sure you take care of yourself."

Zee straightened, wiping her eyes. "I will. And, I'll even put your stuff away. Though I might borrow that gold Valentino dress I bought for you." She picked up the duffel and headed toward the hall. Ursula had the feeling she didn't want anyone to see her cry.

By the window Cera cleared her throat, and Ursula's muscles tensed. *Time to go.*

Chapter 2

𝓤rsula shoved the sword into the Kevlar scabbard and strapped it to her back. She was leaving her clothes behind, but there was no way in hell she'd travel to the Shadow Realm without Honjo.

By the window, Cera turned to her, a wicked glint in her silver eyes. "Are you ready?"

"Not really."

"Have you ever ridden a horse before?"

Ursula shrugged. *Good question.* "I don't think so, but I don't remember anything from before the age of fifteen. For all I know, F.U. may have been a champion rider."

Cera's pale brow crinkled. "F.U.?"

"Former Ursula. My pre-amnesiac self."

Cera flashed her a sympathetic *you-should-probably-take-your-medication* smile.

Ursula forced a smile back. *Right. I sound like a nutter when I talk about the amnesia. Then again, we're about to ride on the back of a giant bat, so a little nuttery is in order.*

"Well," said Cera. "Whatever the case, I'll be guiding Sotz, so you'll just need to hold on." She arched an eyebrow. "I do hope you're not afraid of heights." "Not really." A chill whispered over her skin. *But I'm terrified of Nyxobas.*

Her brush with the shadow void still haunted her nightmares—the god of night filled her with a horrifying, gnawing dread. A painful emptiness that still flickered in the hollows of her mind. She tried to push the thoughts away. Her voyage on the bat would be bad enough without dwelling on the void.

"Climb on." Cera nodded at a pair of leather handles on Sotz's saddle. "Grip there. Then step into the stirrups. Just be sure to hold on tight."

Pretty sure I'll be clutching on for dear life. Ursula pulled herself up to the windowsill, then hooked a leg over the saddle. Gripping the handles, she slipped her feet into the stirrups.

As Cera whispered into the Sotz's ear, Ursula's fingers tightened on the leather. It didn't seem like the safest way to travel. Surely, hurtling through the sky on a giant mammal required a seatbelt or helmet.

In the next second, the bat launched from the window. For a moment, Ursula's breath caught as the creature began a stomach-turning plunge, then the bat's wings unfurled. Their path steadied, and they swooped past West 59th Street and over Central Park.

Ursula clutched the harness in a death grip, her pulse racing. Her auburn hair whipped about her face with each beat of the giant wings. Sotz angled his wings, and they turned sharply. The movement cleared the hair from her eyes, and she caught a glimpse of the Plaza Hotel.

"Where are we going?" she shouted over the wind.

"Brooklyn," Cera said, turning in her direction, her sharp teeth glinting in the moonlight as she spoke.

The Shadow Realm is in Brooklyn? She frowned. It was hard to imagine the terrifying incubus Abrax cramming himself into skinny jeans. Maybe extending his talons to spear a vegan burger at a Park Slope diner.

The night wind whipped over her skin, and she shivered, thinking of the high demon. She had no idea if he'd made it out of the fae realm alive.

Sotz soared over the Plaza's white marble crenellations, then higher above the twinkling lights of New York. Distant car horns floated on the wind, and the bat alternated each wing beat with graceful glides.

Her grip on the harness relaxed. The view was extraordinary.

The great avenues of New York carved between the buildings like golden rivers of light. All around her, skyscraper glass gleamed faintly in the moonlight.

As they flew toward the tip of Manhattan, she breathed a sigh of relief at the quiet of the night air. After four years living in London, she'd grown accustomed to the perpetual background hum of busses, traffic jams and people asking for money. Up here, she heard only the distant beat of a helicopter's blades. Somehow, floating through the dark night sky felt like home.

Before she could get too comfortable, a piercing screech sent her heart racing. Cera screamed in an unintelligible language as Sotz folded his wings into his body. Ursula gripped the harness and they plummeted down, dropping out of the sky—but not fast enough.

As the wind whipped Ursula's hair into her face, something large and scaly slammed into her side, nearly tearing her from the harness. The force of the impact sent them careening toward a skyscraper. Gritting her teeth, she clung to the handles with an iron grip.

Cera shrieked hysterically, letting go of the bat's neck.

"Watch out!" Ursula pulled back on the harness. Her heart pounding hard against her ribs. Sotz's wings snapped out, and Ursula jerked the harness away from the skyscraper. Sotz turned, veering away from the building.

F.U. *had* apparently been bit of an equestrian.

A second screech shattered the night, and she glanced to her right, her blood chilling. She caught a glimpse of an enormous, shimmering outline. A translucent creature, at least the size of a bus. And it was heading right for them. *Bollocks. We're fighting something nearly impossible to see.*

"You need to steer!" she shouted at Cera.

Clenching her knees against Sotz's sides, she drew Honjo from his sheath. The long katana glinted in her hands—and not a moment too soon. She twisted in the saddle, slashing at a long, translucent limb. The blade jerked as it cut into solid flesh.

A howl rent the air.

In the next moment, the creature yanked the sword from her grasp.

Her blood turned to ice. Honjo—her only weapon—had just been ripped from her hands.

Sotz folded his wings, diving lower. Wind whistled in her ears as they raced like a falling meteor toward the East River. Just as Ursula resigned herself to a watery death, Sotz unfurled his wings, redirecting them toward the steel cables of the Williamsburg Bridge.

Somewhere behind them, their attacker screeched, a bloodcurdling sound that shriveled her stomach. Adrenaline surged. *Honjo hadn't killed the damned thing, he had only annoyed it.*

The Williamsburg Bridge grew rapidly larger and Ursula's muscles tightened as she braced for impact. At the last second, Sotz turned, diving between the cables, heading for the tunnel's mouth.

Ursula's heart hammered against her ribs. Lights flashed in its entrance, and a rumbling noise echoed off the walls. *A subway car is heading right for us.* She shouted a warning, but with a single flap of his wings, Sotz cleared the train, flying between the car and the ceiling.

The train raced by beneath them, and she let out a long breath when they cleared it.

Only the flashing red signal lights illuminated the tunnel, flashing off the rows of steel beams and girders on the ceiling. They winged down the tracks as a second train rumbled toward them, its lights glowing brighter and brighter. At the last possible moment, Sotz veered left into a dark corridor.

This tunnel was completely dark, and only the sound of the air rushing by her head told her they were still flying. After what felt like an eternity, Sotz slowed the beating of his wings, and glided to a landing.

Ursula slid off the bat, falling to her knees on a dusty floor. Pure adrenaline pumped through her veins. "What was that creature? I couldn't even see the bloody thing."

Cera pulled something from her pocket—a glowing, violet crystal. From the stone, tendrils of magic snaked into the air, creating a sphere of light that illuminated the space.

Ursula surveyed the derelict subway platform, the space around them covered in broken wood and debris. "That creature," Cera smoothed out her dress, trying to regain her composure, "was a dragon."

Chapter 3

*U*rsula stared at Cera. "But I remember learning that dragons were extinct, and that's why their wyrm-skin hides are so valuable. I was told they were all killed in the ninth century."

Cera brushed the dust off her black dress. "Definitely not extinct."

"I don't understand." She hugged herself, her body still buzzing with panic. "Why did it attack?"

Before Cera could answer, a heavy *thud* reverberated from the ceiling, and bits of plaster drifted down like snow.

Thud. "It's followed us." Cera looked up, shielding her eyes from the plaster dust. "We need to leave at once."

Thud.

White dust rained down on Ursula's clothes.

She scanned the platform, instinct kicking in at last. If there was one thing F.U. had seared into the lizard-part her brain, it was how to find the best escape route when danger closed in. In either direction, two tunnels curved off into the darkness. Her odds were fifty-fifty of choosing the best one.

Thud.

Thick chunks of plaster littered the floor, and her pulse sped up. *We're running out of time.*

"Which way—" she started to ask, but the sight of Cera leaping down from the edge of the platform interrupted her. "Cera?"

"We always keep one of these around in case of emergencies," she called out from under the platform's ledge. Slowly, the oneiroi dragged a child's play-pool onto the tracks. Murky water filled the blue plastic, and faded yellow seahorses and scallop shells decorated its sides.

Ursula gaped. "Are you going to bathe the dragon into submission?"

THUD!

This time, a scratching noise followed the impact. It took a moment for her to realize the dragon was digging.

"Look," said Ursula, raising her voice. "We need to run. It's fifty-fifty odds. We just need to choose a direction."

"Be quiet," Cera hissed. "And take your clothes off."

"I beg your pardon?"

"There is nowhere to run. Not in this realm, anyway." The demon fixed silver eyes on her. "If we don't go now, we *will* be eaten."

Before Ursula could protest, Cera stood, holding up her violet crystal. The rippling water in the pool stilled. Black shadow magic curled over a glass-smooth surface.

Cera turned to hear again, her eyes sparking with irritation. "Why are you still wearing your clothes? I told you to strip."

Bloody hell, woman. Another *thud* sounded from above, and chunks of masonry and plaster poured from the ceiling. *Definitely running out of time. Screw it.* She pulled her shirt over her head.

"Hurry!" Cera shouted, giving an unnerving display of her sharp teeth.

Ursula unzipped her jeans. "Will you at least explain the need for nudity?"

"No clothes may contaminate Nyxobas's water."

Ursula unhooked her bra just as a great crack split the air above them. She glanced up at a shimmering claw tearing through the ceiling. She tore off her knickers.

"Jump in!" Cera leapt into the center of the kiddy pool.

Completely nude, Ursula held her breath, and plunged into the black water.

Her feet didn't hit the bottom of the pool—instead, she plummeted deeper into the inky water, sinking below the surface. Instinctively she shut her eyes, her chest clenching as frigid water completely enveloped her naked body.

How deep was this pool? She opened her eyes, searching for a point of reference in the pitch-black water. Fear tightened her chest—the pool's surface was nowhere in sight.

From the depths, a deep voice whispered, "This one has fire in her veins."

She kicked her legs, moving away from the sound. *Who the fuck is that?*

"The shadow god's enemy," murmured a second voice—a gravelly tone.

The water grew colder, freezing her skin, and shivers wracked her body. Her lungs ached for a breath.

"But there is darkness in her, too," said the first voice.

"And pain. She did a terrible thing," hissed the gravelly one.

"What should we do with her?"

She needed to get away, to get to air and out of the water. She kicked her legs frantically, her fingers clawing for a surface that no longer seemed to exist.

I need to breathe.

"She wants to visit the Shadow Realm."

"But her fire is forbidden."

"Then we take it from her."

"Yessss," said another voice. "Her flames will warm us. It is so very cold here."

Her body shook in the frigid water.

Something cold and slimy brushed her cheek, and the words *deadman's fingers* rang in her mind. She thrashed in the darkness as an ice-cold hand grabbed her foot. *What the fuck is happening?*

More hands grasped her limbs, pulling her deeper. Agony inflamed her lungs, as water began to trickle down her throat. She jerked and twitched in the grasp of the fingers. The hands were all over her, clammy fingers pulling her mouth open.

Cold water rushed in, and her lungs spasmed. *I'm dying.* With each spasm, more water filled her lungs, dousing the flames of her magic.

"Remember the darkness. Only the darkness will save you." the voices whispered. The hands released her, and a light appeared above her.

Am I dying? No, she couldn't accept it. She'd hardly begun to live, and she still had no idea who she really was.

The voices were lying—where there was light, there was air. *Life.*

Fighting her body's desire to convulse, she stretched out her arms, kicking her legs to swim upward. The circle of light grew larger. Her lungs burned.

She kicked her legs, reaching for the light. If she weren't drowning, she would have sighed with relief as one of her hands brushed something solid. A final kick and her fingers broke the surface. Pain ripped her mind apart, and it took every last bit of strength to control her body. She clawed, grasping at an edge. With the last of her strength, she heaved herself up.

And then she was gasping. Coughing. Cold water pouring from her mouth, hot tears streaming from her eyes.

Chapter 4

Ursula lay on a marble floor in the fetal position, as she coughed up another lungful of water.

Cera wiped the wet hair from her face. "Earthly gods below, what took you so long?"

She sucked in a deep breath, trying to find her voice again. "There were dead things in there, dragging me down."

"Oh, dear. The Forgotten Ones found you?"

Ursula rolled onto her back, staring up at a ceiling painted with constellations. Her teeth chattered, and she hugged her naked body. "The Forgotten Ones? Is that what they are? They took my fire."

Cera sighed. She'd already dressed in a cozy-looking black robe. "There wasn't time to warn you, but at least we've escaped the dragon."

Ursula forced herself up on her elbows, surveying her surroundings. She lay in the center of a round room, her feet dangling in a clear, circular pool no more than six inches deep. Was it really possible that she'd been drowning in this shallow water just moments ago? She'd nearly died.

Around the room, thin columns flanked windows that reached from the floor to ceiling. Through the glass, a gray landscape stretched out under a canopy of gleaming stars. Only a few rocks interrupted the flat horizon—no buildings, nor trees or any sign of life. *Where the hell are we?* Her teeth chattered.

Before she could form one of the million questions on the tip of her tongue, the little demon came up behind her and handed her a velvet robe. "Perhaps you should put this on."

Ursula took it gladly, wrapping it around her freezing shoulders. Instantly, her muscles began to relax.

Enveloped by the robe, she glanced out the window again.

She drew in a slow breath, her gaze drifting upward. Above the stark landscape, the pale wash of the Milky Way splashed across the night sky, more vivid than she'd ever seen. Too vivid. *This is not Earth.*

Her breath caught in her throat. "I guess we're not in Brooklyn."

Cera snorted. "No, we're not in Brooklyn. The Shadow Realm is on the moon."

"The moon," she repeated, turning to gape at Cera.

"Of course. Nyxobas's water carried you here," said Cera, crossing the room to a black door. She cast a critical eye over Ursula's bedraggled hair. "Shall I show you to your quarters? You look half-dead."

"Okay," said Ursula absently. Barefoot, she padded over cold marble as she followed Cera, still trying to process the fact that she'd left the earth. She didn't *feel* any lighter. Shouldn't she be floating around the room?

Cera pushed open the door. "This way."

Ursula followed the oneiroi into the cold air, her heart skipping a beat as she realized they were *outside*.

Outside. On the moon. Without a spacesuit or helmet. They stood on a milky, marble bridge, a thousand feet above a deep, cratered valley. The bridge spanned the space between two round towers.

Ursula paused as a bitterly cold wind ruffled her hair, gripping the marble ledge to peer into the crater. Her pulse raced. In the center of the caldera, a towering spire of purple glass loomed above them. Unlike the sleek lines of New York's skyscrapers, this tower was all jagged edges and sharp angles.

All around them, stark palaces of shining, silver towers jutted from the crater's walls. If she strained her eyes, she could see a faint horizon on the far side of the spire, the gleam of distant buildings.

She gazed down at the vast valley spread out below, filled with stone dwellings. She drew in a slow breath. The human race had managed to send twelve people to the moon, and yet here was a vast kingdom no one had ever noticed.

She searched the skies for the Earth—home, something familiar—but only stars twinkled in the black sky. Out here, the air smelled faintly of creosote, and dizziness overwhelmed her. She glanced at Cera, who moved at a fast clip across the bridge, her silver hair trailing behind her.

"Wait!" Ursula called out. "I don't understand. There's a whole colony on the moon? Why doesn't NASA have pictures? And how can I breathe if there's no atmosphere? And why doesn't the gravity feel any different?" Those were just the first four questions that entered her mind, but she could keep going.

Cera paused near the other end of the bridge before a gray door. She pointed at the sky. "Can you see that glimmer there?"

As Ursula walked, she looked up at the dome of stars. At first she couldn't see what Cera meant, but then she noticed a faint shimmer along the horizon. Like the sheen of gasoline on a puddle.

"A glamour of magic surrounds us," said Cera. "It both hides us from satellites and gives us air to breathe. And it takes care of the gravity problem."

"How?"

"Magic."

"Oh," said Ursula, searching again for signs of the earth. "Are we on the dark side of the moon?"

"Yes. The far side, some call it."

A dry wind toyed with Ursula's hair. Shivering, she pulled the robe tighter around her. When she'd left for the Shadow Realm, she hadn't realized it would be *quite* so far from home.

Cera pulled open the black door. "It's freezing out here. Are you quite finished gaping?"

Not yet. She pointed at the spire. "What is that?"

"It's called Asta. Where the god of night dwells."

Ursula looked back at the building, trying to imagine what the home of a god might look like inside.

"Are you quite ready?" said Cera impatiently. "I prefer to walk around clothed and wearing shoes."

Ursula hurried toward the door, her eyes focused straight ahead. As soon as she glanced at the bridge's ledge, she knew dizziness would overwhelm her.

Through the door, Cera led her into an octagonal hall—half of it black marble. The other half lay completely destroyed, as if a giant fist had smashed through the wall, opening it to the night air. *What happened here?* Hugging herself, she surveyed the space.

The hair rose on the back of Ursula's neck. On the mangled side of the hall, sheared steel beams twisted into the air like gnarled fingers. Wind rushed between them, chilling her skin. Shards of glass glinted in the starlight from the remains of old window frames. On the floor, a tile mosaic of a lion's head lay half smashed. Part of the beast's mane had been scorched and half its face smashed to dust. Opposite where she stood, steps climbed to a small platform with a circular black door. Some sort of crystalline stone—obsidian maybe.

"Okay. What happened here?" she asked aloud this time.

"A battle." Cera's eyes shone in the darkness like starlight. "Our lord is very strong. He protected us." She turned, crossing to a door in one of the remaining marble walls. "This way to your quarters." She yanked open the door.

Carefully, Ursula tiptoed over the shards of smashed glass and tile, following Cera onto another towering bridge. She kept her eyes on the demon, refusing to look over the vertigo-inducing railings as she crossed.

At the far end, Cera pushed open a door into a pitch-black room. As Ursula stepped over the threshold, candles in silver sconces flickered to life, casting warm light over a dark hall.

"I will be back in the morning," said Cera, stepping back to the door. "You'll have everything you need here." She pulled open the door, then stepped out and slammed it shut with a click.

Ursula crossed to the door, tugging on the handle, but it wouldn't budge. *Locked in.*

Chapter 5

Ursula surveyed the wide hall. On one side, a spiral stairwell curved upward. The opposite wall abutted a delicate wooden table, adorned with a display of faintly glowing mushrooms.

Beautiful, but slightly unsettling.

Pulling her robe tighter, she followed the hall into a dimly lit, semicircular room.

A great panel of windows curved in the shape of the tower. Through the glass, she had a perfect view of Nyxobas's gleaming spire, jutting from the crater like a jeweled spear. *Guess I won't be walking around here naked.*

A set of marble statues flanked the windows, each at least eight feet tall—nude, athletic men with curly hair and vacant eyes. Ancient Greek, by the look of them.

Arranged about the room, glass cabinets held clay urns and vases, painted with letters from dead languages and geometric designs. Apparently, moon demons had major hard-ons for the Classical era.

Possibly the hots for human men too, given the choice of statues.

She scanned the walls, eyeing the fine glassware. She tried not to stare at the black velvet couches that were nestled into the corner of the room, or she'd give in to temptation and sleep in one for days.

Water portal travel did a number on a person's body.

Her eyes lingered on a silver clock on the wall that looked like an antique ship's clock. It featured a complicated lunar cycle of waxing and waning moons that she couldn't quite figure out.

Before she could move on to another room, her gaze landed on a portrait, framed in silver. The subject—a woman—had gorgeous dark eyes, and long brown hair that curled over a delicate white dress. She wore a solemn, regal expression. Olive skin, sharp cheekbones, full lips. Beautiful as hell. The vulnerability in her eyes seemed remarkably human.

She wasn't exactly an art history expert, but it looked like something from the Renaissance. From one of those painters who depicted gorgeous women—Botticelli, maybe.

So maybe Classical Art Demon was into women, too.

Her rumbling stomach turned her attention away from the beauty. *I'm starving.*

She spotted a small bar tucked in another corner of the room. On it was a platter of cheese, grapes, and a carafe of wine.

Cera might have locked her in here, but at least she'd left something to eat.

As Ursula drew closer to the food, she noticed a beige envelope resting against the carafe. On it was scrawled her name in deep red ink. She popped a grape in her mouth, then snatched up the envelope, tearing it open. She scanned the letter.

I have asked Cera to look after you during your stay. She will be able to provide anything you need. This apartment is yours, and you are free to move about as you wish. For your own safety, I cannot give you free rein of the entire manor at this time. We will speak in the morning.

She crushed another grape between her teeth, letting the sweet juice run down her throat.

Had Nyxobas written this letter? She'd been expecting to meet him here upon her arrival, but now the idea that a god would greet her personally seemed completely stupid.

Then again, she hadn't quite understood Nyxobas's power until she'd come here. Now she could see it, visually represented. Total domination over an entire planetary body, not to mention the demons he controlled on the earth.

Grabbing a chunk of bread, she walked over to the window. Nyxobas's spire glinted in the starlight. She'd been expecting to stay with him, that he had some sort of purpose in mind for her. But clearly, she hadn't been brought to his palace. So what the hell was she doing here?

A hollow opened in the pit of her stomach. She was in some sort of manor, and she had no clue who owned it. And the first name that came to her mind was *Abrax.* The incubus had tried to murder her more than once, and she was pretty sure he was a rapist. He'd pulled some kind of mind-control seduction trick on her. At least, until he'd become disgusted by her and moved on to attempted murder. Clearly, the guy had issues with women.

A chill snaked up her spine. Not only did he hate her, but she had an unsettling feeling she hadn't even begun to witness Abrax's power.

Suddenly, her appetite deserted her. *I want Honjo.*

Her hand was shaking as she placed her bread on the coffee table, and her old, familiar instincts kicked in. If there was one thing that came naturally to Ursula, it was self-preservation.

I need to find a weapon in case Abrax shows up. Her pulse racing, she scanned the room for something that could be used for skull-smashing or organ-puncturing.

Bars had knives sometimes, didn't they?

She hurried across the room and began pulling open the drawers. Coasters, fancy napkins, toothpicks. Bugger all, basically. Not a lot of damage you could do with toothpicks.

She yanked open another drawer. A corkscrew. *Bloody hell. I won't get very far fighting an ancient demon with a corkscrew, but it's better than nothing.*

She shoved the corkscrew into the robe's soft pocket. *Maybe I can find something a bit better.*

She crossed to a door off the living room, pushing through into a bathroom. She scanned the gray tile. The silver, claw-footed bath looked amazing, she had to admit, but she found not a single toilet plunger or towel rack that could be used to smash a head in.

She ran back to the front hallway, her frantic gaze landing on the spiral staircase. She bounded up it, two steps at a time. At the top, more doors lined a long hall. She flung open the first and walked into a luxurious bedroom: floor-to-ceiling windows and a large bed covered with a violet bedspread.

A dresser stood against one wall. Candles and a jewelry box resting on the top, but unfortunately, nothing so handy as a knife. She pulled open the jewelry box, finding only actual jewels. Of course. People didn't tend to keep weapons among their diamonds, but you never knew.

Her pulse racing, she yanked open a drawer, cursing when she found it empty. One drawer after another, each completely weaponless. Not only was this place completely weapon-free, like a psychiatric facility, but she hadn't even been given clothes.

So much for "providing everything you need."

She hurried into the hall, flinging open another door to find another bathroom. An enormous tub stood before the curving windows. *Not a lot of privacy here.*

She crossed to a white porcelain sink, yanking open the cupboard below it. She rifled through a few extra rolls of toilet paper, and some ancient-looking vials of green and blue liquids. Not even a toothbrush she could file down to a point.

Her heart racing, she stood and patted the corkscrew in her pocket. Its thin twist of steel was all she had to protect herself.

Somehow, it did not reassure her.

Ursula trudged down the stairs again. Of course there weren't any real weapons in the apartment. Abrax, Nyxobas—whoever was in charge here—didn't want a hellhound able to defend herself. As a hound of Emerazel's she was simply too dangerous to the night demons.

In the living room, she headed for the bar, then popped the cork off the carafe of wine. She grabbed a wine glass, filling it nearly to the top, then crossed to one of the sofas.

She plopped down onto the rich, velvet fabric and took a long sip. She'd have to keep the glass nearby. In a pinch, she could smash it and stab someone with the shards.

Her stomach tightened. One of these days, she'd like to have a normal Friday night. Though hoping for an ordinary night in the Shadow Realm was probably a bit of a stretch. The alcohol warmed her stomach, soothing the tension from her shoulders.

Abrax or Nyxobas...

Somehow, Nyxobas didn't seem like he'd have a golden lion mosaic in his atrium or a suite of rooms filled with classical art. She shivered. Abrax seemed more like the type to relish intimidation through luxury. He was also the kind of perv who'd put her in a glass cage so he could watch her every move.

She tucked her feet underneath her. If Kester were here, he'd have a clear idea of what she should be doing. He'd stretch out on the sofa, full of confidence. He'd level his green eyes on her and tell her precisely what spells she needed to be practicing and how to evaluate her true threat. Then again, she'd hardly seen him in the past six months. After she'd saved him from Nyxobas, she'd gone to visit him on his tugboat. And that's when she'd learned the truth—that Kester was in this to save his sister's soul. She'd felt so close to him that night, like she'd made a true friend. And yet, since then he'd been a ghost. He'd stopped by the flat once or twice with Zee. He turned on his usual arrogant charm. Flirting, double entendres, references to his prowess with a sword. But when she'd asked what he'd been doing, he'd just shrugged. "On a special assignment given to him by Emerazel," was all he'd said. And then, he'd disappeared again for another month.

When she'd asked Zee about it, the fae girl had shaken her head. "That's Kester for you. Wham, bam, thank you ma'am. It's how he operates."

But that didn't explain it at all. She and Kester had neither whammed nor bammed. Sure, she'd thought about it. How could she not, given his chiseled beauty? But nothing had happened... yet.

And meanwhile, she'd been missing a mentor. Kester was supposed to teach her how to become a hellhound, but there'd been no magic lessons, no practice sessions in the armory to build her skill. In the last six months, she'd learned virtually nothing new about the job.

Sure, she'd kept busy in other ways. There was the mob boss assignment in Hell's Kitchen—a first-rate wanker who'd been forcing his thugs to sign over their souls. Ursula had been tasked with hunting down each of the Mafiosi.

Because they'd signed over their souls involuntarily, her task had been to nullify pacts. She'd thought it'd be easy—who actually wanted to burn in the Emerazel's inferno for eternity?

But once the Mafiosi had tasted Emerazel's power, they seemed to stop caring about eternal damnation. She'd been forced to reap more of their souls than she cared to think about. It had been brutal work, but at least she'd filled a good number of pages in her ledger.

And each page was another step toward freedom. Once she managed to fill her ledger, it was *goodbye* to the hellhound life.

She took another sip of wine, pushing her worries about the ledger to the back of her mind. Right now, she had more immediate concerns. After the dragon attack and the near-drowning with the Forgotten Ones, exhaustion burned her muscles. She propped her wine against the base of the sofa, then leaned back into the velvet. She pulled a soft, white blanket over her body, staring through the window at a perfect view of Nyxobas's palace.

The sharp spire glimmered like a shard of glass. And as her eyelids drooped, dark clouds seemed to whirl around its summit.

Chapter 6

"Ursula." Someone tapped her shoulder.

"Mmgghhft," Ursula groaned, opening her eyes. Cera stood above her. It was still dark outside. Maybe it was always dark here? She still wasn't quite sure how that worked. She pushed up onto her elbows, blinking to clear her mind. "What's going on?"

"You need to wake up. You're to meet the lord in fifteen minutes."

"I don't understand. What time is it?"

"Almost eight p.m. Earth time. You slept all day. You need to get dressed."

"But I don't have any clothes to wear." Ursula's brain was slowly turning on. "I'm supposed to meet Nyxobas now?" Cera held up a white bag. "I brought you a dress. I'm not entirely familiar with Earthly fashions, but I based it on that gold gown I saw in the picture in your apartment."

She straightened. "The Francesco Sforza dress? With the ribbons?"

"Not quite as revealing as that one, but the same idea. The women in Nyxobas's kingdom don't show off their flesh quite so wantonly as Emerazel's women do." She shook her head. "No respect for yourselves."

Ursula frowned. She hadn't been a fan of the ribbon dress, but there was no need for slut-shaming. "There's nothing wrong with female bodies, you know. Or showing them off."

Cera's silver eyes narrowed. "You'll need to adapt to the culture here. I know incubi and vampires flout Nyxobas's rules on Earth, indulging in all sorts of heresies, but you're in the Shadow Realm now." She thrust the bag at Ursula. "Nyxobas believes in denial of bodily urges in order to reach heavenly perfection."

"Right." Ursula peered inside the bag. A lilac dress nestled next to silver shoes and a bag of toiletries.

She stood, then pulled the dress from the bag—an exquisitely delicate fabric that shimmered in the candlelight. She stood, holding it up. It certainly had more fabric than the Sforza dress. This one reached the floor, but it still featured a plunging neckline and tiny shoulder straps. The fabric was practically sheer, but gathered enough around the skirts that she wouldn't be showing too much off.

"Wow," she breathed. "It's gorgeous. Where did you get it?"

Cera's chest seemed to swell. "I sewed it. There aren't any designer shops here, so if you want a pretty dress, you have to make it yourself. I'm glad you can recognize fine craftsmanship when you see it." She beamed. "There's underwear in the bag. I figured a hellhound would like the skimpy kind." She sniffed.

Ursula peered in the bag at a pale blue thong. "Thanks, Cera." Weird as it was to get thongs from a stranger, it was actually very nice of the oneiroi to try to choose things she thought Ursula would like.

"Perhaps you'd like to go into the bathroom to try it on," prompted Cera.

"Sure." Apparently, Cera was horrified by the idea that Ursula might strip right here, even though the demon had already seen her completely naked.

INFERNAL MAGIC

"And while you're at it," Cera called out, "you may as well bathe and beautify yourself for the lord. It will help him warm to you, I'm sure. There are toiletries in the bag."

Ursula frowned. "When you say 'lord,' are you talking about Nyxobas?"

"Honestly, child." Cera chastised her as though it were the most absurd question in the world. "Clean yourself up. You mustn't displease him."

Sighing, Ursula carried the bag into the bathroom and closed the door behind her. A lantern bathed the bathroom in warm light. So, she had to make herself look good for her lord. Whoever he was, she was apparently at risk of provoking his wrath with her bedraggled appearance. This was just getting weirder by the minute. Still, she wasn't going to argue. Makeup was its own armor, and one that made her feel like herself. A war paint of sorts.

Ursula untied her robe, hanging it from a hook on the back of the door.

She crossed to the claw-foot tub, turning a silver knob and letting the bath fill with water. Stepping into the warm bath, she grabbed a bar of floral soap. Steam curled from the water, filling the room with the scent of lavender and mint. Around the bath's rim, candles flickered, casting dancing light over the gray tile. She lathered under her arms, and ran her fingers over her neck to clean up the grime. The water felt soothing over her skin, and she splashed warm water over her shoulders, rinsing off the soap.

She might not understand why she'd been called to the night realm, but she knew Nyxobas had good reason to hate her. She'd forced the high demon Bael, Nyxobas's general, and his second in command, into signing his soul over to Emerazel. A twinge of guilt pierced her chest. Nyxobas had probably ordered Bael's

35

death since then. She didn't imagine the god of night would forgive a tactical failure of that magnitude.

Her stomach tightened. And if Nyxobas *hadn't* ordered Bael's death, the high demon would probably rip her limb from limb. She'd completely destroyed his plans to take over the Shadow Kingdom.

A knock sounded at the door. "Don't take too long in there," Cera cautioned. "We mustn't keep the lord waiting."

Ursula rolled her eyes. Whoever "the lord" was, he sounded like a real prick.

After a final scrub of her legs, she rose, feeling the soapy water drip off her skin. She unplugged the drain and stepped from the tub, grabbing a towel. Goosebumps rose on her bare skin as she dried off.

Cera banged the door again. "You really don't want to make him angry."

Ursula tried to ignore the demon's frantic knocking. Peering into the bag, she grabbed the tiny blue underwear and slipped into it. Somehow, it fit her perfectly. Probably precisely *because* Cera had seen her totally naked and was able to gauge her exact measurements. *No bra, I see.*

She grabbed the dress from the bag and pulled it over her head. The silky fabric skimmed luxuriously over her breasts, hips, and thighs before reaching the floor.

Her gazed flicked to the mirror, and a smile curled her lips. The neckline plunged to her belly button. Braless and with a daring neckline, she was exposing a little more than she normally would. But she *had* just proclaimed the importance of pride in one's body, and she wasn't going back on it now. Plus, she looked damn good.

She slipped into the silver heels, then turned to study her reflection again. She ran her fingers through her auburn waves, trying to tame them into submission. She had to admit—the red of her hair looked stunning against the cool tones of the dress. Cera might be cranky, but the demon was a genius with a needle and thread.

She leaned over, picking up the makeup page to unzip it. As Cera continued to hammer on the door, she lined her eyes with black, rouged her cheeks, and slicked her lips with a rather stunning shade of cherry red. A dusting of shimmery white powder over her cheekbones was the final touch.

If the lord could be mollified by makeup and dresses, she was certain this ensemble would do the trick.

She pulled open the bathroom door into the living room.

Cera beamed at her. Clearly, the woman was proud of her work. "The lord may have a bit of a shock when he sees you. But dark god above, it is gorgeous."

"Well, I wouldn't want to offend the lord with a poor dress choice."

Cera nodded enthusiastically, apparently missing her sarcasm. "Oh yes. Very true. Now, we must go." She looked at the clock, visibly shuddering. "I don't want to anger him," she muttered, turning to hurry for the door. "Please come with me."

Sharp claws of panic gripped her chest. She'd left her only weapon in the bathroom. "Wait," she said. "I need to wee."

"Not now!" scolded Cera.

Ignoring her, Ursula ran back to the bathroom. She gripped the robe, yanking the corkscrew from its pocket. She swallowed hard. *Where the hell am I supposed to hide it in this outfit?*

She didn't have much of a choice. It was going in her thong or it wasn't coming at all. Suddenly, she was no longer so keen on the dress's sheer fabric. She hoisted up her skirt, tucking the corkscrew into the front of her knickers, pointy side up. She didn't want the sharp bit doing any damage to the most delicate parts of her body.

"Hurry up!" Cera wailed.

Ursula smoothed out her hair, pulling open the bathroom door into the living room. She hoped her facial expression conveyed some sense of normality—as opposed to, "I've just shoved a corkscrew in my knickers, and I'm trying not to hurt myself." Plastering a smile onto her face, she followed Cera through the hall and out the front door, trying not to look over the bridge's railings. She didn't need her stomach turning any more flips than it already was. Plus, vertigo and heels seemed like a bad combination.

This time, when they entered the lion atrium, Cera led her across the tiles. The demon climbed the stairs, pausing at the onyx door.

Ursula frowned. "Is this all part of the same manor?"

"Yes. You're about to meet the lord who owns your apartments. He will have control over every aspect of your life for the next six months. So you understand why this is important to get right."

She hugged herself. *And if it all goes to shit, I'll just fight him with the corkscrew in my knickers. Top planning, Ursula. You've really outdone yourself.*

At the top of the stairs, Cera flicked her fingers. The heavy onyx door creaked open, revealing a tunnel.

Cera held out her hand, gesturing for Ursula to enter. "Go along. The lord is waiting for you."

"You're not coming?" said Ursula, her skin growing cold. With a growing sense of dread, she climbed the steps.

"No. He wants to meet with you alone."

The hair rose on the back of her neck. "Can you at least tell me who I'm meeting? Is it Nyxobas? Or Abrax?"

Cera frowned. "I'm not at liberty to say. He's a *lord*. I'm not allowed to call him by any other name, and I'm certainly not going to defy him. Everyone here knows their place, and if you're smart, you will, too. Your life depends entirely on the lord." The little demon backed down the stairs, her milky skin a shade paler than normal. "You're going to be late. You need to go."

Ursula folded her arms, reluctant to plunge into the dark hall without knowing what she was getting into.

She watched Cera hurry across the tile, turning to Ursula one last time before pulling open the door. "Good luck." She disappeared through the door, leaving Ursula entirely alone.

Cold dread bloomed in Ursula's chest. *Well, it's not like I can run away from whoever this lord is.* She was going to be in the Shadow Realm for six months, living in his house. She was going to meet him one way or another. She turned, taking a tentative step into the tunnel. Candles flickered in sconces, their dim light wavering over rocky walls. The tunnel seemed to be carved from a cliff of the moon crater itself.

Hugging herself, Ursula strained her ears for any sound, but she heard only deathly silence.

She walked further into the hall, trying to soften her footsteps on the smooth stone as much as possible. She considered pulling the corkscrew from her knickers, but decided against it. It was too big to hide in her palm, and clearly showing up armed to meet "the lord" would be a major breach of protocol. Still, the bulky feel of sharp metal in her thong was oddly reassuring—a thought she'd never before imagined would cross her mind.

Of course, she never imagined she'd be going to meet a demon on the moon, before.

Goosebumps rose on her skin, and she made her way deeper into the tunnel. Unlike the hard lines and cold steel of the exterior rooms, this part of the manor seemed ancient. Twisting patterns and faded runes adorned the jagged walls. The light changed subtly as she walked, and she glanced down. The illumination no longer came from candles. Instead, glowing mushrooms grew along the floor's edge, and the tarry creosote smell gave way to something earthy and alive.

Ahead of her, the tunnel opened into a large chamber, and a path curved between gray boulders. As she stepped into the hall, her breath caught in her throat. It wasn't so much a chamber as a vast cavern. Huge stalactites hung from the ceiling, their surfaces encrusted with glowing mushrooms.

The path led through the cavern to a thin, stone bridge suspended between two cliffs. No rails, no sides. Just a narrow strip of stone over a vast chasm. Tentatively, she approached the edge. She stepped onto the bridge, her gaze briefly flicking to the stark blackness, the sheer rocky drop into a bottomless abyss.

Her heart hammered against her ribs. *Maybe this is why Cera wanted to stay behind.*

A cold sweat beaded on her forehead, and she took another step forward in her tall heels. *No turning back now.* A deathly silence hung in the air, broken only by the clacking of her stupid heels over the stone.

If there had ever been a time for running shoes, it was now.

She pulled her gaze away from the abyss, glancing at the ceiling. Bioluminescent mushrooms nestled among glowing indigo crystals. The fungi light refracted through the crystals, bathing the bridge in an otherworldly violet light.

She glanced at the bridge again, so she wouldn't lose her footing, and her gaze trailed to the abyss. The darkness seemed to beckon her forward, luring her off the bridge. Her stomach swooped, and a strange sort of terror bloomed in the back of her mind. She wasn't afraid she would fall.

She was afraid she would jump.

She blinked, clearing the disturbing thought from her head. *I'll face forward then, won't I?* A few more careful steps, staring straight ahead, and she cleared the final bit of the bridge, stepping onto a rocky platform. The temperature in this cavern seemed ten degrees cooler than the rest of the hall. She crossed her arms in front of her. She didn't need "the lord" seeing just how cold she was.

After a few more paces, she paused, her heart skipping a beat.

At the far end sat a figure in a jet-black throne, cloaked in shadows.

Night magic curled in front of the lord's features, moving like seaweed caught in an invisible current. He exuded power. And pure menace. Here, in front of the lord, the void called to her. That vast abyss, just a few steps away, beckoned her closer, tempting her to jump.

This was no simple demon's power. This was a god, ancient and wrathful. *Nyxobas.*

It had been a mistake to come here. As if a corkscrew could protect her from this dark hell.

"Ursula." The lord's rough voice boomed through the hall, echoing off the rock.

Fear twisted her gut. She concentrated on straightening her spine. Kester had taught her not to show fear to a demon or god. It only brought out their primal instincts, and the next thing you knew, they were pinning you to the ground, teeth at your throat.

"Why have you brought me here?" She worked to steady her voice.

"You think I wanted one of Emerazel's dogs here? Like *I* had any choice in the matter?" His rage thinned the air.

Despite everything she'd learned about showing confidence, she took an involuntary step back.

"I don't understand." She was trying to make sense of his words. Nyxobas had struck a deal with Emerazel—he'd been a willing part of the bargain. She was supposed to stay with him for six months of every year. "If you didn't want me, why did you make a deal with Emerazel?"

Silence descended on the cavern. Tendrils of black magic gathered around him, undulating from his powerful body like serpents. "You are mistaken," he said at last, rising from the swirling darkness.

Violet light washed over pale eyes, chiseled features, and a body of pure, thickly corded muscle.

Ursula choked down a scream. *Bael.* So *that* was the lord Cera had been talking about. She'd been scared of Nyxobas, but this might be worse. She'd seen him fight, and right now, she could feel his raw power rippling over her skin. Once a demon like Bael decided you were his enemy, that was it. You were dead.

And the truth was—if anyone had a reason to hate her, it was Bael. She'd forced him to sign over his soul to Emerazel. Nyxobas had been furious—in fact, the damage to his manor was probably the night god's doing. Bael was lucky to be alive at all.

And that had all been Ursula's fault.

Cold fury glinted in his eyes, which darkened from gray to black. *That's not a good sign. When a demon's eyes turned black, it usually meant they were about to rip someone's heart out.*

Her back was to the stone bridge. She stood, trapped between an enraged demon and a bottomless chasm. *So that's why he didn't reveal himself earlier.* He'd wanted to wait until she was most vulnerable.

"You stole a soul from me, Ursula." Venom laced his voice. "And left me to die."

Yeah. She was definitely on his enemy list. And now, as she stood before him in a flimsy dress and heels, without a sword to defend herself, he was going to exact his revenge.

Panic sunk its claws into her chest, and a buried memory flitted through the recesses of her mind. Something about his cold fury was familiar. Had she seen him before? Did F.U. know Bael, and was she warning Ursula away?

Run, Ursula. Run before he rips you to pieces.

She turned to run—one step, two—then her heel caught on the hem of her dress. At the edge of the cliff, her arms windmilled in the air as she teetered at the edge of the abyss.

Time seemed to move in slow motion, and the void pulled her over the edge. How long would she fall before she hit the ground? Two seconds? Five? The impact would knock the organs from her body. A burst of light. Then raging fire as she began to burn in Emerazel's infernos.

Or maybe there *was* no ground, and she'd fall forever, trapped in Nyxobas's hell of unending darkness.

As she plunged over the cliff, powerful magic rushed around her, then strong arms enveloped her, trapping her. *Bael.* He pulled her back from the brink, his eyes still black with fury. On the cliff's edge, he pinned her arms to her sides.

He was going to kill her. He just wanted to do it his way.

She brought up her knee, striking his groin, and his dark eyes widened, his grip loosening just enough that she could slam her fist into his Adam's apple. Stunned, he stepped back.

She yanked up her dress, and ripped the corkscrew from her knickers.

If she thought Bael had been surprised before, he now looked like he was about to pop a vein in his forehead.

"Do you mean to attack me, hellhound?" he snarled.

In a blur of black magic, a tattooed arm gripped her throat, powerful fingers encircling her neck. He was about to choke the life from her.

She jammed the corkscrew into his forearm, and he let out a roar, his fingers tightening.

She ripped the thing from his flesh again, before bringing it down a second time. Bael dropped his hand. But in a movement so swift she nearly missed it, he snatched the corkscrew from her grasp. Growling, he flung it into the chasm.

Her heart thudded. *There goes my only weapon.*

In the next second, his arms were around her again, pinning her in a vise-like grip. "Are you quite done?" A cold fury laced his voice.

Adrenaline blazed through her veins, but as much as she strained, she was stuck fast. She stared up at him. Gods, he was enormous. "You know that Emerazel will send someone to avenge me. If you kill me—"

"I'm *not* trying to kill you."

"You're not?" Some of her panic began to ebb, and she studied him. She hadn't quite noticed before, but with his perfect features, he looked a lot like an angel. An angel of death, perhaps, but an angel nonetheless.

"No." He loosened his arms, but he didn't release her. He smelled like the sea, and faintly, of sandalwood. "You have angered me, but I cannot kill you. Nyxobas has tasked me as your guardian while you are in his realm."

"Why you? Did he return your wings?" With his wings and immortality intact, he'd be a powerful protector. If not...

His arms tightened again, crushing her chest.

Clearly, he didn't want to talk about the wings. So that would be a *no.*

He leaned down, his breath warming the shell of her ear. "It would be an understatement to say your kind isn't liked here. You wouldn't be safe in Asta, Nyxobas's spire. So he has burdened me with you. I suspect this is part of my punishment."

"For the whole soul debacle."

"That isn't quite how I'd describe it."

"If you're tasked with protecting me, does that mean you'll stop crushing me?"

He narrowed his eyes. The gray irises were lined with remarkably thick lashes. "Are you going to continue attacking me?"

"No."

Bael loosened his powerful grasp, and she stepped away from him.

His eyes trailed over her dress for just a moment before he glanced away again. "That isn't how most women dress here."

So he was a bit of a prude. Interesting. "Cera made it for me. She warned me it might be a bit shocking."

A muscle tensed in his jaw. "Not quite as shocking as your choice of holster for your corkscrew."

"Well, a lady can never be too careful."

His gaze met hers again. "You're smart to bring weapons with you. You are not safe in this realm. There are many who would like to kill one of Emerazel's hounds. Or worse." He studied her carefully, his magic licking the air around him. "Is it true what Cera told me, that the Forgotten Ones stole your fire?"

Grimly, Ursula nodded. "Yes. And the bastards nearly drowned me, too."

"It is unfortunate that I could not have come for you myself. I should have told Cera to warn you about them."

"I don't think there was time. It was very chaotic when we were leaving. I'm sure it was an oversight."

Bael nodded. "Without your fire, you don't have much to protect yourself. You must remain in your quarters."

Her shoulders tensed. Her quarters were beautiful—luxurious, even—but they were also incredibly lonely.

Bael turned from her, stalking back to his onyx throne. As he neared the stone dais, shadows rose around him. Without looking back, he disappeared into the coiling tendrils of darkness.

Chapter 7

For her return trip, Ursula removed the shoes. Much easier to walk over the stone bridge without them.

As he pushed through the front door into her quarters, she found Cera standing in the front hall, chewing a fingernail.

"Oh dear!" Cera cast a critical eye over her tattered dress, the bare feet, and the silver pumps dangling from her hand. "What in the lord's name happened to the dress?"

Ursula glanced down at herself. It was worse than she thought. The hem was torn up to her thigh, the bodice soaked in Bael's blood. She felt pretty bad about ruining the gorgeous gown—Cera's hard work, now ragged and gore-spattered.

She smoothed the front of her dress, as though trying to reclaim her dignity. "Bael was a little confrontational."

Cera's jaw dropped. "Is that blood?" Her brow furrowed. "Whose blood is it?"

"I'm fine."

Cera's body began to shake. "What did you do to the lord?"

"It was just a little misunderstanding. He'll recover quickly, I'm sure, but I will need another corkscrew at some point."

Cera's hands fluttered in the air like frightened birds. "Of course. The corkscrew. When he asked me to remove all the weapons from your quarters, I didn't even think to take the corkscrew."

Frowning, Ursula crossed her arms. "He asked you to remove all the weapons?"

Cera's hand flew to her mouth, making an audible slapping noise. Given her sharp teeth, Ursula would be surprised if she didn't stab herself.

"Please don't mention this to the lord. He specifically told me not to say anything about the weapons. He said you were prone to violence."

Pot. Kettle. Black. "I won't say a word."

"Thank you." The little demon took a deep breath, then crossed into the living room. "I've brought you dinner."

At the mention of the dinner, Ursula's stomach rumbled. She hadn't eaten anything apart from a few grapes since she'd first arrived. As she crossed into the living room, she saw that Cera had arranged a few folded piles of clothes for her on the sofa. As soon as Cera left, she'd change into them. But right now, she just wanted to tear into the sumptuous-smelling meal.

At the bar, Cera had cleared up the wine and cheese from the night before. In their place stood a silver domed place setting. Cera pulled off the lid. Steam curled into the air, and Ursula's mouth watered at the scent of grilled meat. Cera had arranged fingerling potatoes next to a T-bone steak with a small salad. Ursula pulled a chair up to the bar, a grin curling her lips. "This looks amazing. Did you make it?"

Cera beamed. "I did."

"Thank you so much." Ursula popped a potato into her mouth, savoring the buttery flavor. *Amazing.* She glanced at Cera. "Cera, you are indeed multi-talented. Are you going to join me? It's a shame to eat alone."

Cera shook her head. "I've already eaten."

She picked up the knife and fork. "Maybe tomorrow you could join me."

Cera's brow furrowed. "No," she said with some finality.

"Fine." Ursula picked up her knife and fork. *Guess I'll eat alone.* Still, she didn't want to be completely isolated. She'd lose her mind in solitary confinement. Maybe she could keep Cera here for conversation. "So how does the food get here? Surely you don't have cows on the moon."

"The salad and the potatoes are grown here. The lunar soil isn't very rich in nutrients, but that's easily remedied with natural compost. But you're right about the beef. It is imported."

"And how does that work?" She shoveled in a forkful of salad. "I had to leave all my clothes behind to travel through Nyxobas's water."

"That's right," said Cera nodding. "Since it's impossible to bring anything through a portal with you, we have the lunar bats fly it in."

"Bats like Sotz?"

"Exactly. They can fly between the Earth and the moon."

"They fly through the vacuum of space? Without air?"

Cera shrugged. "They don't appear to need air. They're Nyxobas's creatures."

"Fascinating," said Ursula, carving off a piece of the steak. Red streaks of blood oozed from the flesh.

"Is it okay? We don't usually cook steak. I hope I didn't overdo it."

After ruining the dress, Ursula didn't want to insult the demon. "It's delicious." She cut off a piece from the edge and popped it into her mouth.

Cera's eyes crinkled at the corners when she smiled. "Well, I should leave you to eat alone."

Ursula turned to Cera. "Sotz flew back on his own?"

"Yes. He's in the rookery now. Well, perhaps I—"

It was a long shot, but she had to ask. "I don't suppose you can tell me what I'll be doing here for the next six months. Am I really supposed to just hang out in my quarters?"

Cera frowned. "No. Of course not. And I completely forgot the wine."

Before Ursula could tell her not to worry, Cera was already behind the bar. She slid a glass over the bar and pulled out a carafe of red wine.

Ursula took a sip, letting the rich flavor roll over her tongue. Delicious. It also helped rinse out the taste of raw meat. "If I'm staying here, how often will you visit me?"

"I'll deliver your meals and clothes," said Cera, eyeing the raw steak hungrily. "That's all I know."

"And you'll never eat with me? Even if the food is delicious?"

"That's not how it works. Everyone has their place here in the Shadow Realm. And my place is not at the table with you."

Ursula forked another potato into her mouth. "I don't understand."

"The lord doesn't allow the oneiroi to eat his food."

"You mean Bael?"

Cera frowned. "Yes. The lord."

"I won't tell. You can have the steak, if you want. I don't eat much meat," she lied.

Cera drummed her fingernails on the marble bar for a moment before snatching the plate. "If you insist."

The demon grabbed a fork, lifting the entire steak to her mouth. She opened her mouth, her sharp teeth glinting in the candlelight. She tore into the meat, ripping off a chunk with her teeth.

As Cera ripped into the meat, Ursula crossed to the other side of the bar and pulled out another wine glass. She slid it over to Cera, then filled it. "The steak goes well with the wine."

"You don't mind?"

"Of course not. I don't want to be stuck here on my own. And will you please sit? Make yourself comfortable."

Cera climbed into a chair and continued working her way through the steak, little grunts of pleasure emitting from her throat.

"So tell me about yourself," said Ursula. "How did you come to work for Bael?"

"My mother was the lord's maidservant. When she grew too old to work, I took over the position."

"You seem afraid of him." Ursula sipped her wine, eyeing her new dinner companion cautiously. Maybe she could learn a bit more about Bael while she was at it. "Is he cruel to you?"

Cera stopped chewing, her eyes widening. "Of course not. He's very good to me, but *all* the lords have dominion over the oneiroi. If an oneiroi steps out of line, we can be brought before the council, and—" She glanced out the window, as if Nyxobas could overhear her. "The council demands obedience. Everyone has their place. The lords serve our god. Shadow demons serve the lords. Women serve their husbands. And oneiroi serve everyone."

Lovely. "Can you tell me what happened to damage the manor?"

Cera swallowed the last of her meat. "When the lord returned, we were very happy. He had been away a long time. Having the lord in the manor makes it feel complete. Like we're protected. But he was hurt. When the other lords learned of his injuries..." Cera swallowed, her pale eyes glistening. "They attacked. Our lord—he bravely fought them. He was able to defend the manor, but many oneiroi died. Only a few of us remain now. And he doesn't come out of his quarters anymore."

"What do you think will happen?"

Terror trembled in Cera's voice when she spoke again. "The other lords will find another way to kill my lord. Among the warrior lords, only the strongest are considered fit to live. The weak are sacrificed to the void." Ursula swallowed hard. "I don't understand. If Nyxobas wants me protected, why did he put me with a mortal lord everyone wants to murder?" Cera lifted her tear-streaked face. "No one else knows you're here. My lord is weakened, but Nyxobas trusts him like he trusts no other. When Nyxobas ordered the lord to protect you, he knew he would follow through with every ounce of strength remaining in his body. Even if he doesn't like you."

Gods willing, that will be enough. "I didn't realize I was meant to be a secret here." She nodded at the window. "Can't people see me through the giant windows?" Cera shook her head. "No. The light reflects off them." Cera rose. "Thank you for the meal. I'll return tomorrow."

"I hope you enjoyed it."

Cera's chin glistened with steak juices. "It was the best thing I've eaten in years."

As Cera left her quarters, Ursula stared out the window at Asta. The protection of the night god was the one thing keeping Bael alive. And here, in the Shadow Realm, Bael was the one person keeping her alive. Terrifying as the god of night was, she needed him on her side.

Chapter 8

After Cera left, Ursula tidied away the clothes the little oneroi had left behind. She tucked the knickers into her bureau, then hung the dresses and shawls in her bedroom closet. As she organized, she ran her fingers over the soft fabrics: cotton dresses for home, delicate embroidered tulle for speaking to the lord.

Nothing she could fight in, but apparently that wasn't supposed to be her role here. She just had no idea what her actual role was.

In her bedroom, she pulled off her bloodstained gown and slipped into a black cotton dress that hung to her ankles. And conveniently, the simple dress had pockets by her hips—so she wouldn't need to store anything in her panties.

She glanced around the bedroom—the stark gray walls and clean lines of the violet bedspread weren't exactly inviting. What were the chances Bael would allow her to decorate this place? She needed a reminder of her most calming dreams—of the dusty-blue forget-me-nots and yellow aster, bathed in the amber light. Those beautiful but intangible memories she could never quite grasp... Honeyed sunrise, blue flower petals, tall blades of grass. The warmth of a landscape so different from Nyxobas's Shadow Realm.

With a shawl wrapped around her shoulders, she crossed to the enormous windows. What, exactly, was she supposed to do with her time? There was no TV in this place, no armory where she could hone her skills, not even a bookshelf with a collection of novels.

She stared out at the vast crater. The opposite side of the rim was so far away, its enormity dizzied her. Even Asta, with the strange, gray clouds that swirled around its violet peak, looked thin and delicate from this vantage point.

Ursula glanced down at the houses that clustered around the valley floor. Could she glean anything about the habitants by looking at their homes? In the darkness, it was difficult to make out much. *What I wouldn't give for a telescope right now.*

Still, if she strained her eyes, she could tell the houses were small and built of stone. Among the sea of darkened windows, a few lights twinkled. Did Cera and other oneiroi live in those humble dwellings? From the crater's valley, they could literally look up to their lords in the imposing lunar palaces.

How long had Bael lived here in the Shadow Realm? At the thought of his otherworldly power, a shiver ran up her spine. Instinctively, she reached for her white moonstone—her lucky charm. Her stomach flipped. Of course, it had been left behind when she'd stripped off in the subway. *Bloody hell.* She'd had that thing for as long as she could remember, not that that was very long, but still it had been the one constant that had travelled from her former life to her new one.

She bit her lip. She'd been stripped of everything on her journey here—her magic, her sword, and her touchstone.

She turned, scanning the room. She'd just have to find a new lucky charm. Her gaze landed on a mahogany jewelry box that rested on the dresser.

She lifted the lid, momentarily dazzled by the small treasure inside. Among the silver and diamonds, she found a beautiful brooch. Inset into the silver setting, a cameo stone depicted a lion's head. She ran her thumb over the surface. Somehow, it didn't feel soothing.

She dropped it back in the pile, and picked her way through rings and necklaces. *Too delicate.* She needed something strong and solid.

As she dug her way to the very bottom, she found a ring of solid silver. The thing was enormous—far too big for her own fingers, but heavy enough to feel like an anchor. More importantly, it fit perfectly into the palm of her hand. She stroked the smooth metal, then slipped it into her pocket.

With the ring tucked safely in her pocket, she returned downstairs. She'd already grown more comfortable in the living room than anywhere else in her living quarters.

On the sofa, she curled up into the corner and pulled a snowy blanket over her body. Before she let her eyes close, she glanced around the room. She could still spruce it up a little, bring a bit of life to the place. Some apricot and bronze paints could go a long way...

She let her eyes close, rubbing the solid ring between her fingers. And when she drifted into the dream world, she visited a man with gray eyes, his body hewn of pure muscle. Around them, a room burned and screams pierced the night air...

It seemed like only few moments had passed when Cera tapped her on the shoulder.

"Ursula."

Ursula blinked, slowly waking. Cera peered down at her. Outside, stars still shone in the dark sky. Bloody hell, this place was disorienting. It felt like she'd only been asleep for a few moments.

She sat up, trying to clear the fog of sleep. "How long, exactly, does the night last on the moon?"

"The lunar day lasts twenty-seven Earth days. The sun won't rise for another..." Cera looked at the clock. "The sun will rise in one hundred and eight hours."

Ursula's eyes widened. "It's dark for a month at a time?"

"No, it's only dark for half of that. For just over thirteen days, we see the sun." She gestured at the window. "Lucky for us, the tinted glass blocks out most of the light. Anyway, you need to get dressed. The lord's carriage leaves in thirty minutes. If you want a shower, now is the time to do it."

"The lord's carriage?"

"He has requested your presence. He did not explain why." Cera thrust a silky dress at her.

Of course he didn't. She took the dress from Cera, unfurling it. Deep indigo silk, so dark it almost look black, embroidered with fine silver stitching. This time, a delicate silver bra and panties lay on top of the fabric, plus a pair of indigo flats.

Cera turned her back. "Please hurry."

Ursula stepped out of her clothes, then folded them neatly on the sofa. She slipped into the panties and bra, then plucked the silver ring from her dress pocket, tucking it into the front of her cleavage. "A carriage, you said?"

"Precisely. The lord awaits you. We weren't given much warning."

Ursula stepped into the dress, pulling it up over her hips and sliding the sheer sleeves over her shoulders. From the tops of her thighs down, the dress grew increasingly sheer, sparkling with silver thread. The wide hem gave her more freedom of movement than yesterday's dress. The neckline plunged, giving off a view of her cleavage. Apparently, Cera was enjoying creating fashions for hellhounds with no sense modesty.

She stepped into the shoes. "It's gorgeous."

Cera turned, frowning. "Let me help you." She tugged at Ursula's hair with her fingers, twisting and forcing the waves into submission. When she'd finished, she appraised her work. One of her black eyebrows flew up. "Open your mouth."

Ursula did as instructed, and Cera whipped out a small silver canister, spraying her mouth with a minty liquid. In the next second, Cera was slicking her lips with red gloss. "Perfect. You have everything you need."

"There is one thing this ensemble really needs," said Ursula.

"What?"

"A sword."

Cera snorted. "Fat chance of that. Here, women are meant to please the eye. Not pluck them out with blades. That's men's work. Let's go. The lord awaits you."

Cera turned, hurrying into the hall. Ursula quickened her pace to keep up with Cera as she crossed the bridge, the wind whipping her auburn hair into her face.

When she crossed into the half-shattered atrium, her heart skipped a beat. A metal cage stood in the center, with a hinged door. It looked like something that belonged in a medieval torture chamber. "Um, what is this, exactly?"

Cera yanked open the door. "Don't be afraid. On Earth, I believe you call this an elevator."

Ursula glanced up at the thick steel chain that rose from the cage's ceiling. "Right." As

Cera held the door open, Ursula stepped inside. Without entering, Cera closed the door on Ursula.

"You're not coming?" asked Ursula.

The little demon crossed the smashed tile. "No. The lord only requested your presence."

Ursula wrapped her hands around the elevator's bars, watching as Cera pulled a lever. A great creaking noise pierced the air, and the rattling chain slowly lifted the cage from the ground.

"Good luck!" shouted Cera from below.

Chapter 9

The cage rose slowly, swinging gently from side to side with metallic groans. Ursula laced her fingers through the bars to steady herself. A chilly wind rushed over Ursula's skin, raising goosebumps.

On her journey upward, she passed one balcony after another. This place was *enormous*—practically its own city. Except, as she passed each floor, darkness greeted her. No candles lit the rooms, no voices warmed the air. Starlight shone through cracked glass shards of shattered windows. Instead of art, ragged holes interrupted the sleek walls, and burn marks scarred the marble floors.

The only signs of movement were the pale curtains, dancing in the lunar breeze.

Before the attack, this place would have been stunning, and perhaps teaming with life. As the elevator continued to rise, the walls narrowed. The cage slipped through a narrow gap in the roof, and into the night air.

On the slick roof's surface, the icy breeze blew more strongly through the bars, bringing with it a faint smell of creosote.

A dome of stars spread out above, and Bael stepped from the shadows. Starlight caressed the sharp planes of his cheeks, glinting in his eyes. He wore a dark cloak around his broad shoulders, fastened with a silver lion clasp. Another piece of cloth covered one of his arms. From under his hood, his pale eyes pierced the night like stars.

As he opened the elevator door, his expression appeared grim, almost hostile. The door creaked as he opened it. "Tonight, you will do everything I say."

She frowned. She hadn't expected high-fives and cookies, but there was a hint of rage in his voice she hadn't heard before.

Her stomach fluttered. "What's the matter?"

"Who did you tell about your visit to the Shadow Realm?" Vicious shadows whorled in his eyes.

"No one." She eyed his cloak enviously. Too bad Cera hadn't shown up with a jacket. "The only people who know are Emerazel, Zee, and Kester. None of them would tell a soul. And they certainly don't gossip with shadow demons."

Bael cocked his head. He was doing that creepy demon thing—the eerily still body and penetrating eyes that she was certain could read more than she wanted them to.

He took a step closer, his powerful magic rippling over her skin. "Somehow, someone has told Hothgar about you. He's specifically requested that you show fealty to the council," he snarled. "Your presence here was supposed to be a secret."

"I take it Hothgar is one of the lords?"

"A lord without honor."

Whoever Hothgar was, he'd probably put at least some of those holes in the palace. "Abrax knows I'm here. He wants me dead."

"Abrax wants you for himself. It would not be in his interest to inform the council about you. Once they learn of your presence in the Shadow Realm, they will howl for hellhound blood. The location—the very existence of the Shadow Realm—has been protected for millennia. Outsiders within our boundaries have never left the realm alive. And worse, you belong to Emerazel."

Ursula shook her head. "Nyxobas specifically requested my presence."

"He tasked me with protecting you from Abrax. But he won't risk upsetting the cohesion of his council if they all find out. I cannot protect you from the other eleven lords if they want your neck."

The wind picked up her hair. Maybe this was an opportunity. "Maybe I should return to Earth. You don't want to start a war with Emerazel over me. I'm really not worth the hassle."

"For whatever reason, Nyxobas wants you here. But he's not fully protecting you. If he were, you'd be in Asta or he'd have issued a decree to protect you. He's done neither."

Her forehead crinkled. "So...what's the deal? Surely there are easier ways to kill me than bringing me to the Shadow Realm."

"He hasn't seen fit to fill me in. Whatever he has planned, I view it as my duty to protect you. Tonight, you will come with me to the council." His tone was pure command. "They must understand that you're not here as an enemy, but as a captive. You must convey the message of captivity through acting submissive. It's what they'll understand."

Sounds like a great time. She crossed her arms, shivering. "Can you tell me more about Hothgar?"

"He is the new Sword of Nyxobas." Cold rage laced his voice. "And he belongs in the void."

The cold wind stung her skin and she tightened her fingertips on her forearms. Bael's gaze flicked to her shivering arms. He pulled the dark cloth from his arm, handing it to her. "Put this on."

She took it from him—a black wool cloak, identical to his. She wrapped it around her, savoring its warmth, and fastened it with the silver clasp. A lion, just like Bael's.

"You'll need to cover your head." Bael leaned in closer, pulling up the hood. "It is important you don't draw any unnecessary attention to yourself. And your hair is difficult to ignore." He turned from her, facing the crater, then put his fingers to his lips and whistled sharply.

A shadow crossed over their heads, and Ursula glanced up. Flying above them, a team of lunar bats pulled a black carriage, fastened to the creatures by silver cords. It looked like a gothic chariot from the eighteenth century.

I've either wandered into a nightmarish version of Cinderella, or a hellish Christmas tale, with lunar bats instead of reindeer.

With the whoosh of beating wings, the bats lowered the carriage to the roof, then landed on the slick marble with an ear-piercing scratching of claws.

A male oneiroi hopped down from the front of the carriage, his black hair slicked back off his pale face. He opened the door to the main compartment, then bowed to Bael.

Bael gestured for Ursula to enter.

She tugged her shawl tighter, her gaze skimming over the magic swirling around the carriage's thin, black wheels. *That's what keeps this thing in the air—shadow magic.*

Inside, the indigo seats faced one another. Ursula nestled into the one that faced the front of the carriage. Shutting the door behind him, Bael climbed in the seat opposite. He kept his gray eyes locked on her, and he rapped on the window glass behind him.

With a lurch, the carriage surged into the sky. Through the window, she had a clear view of Bael's manor. Built against the cliff's side, it loomed above the crater, a shining tower of glass and silver. It looked like a skyscraper from a war zone. Jagged holes marred the walls, and great beams of metal twisted into the darkness like metallic innards. Thick dust covered some of the floors, like funeral ash.

Her heart tightened at the sight of it. She didn't know Bael very well, but the loss of all those people must have been catastrophic.

Bael glared at her from across the carriage, not a single muscle moving. "When we get to Asta, you will stay by my side. Keep the hood over your head to cloak your face in shadow. Speak to no one."

Ursula nodded, half-listening. Asta, with its stunning violet glow, came into view through the window. The enormity of the Shadow Realm astonished her. The crater's rim curved around them, and thousands of buildings filled the vast space.

She pointed to the stone buildings below. "Who lives down there? In those small homes?"

"They are the homes of the brethren, and the oneiroi."

"Who are the brethren?"

"Nyxobas's followers."

She shook her head. "So the oneirei aren't all Nyxobas's followers? How did the oneiroi end up here if only followers of Nyxobas are allowed, on pain of death?"

"Very astute." He arched an eyebrow. "The oneiroi dwell within the crater because they were here first."

"I don't understand."

"Nyxobas was imprisoned here one hundred thousand years ago. The oneiroi were here first."

"Wait, so the oneiroi are—" Ursula struggled to process the implications. "They're extraterrestrials?"

He cocked his head. "They're not native to the Earth, so I suppose they are."

The bats' wings beat the air rhythmically, pulsing like a heartbeat. Outside, Asta shone in the darkness, tinging the gray clouds with purple. There really was something odd about the clouds—the way they twisted and writhed, curling high into the air and then diving down in spinning vortexes. Almost like a living thing.

As they approached, a low humming reverberated through the carriage. Her seat began to vibrate, and she tried to ignore the sensation. Especially since it wasn't exactly a *terrible* sensation, but it's not like she wanted to mention that to Bael. Her cheeks warmed, and she could feel her chest flushing.

She was concentrating on blocking out the faint wave of pleasure pulsing through her body, when something *thunked* against the window. A vicious green smudge streaked the glass.

"Watch that you don't fly too close to the moths," Bael called out to the driver.

"Yes, milord."

Bael gazed at Ursula. "We could blow out windows if we flew through one of the murmurations."

"A what now?"

"The astral moths." He pointed at the clouds outside. "They're attracted to Asta's light."

Thunk. A gray wing the size of a dinner plate stuck to the window a moment before peeling off. Ursula pressed her face to the glass, watching the carriage descend. Clouds of moths swirled above them. It took her a moment to realize the low, vibrating hum came from the beating of a million insect wings. Outside, the moths flew in unison, like a flock of birds.

That's why the clouds moved so strangely.

They *were* alive.

"Why do they group and cluster like that?" asked Ursula.

"The murmuration? For protection." He pointed out the window at a gray form gliding toward one of the clouds. "Look."

As the bat approached, the moths dove in unison—a tight spiral of fluttering wings. The bat twisted and jerked. In a gut churning instant, it crushed a moth's body between its jaws. The circle of life, right here on the moon.

When Ursula turned back to Bael, her heart stopped.

The demon lord pointed a dagger directly at her heart.

Chapter 10

She froze, only her eyes moving to scan the carriage for a weapon. Who was she kidding? Of course he hadn't left weapons lying around. "I thought you were my protector."

His eyes narrowed. "You scare easily. The blade is for your protection." He turned the dagger, offering her the hilt. "Take it."

"Oh, I thought—" Ursula cut herself off. There was no need to belabor his point. The fact was, she *did* scare easily. She constantly searched her surroundings for escape routes or weapons. She had no idea what had happened to F.U., but whatever it had been probably wasn't pleasant. Perhaps that burning room from her dreams had something to do with it.

Taking the blade, she rolled her wrist, inspecting the steel. Perfectly weighted. When she held it to the light, she glimpsed strange angular patterns etched into the metal.

"Be careful with it. The dagger was forged from a meteorite, and it's more powerful than you'd think." He reached into his cloak, pulling out a set of leather straps. "Stick out your leg."

"Why?"

His eyes met hers. "So I can attach the sheath."

"Oh." She didn't need his help getting a sheath on her thigh, but something stopped her from protesting. She rested her foot on his seat by his thigh, feeling the heat radiating from him. She pulled up the hem of her dress.

Bael's gaze trailed up her leg, his eyes darkening from pale gray to a deep black. His jaw tightened, his dark magic swirling from his body. He handed her the sheath. "Perhaps you should do it."

She couldn't suppress a faint smile, and she let her leg rest against Bael's as she strapped the leather around her thigh.

Bael kept his gaze fixed firmly out the window. "If you keep the blade strapped to your thigh, you'll have to be seriously comprised before someone finds it."

Ursula slid the blade into the scabbard. "Let's hope it doesn't come to that."

"If it does, I think you'll find it's considerably more lethal than a corkscrew."

In the darkness of his hood, Ursula couldn't tell if he was joking or not.

Outside, Asta's glow burned brighter, washing the cabin with violet light. They seemed to be on a collision course with the spire, and just when she was sure they would crash into it, the carriage veered to the right. It jerked to a stop so abruptly that Ursula lurched from her seat, tumbling into Bael's lap.

Instantly, his powerful hands were around her waist, steadying her. She breathed in. *Sandalwood and sea air.*

"We're here," he said quietly, his breath warming her throat.

"Right. Sorry." She stood, smoothing out her hair.

Bael leaned over, opening the door. Ursula stepped onto a balcony by the side of the spire, pulling her cloak closer around her. Here, the wind felt ten degrees colder, seeming to cut through even the heavy woolen shawl.

As Bael stepped from the carriage, she surveyed her surroundings, trying not to peer over the side of the balcony.

Violet light washed over her, like she was standing in front of an enormous gemstone. On the other side of the balcony, an arched doorway interrupted the smooth crystal. From what she could tell by looking up, they'd landed about midway up the spire. Great walls of purple crystal rose up before her, shimmering in the starlight. Scattered balconies jutted into the air.

When she looked closely, she could see that scars marred the crystal's surface. In other places, great chips had flaked off. When she strained her eyes, she could a jagged scar that bisected the crystal, as if it had been severed and reattached. What the hell had happened here?

They stepped out and the carriage pulled away from the balcony with the great beating of bat wings. Bael crossed to the opening in the wall. Before following him in, she pulled the hood more tightly over her head.

In the door's opening, he turned to her. "Remember, if you want to live, you must do everything I say. Even if it doesn't make sense to you. Do you understand?"

Do I have a choice? "I've got it."

"Good. Now, your first command is to be silent. Absolutely no talking. Keep your hood over your head. Use the dagger only if your life is at risk."

He turned, striding into a dark hall. She hurried after him, keeping her face downcast. Could he tell where they were going? Surely shadow demons had amazing night vision.

A moment later, his strong hand grabbed hers, drawing her next to him. They'd stopped walking.

A voice boomed from somewhere in front of her. "Was that your carriage, Bael?" The tone changed, growing soft and mocking. "I can't imagine getting dragged around in one of those things. You must miss your wings." A chorus of laughter echoed around them, but there was no mirth in it.

Quiet fury tinged Bael's voice. "Yes, Hothgar. It is I."

The familiar urge to identify an escape route began to take hold, tightening her muscles. The Forgotten Ones may have snuffed out her fire, but apparently they'd left her instincts intact.

Too bad she couldn't see anything. As her eyes adjusted to the darkness, she could make out only the faint sheen of gray marble below her, but she kept her head tucked down, hiding her face.

"Then let us convene this council. Do we have a quorum?" said Hothgar.

Another voice answered. "All twelve lords are here, sir."

A cracking noise like metal against stone made Ursula flinch, the sound echoing through the space. It was only after the third crack that she realized someone was banging a gavel.

Hothgar's voice boomed again. "The quorum is convened. Bael, have you brought the cur?"

"I have," he replied. She heard his footsteps circling behind her, and he ripped the hood from her head. In the next second, he had forced her to her knees.

Her stomach clenched. *He did tell me to be submissive, but this is a bit much.* Still, she forced herself to keep her eyes on the floor.

"Good, I see that she is obedient," said Hothgar.

Fury simmered. *I hate these people.* She let her gaze rise, taking in a granite, semicircular table twenty feet in front of her. Behind it sat eleven demons. And not merely mortal demons, like she was. No—these were high demons, ancient and powerful. The dim light of luminescent mushrooms cast their bestial faces in violet light.

At the center of the table sat the man with the gavel—Hothgar, she presumed. He wore a shirt of thin chainmail. His hoary beard and white eyebrows marked him as older than the rest. From his left, Abrax glared at her, his gray eyes glacially cold.

On Hothgar's right sat a literal giant. Snowy skin, horned temples, flared nostrils. Demon-Bull, she'd call him.

She scanned the other lords, trying not to show her alarm at the array of muscled demons before her. Through eyes the color of obsidian, ice, and starlight, they stared at her with a mixture of disgust and hatred.

Mostly hatred.

Terrifying as they were, they paled in comparison to what perched behind them. An ancient throne, shrouded in shadow magic, so thick it almost looked tangible. An enormous form sat there, cloaked in darkness.

There's Nyxobas, the god of my nightmares.

For just a moment, his magic thinned, and she caught a glimpse of his head lolling to one side. *Is he asleep?* No. Not quite. His eyes were open—not their usual pale gray, but black as obsidian.

Hothgar leaned over the table. "Why are you in the Realm of Shadows, hellhound?"

Her chest tightened. Hadn't Bael told her not to speak? Was she supposed to answer Hothgar's question or not? She didn't feel like she'd been properly prepared for this encounter. A soft nudge of her shins from Bael cleared it up for her.

Kneeling, she said, "Nyxobas struck a deal with Emerazel. I'm to spend six months of every year here."

"If that's a lie," growled Hothgar, "I will tear your guts out myself and use them to decorate my mansion."

Ursula's mouth went dry.

"She speaks the truth," said Bael. "I was there."

"Why should I trust your word, *mortal*?" asked Hothgar.

"You don't have to trust it." His voice boomed. "Abrax can tell you."

Dread filled Ursula's gut. Bael had just put her life in the hands of Abrax—the one demon who most wanted her dead after she'd ruined his plans of world domination.

Abrax spoke so softly, it was almost inaudible. "I can confirm Bael's story."

"So it is true?" asked Hothgar. "Your father summoned her?"

"Yes," said Abrax.

"Why would the god invite one of Emerazel's curs to his Realm?"

Abrax's eyes bored into her. "I don't know."

Hothgar studied her carefully with a look that suggested he was still thinking about decorating his house with her entrails. "Let me see her more closely."

Before Ursula could stand on her own, Bael picked her up by the collar of her cloak and threw her on the granite table. Her head smacked the stone so hard, she saw stars. It took every inch of her mental strength to lay still.

Be submissive, Bael had said. At this point, with the concussion he'd just given her, she didn't have many other options. Her head throbbed. Hothgar leaned over her, stroking the side of her face with a cold finger. "She's a pretty one. Maybe Nyxobas wanted her for himself."

"Gross." Dizzy from the blow to the head, the word was out of Ursula's mouth before she could stop herself.

Bael squeezed her wrist.

Hothgar glared at Bael. "But what I want to know is why he put her in *your* care. You lost your wings. Your house is in ruins." He emphasized the next set of words: "You are unfit to hold a manor of the night."

What the hell? Why don't they just ask Nyxobas, who was sitting about ten feet away? He seemed to be in some sort of catatonic state. Asleep or in a mystical trance.

"Nyxobas chooses his lords," said Bael.

"And yet he hasn't given you a new set of wings." Hothgar leaned back in his chair. "We have decided to give your manor to Abrax."

Bael's eyes darkened, and a cold, dark aura whipped from his body like hurricane winds. "No. Only Nyxobas himself may appoint a lord to a manor."

"The choice was unanimous," said Hothgar.

"It's not your province—" Black tendrils of magic snapped around Bael's throat, cutting him short. Ursula's eyes flicked to Demon-Bull, who chanted in Angelic. He was choking Bael with magic.

"We are tired of listening to a mortal," Hothgar snarled. "Your time as lord has come to an end. Prepare to enter the void."

Around Bael's neck, the filaments began to constrict. His eyes were dark as voids, and his fingers strained at the threads twisting about his neck.

Panic stole Ursula's breath, but she lay flat on the stone, trying to go unnoticed. Whatever she was going to do, she didn't want to telegraph her actions.

Her pulse racing, she glanced at Nyxobas, still wrapped in shadows, unmoving. *Why isn't he doing anything?*

Bael hadn't explicitly told her what constituted "an emergency," but she was pretty sure this was it. While the demons watched Bael suffocate, she slowly drew the dagger from the sheath on her thigh. Just as she managed to extract it, she felt Hothgar's fingers grab the corners of her cloak. In a single motion he picked her up and heaved her across the room. She slammed into a crystal wall with a bone-jarring smack. Her dagger clattered on the floor.

Bollocks.

"The hound had a blade," Hothgar roared.

Demon-Bull flicked his wrist, and black tendrils raced across the room. She ducked, diving for the dagger. Just as she gripped its hilt, dark magic slammed into her chest. She flew back against the wall, grunting from the pain.

Pinned to the wall, shadow magic coiled around her chest. Demon-Bull was crushing her lungs, her blood roaring in her ears. *Air. Please.* How long would it take for her ribs to shatter and pierce her heart? *Please. I can't die here.*

Ten seconds, maybe twenty.

"You have disrespected our hospitality," Hothgar roared. "You tried to assassinate the Sword of Nyxobas."

She opened her mouth to speak, but the pain ripped her mind apart. She doubled over as the magical bonds began to crack her ribs. Across from her, Bael hung limply, suffocating. He dropped to the ground, his large body twitching.

Air.

Her vision darkened, and for just a moment, she caught a glimpse of a woman with vibrant nectarine hair, wielding a sword with expert skill—her face like Ursula's, but her eyes a deep shade of brown...

A voice in the hollows of her mind whispered, *Kill the king.* A clear voice, ringing like a bell, reverberating off her skull. A voice so familiar, it was like a part of her soul. *Kill the king. Kill the king.*

With the last of her strength, she lifted the blade.

Hothgar laughed. "We are immortal—you cannot hurt us with that."

It's not meant for you, fuckwit.

It's for the king.

With the last of her strength, she hurled the dagger at Nyxobas's slumped body.

Chapter 11

The blade sank into Nyxobas's chest. The lords froze, staring at the god of night. Time seemed to slow, and the temperature in the room plummeted.

The filaments around Ursula's chest loosened, and she gasped. *Air.*

She sensed the terrifying presence of the void, flickering in the edge of her consciousness. Watching her.

"Who has done this?" Nyxobas's voice boomed through the silence. His eyes had shifted from black to a glacial gray—the icy gaze of her most terrifying nightmares.

Black blood bubbled around the hilt of the dagger in his chest.

Hothgar slowly turned, pointing at Ursula.

"The hound?" Nyxobas roared.

At the sound of his voice, a vast emptiness filled her mind. She stood at the edge of the precipice. Black and bottomless, it drew her closer. She only had to step off the edge, to give herself into eternal descent.

No sound, no light, no sensation. Just Ursula and the unending darkness.

Distantly, she felt the pain of her broken ribs. *I can leave this wrecked body behind, this withering carcass.*

Is this what the Forgotten Ones had meant when they told her the darkness would save her? She could join Nyxobas now. Supplicate herself to him—become one of his brethren. He would give her power she couldn't begin to imagine. She just needed to accept the void, to give up this decaying flesh.

To give up the broken ribs and burning walls, the rapacious hunger that could eat her alive...

Give up the tall grasses, beams of light through yew trees, the salty taste of sea air on her lips...

No, she thought. *I want to live.*

Before her, the darkness thinned. Her heart thrumming, she stared as Nyxobas slowly drew the blade from his chest. He crushed it between his fingers. "Why have you roused me?"

"They were murdering Bael." Her voice was rough and strained. Agony still pierced her chest where the cords bound her.

From the floor, Bael moaned, no longer enshrouded by dark magic.

Still alive.

Nyxobas turned his gaze on Hothgar. "You chose to murder one of my lords?" Ice tinged his voice.

Hothgar straightened. "He has lost his wings. Since we last spoke with you, he has proven himself unable to protect Albelda Manor. The palace has been destroyed, half his men slaughtered. As a mortal, he has been unable to fulfill his duties as lord. Abrax, your son, can hold the manor until another lord is appointed."

Nyxobas's glacial eyes bored into him. "Is this true?"

Bael pushed up onto his elbows, blood dripping from his lips. "The other lords attacked. I defended. Albelda Manor stands, and I live."

Hothgar's eyes flicked to Ursula. "He wasn't able to control his captive very well either. The hound is out of control, as you have seen."

Ursula's mouth went dry. *This is not going well.* "Isn't there a way for Bael to get his wings back? When I became a hound, I was offered a trial—"

"A trial," said Nyxobas, lifting a finger. "The wretched hound has the blood of a warrior."

Hothgar and Abrax both turned to glare at her. *Shit. What did I just suggest?*

Shadows coiled around the god of night. "The code of the warrior has always allowed for a trial. If Bael wishes to keep his manor, he must fight for it. Win, and all is forgiven."

Bael rose to his feet. "I will kill whomever I need to. I may be mortal, but you know my strength."

The god's silver eyes narrowed. "There will be a tournament. The lords may nominate five champions each—their greatest warriors. For the tournament, all demons shed their immortality. And if you, Bael, wish to reclaim your status, you must win the trial."

Bael nodded. He spoke through bloody teeth. "So be it."

"Then it is settled," said Nyxobas. "When the shadows grow long above Lacus Mortis, and the sun sets, we will conduct a melee. Those who survive will join the race. Finally, a duel. The prize is the remnants of Albelda manor, and a position as lord. If Bael wins, I return his wings."

An icy silence fell over the room, then Hothgar slammed his gavel onto the stone. "A trial for all the lords. A just ruling." His voice boomed, echoing off the crystal ceiling. After a moment, the room filled with rumbling cheers.

Hothgar stood. "Before the melee, we will hold a feast. We will present our champions. Then, the bloodletting begins."

Bael stared out the window of the carriage, his jaw set tight. He kept his eyes fixed on the gray horizon. In the distance, his ruined manor glittered faintly.

The bats' wings beat the air, an oddly soothing sound after her close brush with death.

Bael hadn't spoken for the entire carriage ride. He'd regained his regal bearing, and blood no longer dripped from his mouth. But his demonic stillness sent a chill up her spine.

She was quickly learning that the stiller a demon's body, the more unquiet his mind.

"Are you okay?" she asked.

Bael fixed his eyes on her, his irises shading over. "I *told* you to be subservient," he spoke in a guttural growl. "Not to put a dagger in the god of night." Dark magic whorled from his body, skimming her skin like an ice breath of wind.

Anger inflamed her cheeks. "I was about to die. And if you hadn't noticed, I saved you from suffocating to death. If stabbing Nyxobas is what it took to save us both, then so be it. I owe him nothing. He might be your god, but he's not mine."

It took only a second for Bael to cross the carriage in a blur of black smoke. He boxed her in, one hand on either side of her head. "That's right. You worship Emerazel, the wretched beast of hell. You have bathed in the fires of her evil heart."

Anger simmered. She'd never had a choice in aligning with Emerazel—at least, not one she could remember. She lifted her legs, kicking him in the chest. He slammed against the other side of the carriage, emitting a low growl.

Ursula's lips curled. She no longer had Emerazel's fire in her veins, but her own rage blazed through her blood. "I do not worship Emerazel. I'm a pawn in the game of the gods. Like we all are. I don't remember carving the mark in my chest, or why I thought it was a good idea, or anything about my life before three years ago." She pulled down the shoulder of her dress. "The only thing I know is that this stupid scar is the worst mistake I ever made." She yanked it up again. "I'm not Emerazel's worshipper. I'm her slave, and I don't know why. That's the truth."

Shadows still clouded his eyes, and his nostrils flared. His cold magic thrummed over her skin. "You don't belong here. The god of night has asked me to protect you, but I hate this job with every fiber of my being. He's making a mistake. As a fire demon, you're naturally inclined to destroy Nyxobas. To destroy all of us. Tonight proves it. You do not deserve my protection."

The coldness of his words pierced her chest.

Brilliant. Her only true ally here hated her. Tears stung her eyes, and she blinked them away. *I'm not going to cry in front of him.* "I was about to die," she said through clenched teeth, trying to gain mastery over herself.

"You could have thrown the knife at Bileth, the one whose magic assaulted you. But you're Emerazel's hound, and even without her fire, you are destined to fight the darkness. Her flames have tainted your soul."

"It wasn't like that." She swallowed hard. It *wasn't* like that, was it? She'd heard a voice in the back of her mind telling her to "kill the king." Was it simple self-preservation, or the voice of Emerazel?

Flustered, she waved a hand. "I didn't have a lot of time to think about the options. And it was eleven against one. If I weren't a hellhound, you'd be thanking me right now."

"But you are a hellhound. You don't belong here. Every time I look at you, I'm reminded of the hell-beast and the evil that runs through your blood."

"And Nyxobas isn't evil?" Her fingernails dug into her palms. "Are you really that loyal to the god of night, so devoted you think there's a vast difference between the gods of night and fire?"

He cut her a sharp look. "It's not because of my loyalty to Nyxobas that I hate her."

"Then what's your deal?"

"Her mind has been twisted by the flames, and has been since the dawn of civilization. She is an abomination. I owe her vengeance, and I will not rest until I have ripped her heart from her chest." The hatred in his eyes cut Ursula to the bone, warning her not to ask any more.

A pit opened in the hollow of her stomach. He hated Emerazel with a ferocity that literally chilled the air. And here she was—wearing Emerazel's sigil on her skin. A hellhound, loyal to his nemesis. Suddenly, she didn't feel so safe around Bael. He might be mortal, but he could still kill her.

Still, she knew how to handle men with rage problems. A year surrounded by drunks in her London bar had taught her how to manage that.

Stalling and distraction were her greatest assets.

She sighed, schooling her face to serenity, and drummed her fingernails. "So what happens now? What's this trial all about, and the code of the warrior?"

His steely gaze met hers. "You've manage to buy yourself some time. But you should know you've made some dangerous enemies tonight. The pale one, Bileth, is a psychopath. And while Hothgar might look old, he is the most powerful of the lords. You humiliated him in front of Nyxobas. He will want revenge." The ash-gray returned to his eyes.

"I thought you were the most powerful of the lords."

A rueful smile curled his perfect lips. "Before I lost my wings, I was Nyxobas's Sword. The leader of his legions, but now—" He coughed and Ursula saw him wipe blood from his lips. "I am still a warrior, but I am a mortal. A mortal's power is not the same. Still, I will fight in the tournament. And I plan to win."

"You certainly don't lack for confidence." *And I hope to hell you're right.*

"I am the best fighter the world has ever known." His pale eyes slid to the window again, the chiseled lines of his profile showing silver in the starlight.

She crossed her arms, sitting back in her seat. *Biggest ego the world has ever known, too.*

Chapter 12

The rest of their journey passed in silence as Bael brooded over whatever nightmares plagued his mind.

After their elevator had touched down, he'd disappeared into the shadows without a goodbye.

When she finally reached her quarters, her ribs were throbbing. Gingerly, she sat on the sofa, staring through the window.

The crater looked the same as it had when she'd left. In this desolate place, loneliness gnawed at her. Bael was right about one thing—she didn't belong here. And now, she'd landed herself in a whole new shitstorm.

Tension turned her stomach. Hothgar, Abrax, and Bileth would want vengeance. Worse, she'd attacked a god. Obviously a major breach of protocol. And what if Bael was right—that Emerazel could still somehow control her? It would make sense. Help explain why Emerazel had been willing to give her up in the first place. Though it didn't explain what Nyxobas wanted from her.

What she needed was a stiff drink. She rose, sucking in a short breath as she was greeted by a jolt of pain in her chest. Her ribs felt like they were on fire where Bileth's black tendrils had crushed them. Wincing, she carefully pulled off her dress, inspecting the damage. Deep bruises encircled her ribs.

Grimacing, she searched her mind for the Angelic spell—Starkey's Conjuration Spell. She remembered how it would feel—the familiar burst of pain as the spell knitted her bones back together, then blessed relief.

Only, she couldn't remember the bloody thing.

What the hell? She'd properly memorized it, having used it dozens of times to heal herself.

In fact, when she closed her eyes, she couldn't bring to mind a single Angelic word, the divine language of magic. Not even the spell for light.

The Forgotten Ones hadn't just stolen her fire magic. They'd ripped all the magical knowledge from her mind.

Dead-fingered bastards.

When she touched her ribs again, pain shot through her chest. She winced. She'd have to find some other way to heal.

A banging noise at the door turned her head, and she practically jumped out of her skin. Rising, she lifted the dress from the couch and slipped it over her head. If Bael were at the door, she didn't need to shock him by the sight of her naked flesh, though something about the idea amused her.

As she crossed the room, a part of her actually *hoped* it was Bael, even if he hated her. Suddenly, she had a deep desire to know why he hated Emerazel so much.

But instead, when she pulled open the front door, she found Cera, dressed in a woolen cardigan and holding a dome-covered tray. The rich smell of meat wafted into the room.

Ursula's mouth watered, and she gripped her chest. "I'm starving."

Cera's pale brow furrowed. "Oh my, what happened to your dress? It's been rumpled and torn."

"Bileth attacked me."

Cera's jaw dropped. "What happened?"

"Hothgar demanded my presence at the meeting of the lords. Bileth attacked Bael—"

"Is the lord okay?" Cera pushed inside. The door slammed behind her.

"I think he's okay. His throat is injured. He nearly died, and so did I. I did end up stabbing Nyxobas, which I realize overstepped a boundary or two. But in my defense, it was an emergency."

The tray in Cera's hands trembled violently. "You did *what*?"

"Did you hear the bit about the emergency?" Ignoring the throbbing pain in her chest, she grabbed the tray from Cera, carrying it to the bar. Her stomach twisted with a mixture of panic and hunger. "Anyway, now, in order for Bael to get his wings back, there's got to be a tournament. When the sun next bleeds into the sky. Bael must fight and win if he wants to live and get his manor back." She dropped the tray on the bar, cautiously eyeing Cera for her reaction.

"This is a disaster." Cera's eyes were wild. "If he was injured tonight, he won't have much time to heal. How will he fight?"

"He can't use magic to heal himself?"

Cera shook her head. "No. He must keep the wounds on his back fresh so he can reattached the wings when he wins them back."

That didn't sound good. "Can't he choose five champions, like everyone else?"

Cera shook her head, her eyes glistening. "Who would he choose? His men have all been killed."

"So each lord gets five champions, and he only has himself? That doesn't seem fair." She cocked her head. "Given those odds, he seemed pretty confident, though." She winced as a sharp spear of pain stabbed her ribs.

Cera studied her. "Are you injured?"

Ursula touched her ribs. "It hurts. I think I may have cracked a rib. Or three. And those Forgotten Arseholes erased all the healing spells I memorized."

Cera hurried to her side, her features pinched with concern. "Let me see. Lift your dress."

Ursula pulled her dress over her head, draping it over a chair.

Cera bent lower, letting out a low whistle at the purple bruises darkening her skin. "A lord did this to you?" Ursula could hear the hatred in Cera's voice.

She nodded, wincing as Cera gently she palpated her chest.

"It doesn't seem like a complete fracture, but I think you're right about it being cracked. I can heal it for you."

"Thank the gods." Ursula exhaled.

Cera reached into her sweater pocket and pulled out a purple crystal. It shimmered in the darkness.

Ursula took a step back as an icy wave of shadow magic washed over her skin. "What are you doing?"

"This is a lunam crystal. I keep it with me at all times in case I need to perform a spell. I can control the shadow magic within it. Even without knowing Angelic."

"You've never learned Angelic?"

"The oneiroi are not allowed. I'm not one of Nyxobas's brethren."

Ursula leaned closer, studying the crystal. It looked exactly like the ones she'd seen on the ceiling in Bael's cave. Shadow magic swirled from the violet rock, buzzing over her skin.

With a faint smile, Cera said, "The lord gave it to me. It's from the druse that grows in his cavern. It contains some of Nyxobas's magic."

She gripped it between her fingers, closing her eyes. Ursula stared as powerful shadow magic wafted from the crystal, curling around her ribs. The magic caressed her body, soothing her and exiting her at the same time. And most importantly, it leached the pain from her body, drawing it out as her bones fused together.

Ursula took a deep breath, sighing as the magic curled back into the crystal.

"Did it work?" asked Cera.

"Beautifully." Ursula grabbed her dress, pulling it back over her head. "Thank you."

Cera smiled. "Excellent."

Ursula pulled the dome off the tray, revealing a steaming meat pie with a side of mashed potatoes. "Will you join me?"

Cera wrung her hands. "I am quite hungry..."

"Please, eat with me."

Cera plopped down on a stool, grabbing a fork to delve into the pie.

Ursula speared a potato and bit into it, letting it melt in her mouth. "I'm confused. Nyxobas said the melee begins when the sun sets over Lacus Mortis. But the sun has already set. It's night."

"Lacus Mortis is on the other side."

"I see. Seems a long way to go."

Instead of answering, Cera shoveled another forkful of meat into her mouth, gnawing away.

She had to wonder who Cera would have shared a meal with before the Abelda Manor massacre. This place was almost entirely deserted now. Ursula couldn't be the only one plagued by loneliness. "How many oneiroi lived here before the attack?"

Cera's face fell for a moment. "Hundreds. Most died. The rest ran away."

"Why didn't you?"

Cera's face contorted with anger. "Serving in a lord's manor is a lifetime appointment. Without loyalty, we have nothing." She shoved a hunk of pork into her mouth.

"I see."

"And besides, if my brother's lord learned I'd failed in my duties as a servant, it would be very bad for my family."

She scooped a piece of buttery, flaky crust into her mouth. *Gods below. This woman can cook.* "You never mentioned you had a brother."

"Yes, it's just me and Massu now. He's a soldier. Even if I wanted to desert the lord, I couldn't, for his sake. I must protect Massu by remaining loyal to my lord." Savagely, she tore into a hunk of meat, swallowing quickly. "Of course, I don't hear much from him these days. I'm not sure that his lord would find out if I ran, but it's better to be safe than sorry. I worry about him terribly."

"Are you close?"

Cera nodded. "We were, before we were split into different manors. He was the sweetest boy. He always wanted to dress up like a lord, and he'd parade around with his little toy sword in secret. And he used to draw little pictures for me, of moths and bats and ships that flew in the air."

Ursula smiled. "He sounds adorable."

"He certainly was. All grown up now, but I'm sure the same sweet boy inside, even if he serves another lord."

So which one of those sadistic arseholes does Massu work for? "Which lord are we talking about?"

Cera shook her head. "I'm not allowed to say the name of any lord."

"Can you write it down?"

Cera shoveled a forkful of potatoes into her mouth. "Why is this so important to you?"

Because I watched Abrax bring an army of oneiroi into the fae realm, and I killed dozens of them. "I just like to know the lay of the land. And I may have seen him in the fae realm."

Cera silently nodded, swallowing her food. She placed her finger on the granite countertop, slowly tracing out letters. Ursula followed along, tracking the movements as Cera spelled out a name:

A... B... R... A... X

Ursula's blood went cold. *Fuck. Fuck. Fuck.* Cera's brother *was* a soldier in Abrax's army. Had Ursula killed him—murdered the brother of the only person she actually liked here? Had Bael killed him?

"You think you saw him in the fae realm?" asked Cera hopefully.

Ursula's chest tightened. *I can't tell her now—not until I know the truth. It would only worry her.* "I can't be sure." Feigning calm, she plucked a fingerling potato from the plate, biting into it. "When was the last time you heard from him?"

"It was before the attack on the manor. He said he was going on a special mission. He wouldn't say where."

Sweet mother of hell. I could have slaughtered Massu, the boy with the spaceship drawings.

Cera cocked her head. "Are you okay? You look ill."

"I'm—I'm okay." Ursula put down her fork, staring at the now empty tray of food. "I'm just feeling a bit queasy from everything that happened today."

"Of course." Cera plopped the dome back on the tray. "I'll let you get some rest."

"Thank you."

"I'll be back later with some food. I must check on the lord now." Tray in hand, Cera slipped out of the room.

But Ursula knew she wouldn't get any rest, not with her thoughts roiling like storm clouds. Bael hated her, the lords wanted her dead, and she may have killed the beloved brother of her only ally.

And what the hell had happened earlier, with that voice in her head? *Kill the king?* It had sounded so familiar, like it was a part of her very being.

Ursula pulled off her dress, dropping it on the floor, then kicked off her shoes. Exhaustion burned through her body, and she longed for sleep. In her underwear, she curled up in the corner of the sofa and pulled a downy white blanket over herself.

Loneliness tightened its fingers around her heart. If she'd been a normal person—one with memories—she'd probably take this opportunity to recall the times that her mother had looked after her, bandaged skinned knees or quieted her fears. Those sort of memories would soothe her soul, she imagined.

Instead, the best she could do was think of Zee, with a champagne cocktail and a fashion magazine. She missed her friend terribly.

In the darkness beyond the windows, Astra glowed faintly, and the clouds still twisted and writhed around it. Now that she'd learned what they were, the clouds no longer seemed quite so beautiful. Each vortex, each tendril, was a flock of moths fleeing in terror from a hungry bat.

She closed her eyes, and in her mind's eye, streams of moths whirled in frantic eddies.

She was one of them now—a moth hunted by Nyxobas's creatures.

Chapter 13

Curled up on the sofa, Ursula awoke with a start, adrenaline flooding her veins. What had roused her?

She scanned the room. Nothing seemed amiss—nothing had moved, not a single Grecian urn out of place. And yet, the hair on her neck stood on end.

An uneasy feeling licked at the back of her mind, telling her that someone was *watching* her.

Could someone have entered the room while she'd slept? She lay perfectly still, pretending to sleep, searching the darkness through slitted eyes. Had one of the demon lords come for revenge?

You're just paranoid, Ursula. Probably Emerazel's mind tricks, fucking with you.

Then, she caught a flicker of movement in the darkness outside her window. *Shadow magic.* Her pulse raced.

Not paranoid after all.

She opened her eyes wider, straining to see through the swirls of magic. She pushed up onto her elbows, desperately searching for a plan. Without so much as a corkscrew, what would she use to fight? Urns? Not to mention the fact that she was wearing nothing but lace knickers and a bra under her blanket. *Please don't let it be Nyxobas or any of the other perverts.* As she stared outside, the magic thinned, revealing an enormous lunar bat.

It hovered in front of the window, wings beating silently, blood-red eyes and wings of the color of bone. Something moved on its back—a rider dressed in gray. He straightened, then flung a sticky black substance against the window in front of her. Then, in a single silky motion, he aimed a small crossbow at her.

Panic stole her breath. *What the fuck is going on?*

She threw herself from the sofa.

The black tar exploded, shattering the window in a spray of glass that ripped into her skin.

Curling into a ball, Ursula tried to shield her body from the crossbow. Her stomach clenched as she heard the soft *whirr* of the arrow flying through the air.

Her heart raced. She waited for the thunk of the bolt when it struck her, the searing jolt of pain, the tearing of her flesh.

Instead, she felt only the sharp ringing in her ears from the blast.

When she opened her eyes, the rider had disappeared into the night. She gaped at the remaining shards of glass. The bolt had missed her. Why? It's not like she'd been a moving target.

She rose to her knees and glanced down at her body, at the crimson streaks cutting across her pale flesh. She'd been cut all over by the glass. But at least that was the worst of it.

Still, she couldn't exactly forget about it. The rider had left a gaping hole in the bottom of the window, and anyone could return to finish her off. She slipped into her shoes, then slipped behind the sofa. Blood dripped from her cuts, staining the floor. Injured or not, she had to protect herself. Now.

Using the couch as a shield, she pushed it closer to the window, grunting as she shifted it. *Not only can they enter into my quarters,* she thought, *but they can see me here, too.* Suddenly, she felt very exposed.

When she'd finished pushing the couch, it blocked the bottom of the hole, but she still had more work to do. A thin sheen of sweat rose on her forehead. *A moth hunted by the creatures of Nyxobas.*

With one eye on the window in case the rider returned, she crossed to an armchair on the other side of the room. She pushed it across the floor, straining her muscles. Sweat dripped down her skin, mingling with the blood. A combination of adrenaline and brute strength allowed her to lever it on top of the sofa with a pained groan.

The sofa and chair together covered most of the window, and a second armchair added extra support to the structure. *Not ideal, but better than nothing.*

She stepped back and took a shaky breath. With the adrenaline draining from her system, the cuts in her skin began to burn. She ran a hand over her bare abdomen, smearing blood across her fingers.

What the hell had just happened? The rider had practically been at point-blank range, but still missed. Could this be only the first volley before a second attack?

Or maybe, someone wanted to frighten her, to flush her out of the quarters. Nothing protected the bridge to the lion atrium—an ideal spot for an assassin to hide.

Ursula turned in a slow circle, searching for the bolt. She'd heard it fly from the crossbow. Maybe it would hold some sort of clue.

As she turned toward the portrait of that dark-eyed woman, she froze. There, in the center of the painting, a bolt jutted into the air.

She crept cautiously closer, examining the weapon. It was carved from black wood. Ebony maybe. As she stepped closer, she could see that something had been wrapped around it—parchment.

This hadn't been an attempt on her life. Someone had wanted to deliver a message.

Ignoring the pain that seared her skin, she pulled the bolt from the wall and peeled off the parchment. When she unfurled it, she found a message scrawled in black ink:

YOU ARE NOT WELCOME HERE, HOUND. THIS IS YOUR ONLY WARNING. NEXT TIME, WE WILL NOT MISS.

Chapter 14

The door to her quarters flung open with a bang.

Instinctively Ursula dove behind the bar, her knees and palms scraping over glass shards. She groaned in pain.

"What in the seven hells is going on in here?" Bael's voice boomed through the room. Ursula exhaled, rising unsteadily. Maybe Bael hated her for being the enemy, but he viewed it as his job to protect her. She rose unsteadily and crossed in front of the bar.

He stood in the living room, dark magic swirling around him, wearing nothing but a pair of black shorts. He held an enormous broadsword, and the cold battle fury blazing in his eyes made her stomach clench. "Are they gone?"

"Yes. I think so."

His chest was bound in bandages, but it didn't hide his perfect, chiseled body. And peeking out from the bandages, she could see glimpses of his tattoos—a crescent moon, a pointed star, a lightning bolt, sharp as a blade. Terrifying—but magnificent to behold nonetheless.

He gazed at her, some of the fury fading from his eyes. Concern flickered across his features. "You're hurt."

She nodded. As the adrenaline left her body, her teeth began to chatter. "There was a lot of broken glass."

He crossed the room in a blur of shadow, dropping his sword on a chair. In the next second, Bael's strong hands were around her waist.

Surprise flickered through her. Gently, he lifted her onto the top of the bar, careful not to touch her wounds. He examined her skin, pulling out a shard of glass from just below her ribs. She clenched her teeth, trying not to cry out at the pain. A warrior like Bael wouldn't be impressed by a load of whining. For a man with such large hands, she had to marvel at the nimbleness of his fingers as he plucked one tiny shard of glass after another from her skin. A deep concentration furrowed his brow, and he worked silently, like an expert craftsman.

When he'd finished, he gazed into her eyes, resting his hands on the counter on either side of her legs. For the first time, she saw a hint of softness in his glacial eyes. "You're withstanding the pain remarkably well."

She swallowed hard. His otherworldly beauty was distracting, and she could feel the warmth radiating from his body. If she hadn't been covered in blood and cuts, she wasn't sure she would have been able to stop herself from pressing herself against him.

Flustered, she blurted the first thing that came to her mind. "I'm quite badass, actually."

She cringed. *Idiot.*

His brow knitted with confusion. "Right. Well, I'm going to heal you with my magic. When I'm done, I want you to tell me exactly what happened."

She nodded, watching as he traced his fingertips just below some of the cuts in her skin. His magic caressed her skin, soothing her pain. As she closed her eyes, the shadow magic licked at her skin, then seeped deeper into her body. Her heart sped up, and the waves of pleasure dizzied her. An image rose in her mind of a sandstone temple, gleaming in the sun.

Her eyes fluttered open, and before she could think better of it, she touched the palm of her hand to his cheek.

Nearly imperceptibly, he leaned into her. His gray eyes roamed over her bare skin. With a hoarse voice, he asked, "What happened? What did they do to you?"

She dropped her hand. "A bat flew up to the window and threw some sort of bomb against it."

His brow furrowed. "A bat threw a bomb on your window?"

"No... No, I mean." Bael's bare skin and his closeness was distracting. Her pulse raced, and her cheeks flushed. Could a demon tell when you were turned on? *Probably.* "Someone rode it."

"The rider didn't come in to attack you?"

"No. He just sent a bolt through the window with a warning about how I don't belong."

Bael backed away from her, glancing at the punctured portrait. "What happened to your clothes?"

She shrugged. "I was asleep. I wasn't expecting any visitors."

"Are you okay now?"

"Completely knackered, but unharmed. Now that you've healed me."

He turned, studying the broken window. "You made a barricade from the sofa and chairs."

"I was worried they might try to come in, and I didn't want them to see me."

"That was smart." Suddenly shy, he wouldn't meet her gaze. Without the cuts, her nudity seemed to bother him. "Where's the note?"

She slid off the bar, then pointed at the floor where she'd dropped it. "It's right there."

He reached down, snatching it off the floor, along with the bolt. "I hope you didn't touch it. It could be cursed."

"But it's okay for you to hold it?"

Ignoring her, he inspected the wood. "So he blew out the glass and then shot at you with the crossbow."

"Exactly." *Why do I get the feeling that Bael knows more about this particular method of assassination than he's letting on?*

"And he didn't hit you?" Bael scanned the room.

"No."

He shook his head, still searching the floor for something. "That rider is a dead man."

"You're going to kill him for trying to murder me?"

"I don't need to. His lord will." He glanced again at the painting of the dark-eyed beauty.

"For not assassinating me?" Ursula asked. Blood still covered her body, and a chill washed over her skin. Shivering, she crossed her arms.

"It is the law here. Failure to complete a mission is punishable by death." For a second, his gaze flicked to her, then he sucked in a sharp breath, glancing at the painting of the beautiful woman. His pale eyes shined in the dim light of the candle.

"Have you executed any oneiroi because they didn't complete a mission?"

"I follow the law." Slowly, he crossed to the painting. He reached out to touch the canvas, running his fingertips over the tear.

Ursula frowned. "Why are the laws so draconian?"

"Nyxobas provides order in the chaos. Before he arrived here, the oneiroi were lawless. Vengeance and blood feuds ruled the darkness. The god of night has civilized them."

"Yeah, it seems really civilized here, with all the murder and assassinations."

"We have our own code." His fingers traced over the hole in the painting.

"Why can't the oneiroi speak your name? I don't see what that has to do with security."

His gaze slid to Ursula, his eyes so black they might have been direct conduits to Nyxobas's void. "My name was given to me by the god himself. Only the brethren may utter it." Bael crossed his arms over his mammoth chest. "The bolt tore the painting."

"Right. I hope it wasn't valuable."

He fell silent for a moment, his jaw working. "Perhaps you should get dressed."

"You're not dressed, either," she pointed out. She glanced down at herself, at the sticky blood still covering her skin. "I need to bathe before I put anything on. But I still have questions for you. Come with me."

"You want me to bathe with you?"

Her cheeks flushed. "That's not what I meant. I'll leave the door open. You can stand outside."

He nodded curtly. "I'll be staying here tonight. To stand guard."

A wave of relief washed over her. "Perfect. Thank you." She crossed to the bathroom, leaving the door partially open. Bael's presence both unnerved and calmed her at the same time, but she still had a million things to ask him. She leaned over the bath, turning on the water. Steam filled the room, and she unhooked her bra, sticky with blood, then stepped out of her knickers.

As the bath filled with warm water, she stepped in. "I saw your bandages," she said, calling to him. "Are you hurt?"

He paused a moment before answering. "Without my wings, I can't use magic to heal myself."

She grabbed the bar of lavender soap, lathering her arms. Bael's healing magic had left not a single scar on her skin. "I don't understand how you plan to fight the champions with two bloody holes in your back. You know you're not invincible. You could die trying to keep your manor."

"It's not like I have any other choice. If I lose, Hothgar and Abrax will hunt me down. My existence will always be a threat to them."

She splashed the water over her soapy skin, and her blood stained the water pink. Suds dripped off her shoulders and breasts. "Why would your existence be a threat to them?"

"Because Nyxobas chose me to be his Sword. He didn't chose them. And I am the strongest warrior the Shadow Realm has ever known."

"Not really big on humility, are you?" He was silent for a moment. "I'm starting to learn. I'm no longer as strong as I was." He cleared his throat. "I'll return in a moment."

Outside the bathroom, the faint sounds of tinkling glass filtered through the air.

Ursula's mind churned. Bael was obviously trying to fulfill his role as protector—whether he liked her or not, it was his duty. But how much could he really do—especially with this tournament hanging over his head? He might have been the best fighter the shadow world had ever known at one point. But now, he wasn't a match for immortals.

She pushed the thoughts to the back of her skull, and rose from the bath. Water trickled from her skin. She leaned over, unplugging the bath.

As goosebumps rose on her skin, it occurred to her that she'd failed to bring any clothes inside the bathroom. *Idiot.*

She grabbed a towel, drying off. "I don't suppose you could grab me some clothes?"

He cleared his throat. "Right. Clothes."

Clearly, a lord of Nyxobas was unused to fetching women's dresses.

She shivered. If the lords were going to keep coming after her, maybe she'd have to find a new place to live. The manor was huge—surely there were some hidden depths where she could remain unnoticed.

The door creaked open another inch, and Bael thrust a dress through.

She grabbed it from him. "Thank you."

She unfurled the dress—black lace with embroidered swirls that climbed up the sheer bodice. Way too fancy for hanging around in a half-demolished house, but she couldn't expect Bael to be an expert on women's clothes. Nor could she have expected him to include knickers and a bra—which he didn't.

She stepped into the living room, eying the floor. He'd cleared up all the glass. Starlight washed his deep golden skin in silver.

For just a moment, Bael's eyes roamed over her body, then he nodded at the remaining sofa. "Get some rest. I'll keep watch to make sure no one returns for you."

"This place is huge. Why don't we go to another part of the building?"

"You're safe as long as I'm here."

"You need to sleep, too."

He cut her a sharp look. "I have lived over twenty-two thousand years. I can survive a night without sleep."

As she crossed to the sofa, he sat in an armchair facing the window, arms folded.

She dropped into the sofa, pulling a soft blanket over her body. "Twenty-two thousand years?" The number made her dizzy. "Where do you come from, anyway?" "Canaan."

Okay. Bael was maybe a few millennia behind the times, but it must be hard to keep up with things when you're twenty-two thousand years old.

Still, despite his staggering age, he wasn't one of the original fallen. They'd arrived on Earth a hundred thousand years ago. "Was your father a high demon? Or your mother?"

"You have a lot of questions for someone who is supposed to be sleeping."

Her muscles ached, and she pulled the blanket tighter over her shoulders. "I can't answer the questions about myself, so I have to satisfy myself with learning about other people. And you have a lot of history to cover."

"We're not going to cover my history," he said tersely.

"Fine."

A silence fell over the room, and she closed her eyes, trying to sleep, but her tense muscles wouldn't relax.

After another moment, Bael spoke again, more softly this time. "What do you remember of your youth?"

She shook her head. "Only brief flickers, like an old film strip. Fields with aster and blue wildflowers. I usually try to paint them in the places where I've lived, to remind me of... wherever I'm from. Must be some rural part of England, because there aren't exactly many fields of wildflowers in London. But the flowers feel like home."

"I saw them in your room. In New York, after you roused me from a very long sleep in your attic."

What she didn't add was that there was another side to her. The flowers were home, but sometimes she longed for the night sky, to feel the cold wind over her skin and to escape into the darkness. To hide from the world.

"Is that all you remember?" he asked softly.

"A few more things. Burning walls. Sometimes I remember a woman who could use a sword, like me. I'm guessing that was my mum."

"A warrior woman."

"Just like me."

"Warrior women are a rarity in the Shadow Realm. Perhaps that's why Nyxobas is so interested in you."

"Maybe. Though I'm not doing much fighting here."

"It seems you have no family now."

"Nope. None that I know of."

He glanced at her. "Sleep. I will watch over you."

Her eyes began to drift closed, and as she fell asleep, she dreamt of soft grasses tickling her ankles, and air thick with humidity.

Chapter 15

The clinking of glasses jolted Ursula awake.

In the pale starlight, Cera stood over her. "It's time to get up. I've brought you breakfast."

Ursula rubbed her eyes, trying to bring the room into focus. A familiar, delicious scent wafted through the air.

"Is that...coffee?"

Cera flashed her a toothy smile. "I thought you might like some. The lord said you had a difficult night."

"You're the best." She sat up, stretching her arms above her head. She glanced around the room. Surprise flickered through her. She no longer lay on the sofa in the living room. Someone had brought her up to the bedroom while she'd slept and tucked her under the violet duvet.

"How did I get here?"

Cera dropped a flannel robe next to her on the bed. "How should I know?"

"Did Bael carry me up here? I don't remember it."

"The lord is very strong and swift. I'm sure he could have carried you while you slept." She frowned. "Are you sleeping in one of your finest gowns?"

"Bael chose it."

Smirking, Cera arched an eyebrow. "Did he, now?"

"Just—I needed something to wear. I was in my—never mind." Ursula pushed off her blanket and grabbed a cup of steaming, black coffee. She took a sip of the hot brew, letting it energize her. Beside the carafe of coffee lay a basket of warm bread and butter. Her mouth watered, and she bit into a fresh roll.

"Fill your belly," said Cera. "Then come downstairs when you're dressed in something more appropriate."

Ursula ate her way through several rolls and another cup of coffee, taking care not to get crumbs all over the bed. When she'd had her fill, she pulled off her gown and selected a simpler dress—gray cotton with a deep V neck.

As she made her way downstairs, she combed her fingers through her hair to tidy it.

In the middle of the living room, she found two oneiroi men standing next to Cera. Just outside the window, a third rode on the back of a lunar bat.

Ursula's muscles tensed. "What's going on?"

"It's only Sotz," said Cera. "He's helping with the window replacement."

Ursula nodded, staring as Sotz clutched a rope in his feet. As she moved closer to the window, she saw that a large plate of glass dangled at the other end of the rope.

At the direction of the oneiroi workmen, Sotz flew higher, lifting the glass. With a volley of shouts and frantic gestures, the men were able to maneuver the pane into the room. Ursula watched as the workmen carefully fitted the window into place, Sotz hovering just outside. The rider on Sotz's back slowly adjusted his position in a fascinating display of control.

"Ursula." Cera touched her arm. "I brought you a present."

Ursula smiled. "You did? What for?"

"Not my idea. The lord told me to give it to you. He thought it might keep you busy."

"Right. So I won't stab anyone else, presumably."

"That would be for the best." Cera scurried off toward the hall. When she returned, she carried a shiny black bag.

Ursula's eyebrows rose. *More clothes?*

"The lord said you liked to paint."

A smile curled her lips. "The lord is right."

Cera reached into the bag, pulling out brushes and tubes of paint. Lastly, she pulled out a small canvas stretched over a wooden frame. "He said if you want a larger canvas, you should let him know."

"This is such a lovely present."

"The lord provides," said Cera.

The two oneiroi workmen approached. The smaller of them met Ursula's gaze. "The window is in—airtight. The lord protected all the windows with his magic. Nothing will destroy the glass now. You're safe inside here."

"Thank you so much," she said. *Thank the gods.* She wouldn't have been able to relax in here, knowing that a man on a giant bat could shatter the glass at any moment.

As Sotz flew off outside, the two workmen left the apartment.

Cera turned back to Ursula with a mischievous grin. "The lord spent the night in your quarters."

"Not like that."

Cera's eyes widened. "He hasn't come in here in centuries. I think it's because it pains him to see the portrait."

Ursula frowned, glancing at the spot on the wall where the portrait had hung. Someone had removed it during the night. "Of the woman? Why?"

Cera's hand flew to her mouth. "I should not have spoken."

Well, now I have to know. She touched Cera's arm. "You can tell me. Who else am I going to tell? You're my only friend here."

Cera's eyes shifted frantically from side to side. She was obviously trying to decide how much she was allowed to tell Ursula.

Finally, she whispered, "The lord's wife, gods protect her soul."

Her jaw dropped. "He was married? I had no idea. Did she die in the attack?"

"No. It was long ago, long before my time. I should never have said anything." Cera backed toward the door. "It's not my place to talk about the lord's life."

Her face even paler than usual, Cera hurried out the door, slamming it behind her.

Chapter 16

On the day of the Selection of Champions, Ursula's stomach was twisted in knots. She filled the bath with warm, lavender-scented water, trying to soothe away her nerves, but one terrifying thought rang loudly in her skull.

Today, she would find out exactly who Bael had to kill.

If he failed, he'd forfeit his life. Terrifying and gruff as he might be, she didn't want him to die. And moreover, if he lost, she'd be joining him in the afterworld.

Or worse—Abrax would enslave her for an eternity of sadistic torment.

As she soaked her body in the bath, Cera's voice rang out from the living room. "Hello? Ursula?"

"In the bath!" she shouted.

"Good. You've started preparing yourself. I've brought you a new dress for the ceremony. Everything must be perfect!" she shouted. "We must help the lord by making everything perfect!"

Ursula winced at the shrill tone. *Apparently, I'm not the only one plagued by nerves.* She rose from the bath, grabbing a towel. She wrapped it around herself and then stepped into the living room.

Wearing the gray coat, Cera stood in the center of the room, her knuckles white as she clutched a box. A bag hung over one of her arms. "I have pressed the lord's clothes to perfection. He will have not a wrinkle on him before the other lords. Mortal or not, they will know his glory through his divine beauty." Her eyes were wide, slightly frantic.

Ursula held up the towel with one hand, taking the box from Cera with the other. She flashed a placating smile. The little oneiroi was losing it.

Still, Cera wasn't kidding about Bael's divine beauty, though Ursula wasn't going to admit it.

She dropped the box on a chair. "Why doesn't Bael look like a demon, like the other lords? They all have horns and creepy eyes."

"Nothing creepy about silver eyes," snapped Cera. "But as for how the lord looks, you'd do best to mind your own business. Open the box."

With one hand, Ursula pried off the top of the box. Tucked neatly inside were tiny silver knickers, and a dress of a gorgeous midnight blue, the fabric so thin and sheer it almost seemed enchanted.

"Wow," said Ursula. "This looks amazing."

She saw the beaming smile on Cera's face before the oneiroi turned around to give her privacy. "All the great ladies will be dressed in their finest clothes. I wouldn't want Abelda House to fall short."

Ursula pulled off her towel, the stepped into the lacy silver underwear. When she picked up the dress, she gasped. It was stunning—a delicate gown, dappled with silver gems around the belted waist. She pulled it over her head, and the silky fabric brushed over her thighs. Like the dress she'd worn before, a

V-neck plunged down to her belly button. The sheer fabric gathered at the waist, providing just enough coverage for her lower half. But if she extended a leg, she saw that the dress had a slit all the way up to the top of her thigh.

"Gorgeous," she said.

Cera turned, grinning. "I knew it would be perfect. It's skimpier than the ladies of the Shadow Realm wear, but you're a hellhound. Everyone will expect you to be a harlot anyway," she chirped, rifling around in her bag.

Before Ursula could come up with a retort, Cera was standing before her, wielding eyeliner. "Sit."

Ursula did as instructed, and Cera spent the next two minutes attacking her face with eye makeup, blush, and a berry lipstick. When she'd finished, she packed away the makeup, and pulled out a pair of black heels and a new cloak made of dark silver feathers that shimmered as it moved. Ursula pulled the cloak around her shoulders. She plucked the silver ring off the bar, shoving it into the cloak's pocket.

"What was that?" Cera asked suspiciously.

"Just my lucky charm. I think I might need it tonight." Her eyes flicked to the window, searching for signs of the rising sun. Dread welled in her chest.

When the sun sets over Lacus Mortis... For the finishing touch, Cera slid a sparkling silver headband onto Ursula's head. "Splendid," she purred, stepping back to admire her work.

Ursula slipped into the heels. Somehow, she felt at home in these clothes.

Cera arched a cautionary eyebrow. "My only request is that you don't destroy the clothes through bloodshed and mayhem."

Ursula grinned. "I'll do my best."

Cera scowled. "Please try to behave appropriately when you meet the lords' wives."

111

Cera tilted her head. "Do they all have wives apart from Bael?"

"Most do. It can get pretty lonely on the crater's rim."

"I've noticed, I was going to ask if there were any books I could read. I don't think I can make a shank from the pages of a novel."

Cera frowned. "A what?"

"A shank, you know, like what prisoners make to stab—" *Abort, Ursula. Abort!* "I mean, since Bael said to remove anything I could use as a weapon. Surely books are harmless."

Cera nodded slowly. "There's a library I can take you to tomorrow, if you like." She glanced at the clock. "It's time for us to leave. You can eat at the ceremony."

Ursula's stomach rumbled. The last thing she'd eaten was a soup made from those strange, glowing mushrooms.

Cera crossed over to the door, flinging it open. "Come along!"

Ursula hurried to keep up with Cera as she made her way across the windswept bridge and into the atrium. There, the elevator waited for them.

Cera gave a little bow outside the elevator. "Good luck."

Ursula pulled open the door, stepping inside. The door clicked shut. "Thank you, Cera."

As the cage rose slowly on its chain, her chest clenched. Tonight, she'd be facing all the lords again, and getting an eyeful of the champions. She didn't know what to expect, but she imagined they'd be terrifying.

She shoved her hand into the cloak's pocket, running her fingertips over the smooth silver ring. It seemed to center her.

The elevator creaked up past one flight after another of shattered glass, twisted steel beams, and layers of gray ash.

Bael was an ancient, stunningly powerful demon. And maybe he was mortal right now, but he had enough magic and brute strength on his side to fix this place up. Still, he'd chosen to leave the damage untouched.

Perhaps he wanted to leave it as a testament to his rage, fuel for his fury.

Ursula could only hope that was enough for him to win in a battle against the champions.

The elevator lifted onto the roof. Bael stood before her, the cold wind feathering a few strands of hair across his face. He pulled open the elevator door, and she stepped out.

He wore fitted black clothes with a high mandarin collar. A dark cloak—feather at the shoulders—was held together over his enormous chest with silver chains and a lion insignia.

Starlight glinted in his pale eyes.

He looked every inch the military leader. At the sight of him, hope sparked in her mind. *He looks like he can actually win this thing.*

As she stepped onto the roof, a frigid wind toyed with the hem of her dress, lifting it into the air. The delicate fabric floated in the breeze.

"You look..." he said, his gaze trailing down to her leg, exposed in the breeze. "Exactly as you should."

That... might be a compliment. "And how is it that I should look?"

"Stunning."

A blush warmed her cheeks. "Thank you. It's nice to see you in some clothes, after you were traipsing around in your smalls all night."

Bael's mouth twitched with the hint of a smile before he lifted his fingers to whistle for the carriage.

The faintest hint of purple stained the sky, and she shuddered, watching as the team of bats whisked the carriage before the moon.

Ursula bit her lip. "So am I to be subservient again, or do I get to act on my own volition this evening?"

With a gentle scraping noise, the carriage landed on the rooftop.

Bael's jaw tensed. "You must act subservient. All the women are, and you mustn't draw attention to yourself."

Of course they are. She heaved a deep sigh, fighting the urge to ask him about his wife. Even in the painting, the determined look in the woman's eye told Ursula she had never been subservient.

Bael pulled open the carriage door, and she stepped inside.

"Can you tell me what to expect tonight?" she asked.

Bael climbed in, sitting across from her. "As you wish. We're going to the hall of lords. There will be a feast. The lords will choose their champions, apart from me, of course. Hothgar will announce the rules of the melee. Then we will leave. Hopefully alive."

Well, that inspires confidence.

"Do I get a dagger again?"

One of Bael's eyebrows rose. "After last time? No. Absolutely not."

She rubbed the solid ring in her pocket. "You're going to leave me entirely unprotected, then. And if Abrax decides he wants to get me alone—"

"I'll protect you."

"You said I don't deserve your protection."

He winced. "I will protect you," he said again.

She leaned forward, studying him. "Why don't you choose me as your champion?"

Surprise flickered across his features, his eyes widening. "Why in the name of the dark god would I do that?"

"The other lords have better odds with five champions each. You've only got one. If I fight with you, it doubles our chances of winning, right?"

He shook his head. "You misunderstand. There will only be one left alive at the end," he said. "None of the other champions will be left alive by the end of the tournament. I would have to kill you."

She swallowed hard. "You're injured. I could take your place, then. I may have a better chance than you."

His eyes bored into her. "Don't be absurd."

Maybe he has a point. She might be pretty good with a sword, but she was no match for someone who'd been fighting for twenty-two thousand years. And moreover, she lacked a weapon and her firepower.

His eyes darkened. "Tell me you won't call attention to yourself this evening. That you won't attack anyone."

"I can see you're still upset about the kerfuffle with Nyxobas."

"Tell me."

"Fine. I'll do what you say." *Within reason.*

Chapter 17

The carriage plunged lower and lower through the air, and Ursula gripped the seat to steady herself. They were descending all the way to where Asta met the crater floor.

With a lurch, the carriage touched down on a rocky avenue.

She peered out the window at a long line of carriages. As the bats inched forward slowly on their claws, Ursula gazed out at the desolate lunar landscape. Apart from Asta's violet light, darkness shrouded the land. Deep fissures cut into the stone around the base of the spire.

Their carriage slowly pulled forward to a covered entrance, and two footmen in gray jackets hurried out to open their door.

Bael stepped out, holding open the door for her. He offered her his hand as she stepped out.

Ever the gentleman.

This close to the ground, Asta's crystal was a deep mulberry, the color of a bruise. Above them, gray clouds of moths swirled and danced, blotting out the stars.

"This way," said Bael.

A walkway, lit by glowing mushrooms, led to the arched entrance. Ursula walked by Bael's side, rubbing the silver ring between her fingers.

Through the doorway, she stepped into an enormous hall, carved from the purple crystal. The walls arched at least two hundred feet above them, and great clusters of glowing mushrooms hung from the ceiling like chandeliers. Long, onyx tables, populated by demons filled much of the hall. An open space had been left in the center, like a dance floor. By Bael's side, she walked further into the center of the hall.

At the far end of the massive room, a single table stood on a dais. Eleven lords sat at the table, proudly enthroned in silver chairs. Abrax glared at her, licking his lips, and a shudder ran up her spine. No one here seemed to know or care that he'd tried to overthrow the entire Shadow Realm. Apparently, losing your wings was unforgivable, but a full-fledged divine coup was okay, assuming you were a demigod.

In the center of the table, in the largest chair, sat Hothgar. A gavel lay on the table before him.

Ursula frowned. *That should be Bael's spot.* Until Abrax had stolen his wings, Bael was Nyxobas's Sword, the most senior of all the lords.

Ursula looked at the whorls of shadow magic behind the table. *Nyxobas.* Behind the powerful clouds of magic, she'd nearly missed him. He sat in a silver throne, half-shrouded by writhing shadows. As a swirl of magic cleared, his eyes—two dark abysses—seemed to stare right at her. At the sight of him, dread tightened its grip on her heart.

A small oneiroi hurried up to them.

"Milord," she said with a deep bow to Bael before turning to Ursula. Her eyes trailed down to Ursula's dress, and the shockingly sheer fabric that hung below her cloak. The oneiroi scowled, then plastered a smile on her face once again. "Please follow me, milady. The lord will be seated at the table of nobles."

Ursula looked to Bael for help, but he was already moving toward the dais, leaving her behind.

"Right this way," the oneiroi chirped, beckoning her forward.

Ursula took a deep breath. *Let's do this.*

She quickened her pace to keep up with the oneiroi, who navigated between the sea of demons, seated at the tables. Some appeared entirely human—and shockingly beautiful. Others sported more demonic features: horns, talons, or even eyes the color of blood. And yet they were beautiful in their own ways, too. Men with chiseled features, women in glittering gowns, their bodies lithe and delicate. Since arriving here not long ago and spending time with Cera, her definition of beauty seemed to be expanding.

She surveyed the guests—gowns of dusky purple, midnight blue, or shimmering black seemed to be the favored colors. Some women had jewels threaded into their hair, and many of the men wore dark suits with silver accents.

And each one of the demons stared at Ursula as she passed their tables.

Obviously, word had spread about her presence. The hellhound harlot. *Wait till they see the whole dress.*

Avoiding their stares, Ursula followed the oneiroi deeper into the hall, closer to the platform. Finally the oneiroi stopped, and gestured to an empty chair at a long table, filled with female demons sporting totally demonic features: horns, talons, white eyes, sharp teeth. All beautiful. All dripping with diamonds. And all staring right at her.

The oneiroi pulled out a chair by a striking woman whose jet-black hair tumbled over a white gown.

"Your seat, milady." The oneiroi held out a hand. "May I take your cloak?"

Ursula unclasped the cloak, pulling it off. Before she handed it to the oneiroi, she snatched the silver ring from her pocket.

As the other women took in Ursula's daring gown, they gasped audibly.

Ursula's shoulders tensed. *That's me. The hellhound harlot.* She rubbed the ring between her fingers.

She tried to force what she imagined was a pleasant expression onto her face and sat down next to the raven-haired woman. Immediately to the right of her sat a striking woman with flowing black hair. Her skin was so pale, it could have been carved from marble or alabaster. Ursula almost mistook her for human until she glimpsed a flash of sharp fangs. *A goth princess.*

To Ursula's left sat a woman in a dark blue dress. Two long blond braids draped over her formidable bosom—appropriately covered in opaque fabric. *Unlike my gown.* But what most drew Ursula's eye were the delicately curled horns growing from the woman's forehead. Their tips had been capped with gold. Overall, she looked like some kind of terrifying Viking.

As Ursula sat, the women turned away from her. Her eyes flicked up to the dais, and she watched Bael take his seat at the end of the nobles' table. It must really irk him to watch Hothgar steal his role as Sword.

The goth princess raised a delicate white arm. "So who will be joining the pool?"

Around the table, the demonesses began plucking off their jewelry, tossing them onto a plate in the center of the table—enormous diamonds, black opals, and deep violet gemstones so rare, Ursula didn't even know what to call them.

Her eyes widened. There, on a silver plate in the center of the table, lay a pile of carelessly discarded jewels that were probably worth more than the GDP of a small nation.

Goth Princess rubbed her hands together. "Is everyone clear on the rules?"

The Viking raised a hand. "The one who picks the winner gets the whole pot. Yes?"

Goth Princes sighed. "No, a quarter of the pot goes to whomever chooses the most finalists in the melee, a quarter goes to the one who picks the winner of the race, and the remaining half goes to whomever picks the winner of the duels."

The Viking grinned. "This is going to be so exciting. We haven't had a proper tournament in ages."

A woman whose silver hair tumbled over a black gown narrowed her eyes at Ursula. She drummed long, pearly talons on the table. "Did you want to join the pool, hellhound?" The woman's eyes were nearly as pale as her skin, framed by black lashes. "You'll have to contribute if you want to join."

Ursula tried to flash a friendly smile. She knew how rich, glamorous chicks worked. They were perfectly happy to be your best friend, as long as you never threatened to outshine them. *Best to be humble in this crowd.* "I'm afraid I have nothing of value to offer."

Talons nodded approvingly.

The Viking's brow furrowed. "So what do we do about Bael?"

"What about him?" asked Goth Princess.

Viking cocked her head. "He's already won a tournament before. He's older than the rest. I don't think it's fair to pick him for the final winner."

The princess nodded. "Excellent point. Can we all agree to leave the Lord of Albelda off the ballot, mortal as he might be?"

Around the table, the women nodded. No one wanted to annoy Goth Princess.

Viking flicked one of her braids behind her shoulders. "I still can't believe that he lost his house. Such a shame. From what I understand, he was the only one of the lords who actually knew how to pleasure a woman."

"Not that his skill in bed made a difference." Talons sighed, eying Ursula. "He was never going to marry again. I believe he never quite got over Elissa."

Viking's eyes widened. "I heard one of Borgerith's ogres ripped his wings out. Two millennia, and he was felled by an idiot ogre."

Ursula's chest clenched. *It was Abrax, you twats. Abrax ruined him.*

Goth Princess took a sip of champagne. "I'm not sure it was a wise decision for Nyxobas to appoint him Sword in the first place. You all know his background, I'm sure." She let her dark eyes wander to Ursula. "He was bound to snap at some point."

Ursula's face heated. *This arsehole knows he hasn't told me about his background. She is throwing some serious demon shade.*

The princess cocked her head, staring right at Ursula. "Bael might be a legendary warrior, but he's broken inside. Always has been."

They all nodded, then clinked their glasses in some kind of fucked-up toast.

Please get me out of here. She was quickly getting the impression that it was going to be *very* difficult to get through the night without hurting someone. For Bael's sake, she kept her mouth shut.

Viking stroked one of her braids. "Worst of all, my husband lost a third of his legion trying to drive Bael from his manor."

Goth Princess twirled the delicate stem of her glass between her fingers. "A travesty we weren't successful. Bael should have been sent to the void months ago—"

A loud banging from the dais interrupted her. All heads turned as Hothgar slammed his hammer down again, his eyes flicking to the Viking for just a moment.

"Tonight, the lords select their champions to determine who is worthy of Abelda mansion," he roared. "But now, it is time to feast!"

Chapter 18

A crew of oneiroi waiters bustled into the hall, carrying silver platters laden with food. A waiter pushed one of the trays between Ursula and Goth Princess, and her gaze slid to the roasted meat, seasoned with rosemary and garlic. *At least they know how to eat here.*

Her mouth watered at the sight of meat and potatoes—and the bowls of luminescent mushroom soup.

The waiter placed a bowl in front of Ursula, and she breathed in the rich, earthy scent. It looked terrifying, but smelled amazing, and her mouth was already watering. As he dropped a bowl before Goth Princess, he leaned in to ask, "Would you like bottle of wine for the table?"

Goth Princess's lip curled back from her fangs, and she snarled, "Would you like a bottle of wine for the table, *milady*."

The waiter nodded frantically, avoiding eye contact. "Milady, I'm sorry—"

"Stop talking and fill my glass," she snapped.

"Of course, milady."

Ursula glared at her. *Wanker.* Too bad there would be no tournament between the women of this table.

Ursula focused all her energy on keeping her mouth shut. A waiter bustled around the table, slicing up the meat and serving it on plates. Ursula waited until Goth Princess began cutting into her food and then followed suit. The meat tasted as delicious as it smelled. Roast beef maybe? It wasn't ham, she was certain.

Viking raised her hand, snapping her fingers at one of the waiters. She pointed to her plate. "Is it from Nyxobas's stables?"

The waiter bowed. "Yes, milady. Strictly moth-fed around Asta, no supplements or additives."

Ursula stopped mid-chew, her stomach turning. "What kind of meat is this?"

The waiter bowed again. "Milady, it's bat-shoulder. Just slaughtered this afternoon." He flashed a proud smile.

She swallowed the lump of flesh in her mouth. *Maybe I'll just stick to the mushroom soup.*

She lifted a spoonful into her mouth, savoring the woodsy, garlicky flavor. *Perfect.*

She tried not to stare at Viking, who ripped through the bat-shoulder with the terrifying ferocity of a pit bull. *Maybe it's for the best we're not part of a tournament.*

Talons leaned across the table, her eyes locked on Goth Princess. "How was your vacation on Earth?"

"Glorious. We rented a little cottage on a private atoll in the Maldives. The water was amazing—beautiful night swimming. The locals were delicious."

"I'm so jealous," Viking cut in. "Hothgar's idea of romance is drinking five pints of blood and asking me to watch him rut with a human in a hayloft. He likes to control their minds, you know. Make them supplicate themselves before him. He makes them call him Nyxobas and praise his lunar staff."

"We know," said Talons. "The entire Shadow Realm knows."

Goth Princess shrugged. "Abrax does that, too. It's just what demon males do. Especially incubi, of course. He can't get enough of his little human playthings."

"I hate Hothgar," muttered Viking. "The last time he showed me any affection was our claiming ceremony. But it isn't a woman's place to complain to a husband. At least, not to his face."

"All demons want to dominate humans," said Goth Princess. She turned to Ursula. "You're basically human. I mean, you're a mortal demon. You have no powers here in the Shadow Realm."

Ursula paused, mid-spoonful. "What, now?"

"We know you're here to be someone's whore." Talons poked a finger in her face. "Is it Bael? Are you his consolation prize for the loss of his wings and his manor?"

Ursula cringed. "Can we go back to when you were ignoring me?"

Goth Princess narrowed her eyes. "What depraved things has he been making you do in that ruined manor of his?" She licked her fangs. "He is quite gorgeous, so I'm not sure that I'd mind if I were you."

Talons licked the soup off one of her curled claws. "He is reputed to be an amazing lover, you know. Not like Hogarth. Long ago, he was worshipped as a god in his home country. It could be worse for you."

Ursula frowned, and she glanced at Bael on the dais, sitting silently by the other lords. "I have no idea what you're talking about. He's a perfect gentleman."

Viking snorted. "You're an idiot. They don't exist."

Talons raised her champagne flute, smiling. "Demon males view all women as their property and playthings. And when it comes to weak little human women, that goes double. You're here as a harlot, my dear. We all know that."

Ursula could feel her face heating from anger. Just as she was about to indulge in a tirade, Hothgar banged his gavel from the dais.

"It is time to begin the Selection of the Champions. We will start with the most junior lords." He turned to the lord furthest from him, a cloaked man with milky-white skin and eyes like black pearls.

Hothgar raised his gavel. "Lord Vepar. you may nominate your five."

Vepar stood and spoke in a firm voice. "I nominate Inth from my legion."

A lanky demon in a full suit of silver armor entered from a side entrance, gripping a long spear. He strode into the empty space in the center of the hall, then bowed deeply toward the dais.

"Inth of the Vepar Legion. May Nyxobas grant you the grace of a shadow and the strength of a warrior."

As Inth finished bowing, inky tendrils of magic lifted from his body, curling toward Nyxobas.

"What is that?" asked Ursula.

"His immortality," said Talons. "It's not much of a fight to the death if no one can die."

"He'll get it back if he wins," said the Viking. "Except, he won't win."

His voice booming through the hall, Lord Vepar nominated the rest of his champions—all enormous men, shielded in silver armor.

Without seeing them fight, she couldn't quite gauge their prowess. Somehow, none of them seemed quite as formidable as Bael, but you couldn't always tell just by looking at someone. Some skinny men were just psychotic enough to put up a terrifying fight. In London, she'd once seen a slender Millwall F.C. fan bite the ear off a man in a Chelsea Football Club shirt.

Hothgar called upon one lord after another to nominate their five, and Ursula stared at the stream of muscled champions filling the center of the hall with a growing sense of dread. *Bael must kill all of them. He must cut through each warrior, and he's not even at full strength.*

Her panic only worsened as Hothgar called on the senior champions, whose warriors grew in stature. One—a near giant—sent trembles over the floor as he walked.

When Hothgar reached Bileth—the Demon-Bull— he paused for just a moment. "Lord Bileth. Are you prepared to nominate a champion?"

"I am," said Bileth, his deep voice filling the room. "I nominate my son, Sallos."

An enormous beast of a demon strode into the center of the room. Like his father, his white skin had an almost bluish tinge. He wore only a white fur kilt about his waist, revealing a muscled torso. In one hand, he gripped a massive axe. Ursula's stomach flipped. His weapon was as least five feet long, with a head of blue steel. She'd never seen Bael wield a weapon like that.

"Congratulations, Sallos. May Nyxobas—"

A door slammed open at the other end of the hall, cutting off Hothgar. Completely dressed in gray cloth, a stranger strode through the hall. A scarf covered most of his face, apart from a thin slit for his eyes. The entire hall stared.

"What is this interruption?" Hothgar bellowed.

He strode into the center of the hall, taking his place among the champions. "I wish to compete in the tournament." His scarf slightly muffled his voice, but his words were clear nonetheless.

"Who are you and on what grounds do you claim the chance to compete for Bael's manor?" roared Hothgar, rising from his chair. His cheeks had reddened, and fury sparked in his eyes.

"This tournament is only open to the champions of the lords of Nyxobas."

"I am not a member of a lord's legion," said the intruder. "But by the law of the warrior, I request the chance to challenge a champion. I will take another's position." He turned to Sallos. "If there are any here brave enough to take on this challenge."

Before Hothgar could respond, Sallos raised his axe. "I accept."

Sallos circled the stranger, swinging the massive axe around his head like a drum major's baton. Ursula held her breath. The intruder didn't even have a weapon. What was he thinking? As Sallos neared striking range, the stranger dodged back. Sallos lifted his axe to strike, but the stranger dodged again.

"Fight me, you coward," Sallos shouted.

The stranger remained silent.

Sallos continued circling, thrusting, striking—while his opponent weaved and dodged, just out of reach.

Fascinated, Ursula stared. She had a perfect view of the fight from here. She could see the sheen of sweat on Sallos's forehead, but he continued to press his advantage.

From the lords' table, Hothgar called out, "You won't win by the grace of your dancing. A challenge can only be settled with blood."

A few of the lords chuckled. Apparently that comment passed for a joke in the Shadow Realm.

Dodging another strike, the intruder leapt backwards in a perfect backflip. When he landed, he'd deftly produced two daggers, one in each hand.

Ursula's throat tightened. *Bloody hell. He may be small, but he's agile as a gymnast.*

Sallos didn't seem to understand the threat. He threw back his head, laughing. "You think you're going to hurt me with those children's toys?"

The stranger merely stared at him, gripping his daggers.

Sallos advanced again, swinging the ax in great curving arcs. As he closed in on the intruder, he drove him closer to Ursula's table—so close, she could actually hear the whoosh of Sallos's blade as it sliced the air. She turned in her chair, her eyes locked on the fight.

When the stranger stood only a few feet away, he dodged toward Ursula. His foot caught on the fabric of her dress, tearing it. Her heart jumped into her throat as she watched the intruder fall to the floor. *Please don't die because of my dress.*

Instantly, Sallos charged, thundering at the fallen man like a bull at a toreador. Lifting the axe above his head, he prepared to strike the coup de grâce. But as the axe descended, the stranger rolled away.

He dodged the swing. Then, with a perfectly timed stroke, he slashed at Sallos's foot.

Sallos's face reddened, and he bellowed in pain. He spun to face his assailant, but the stranger was already on his feet, already out of reach.

Sallos charged forward, but stumbled as his foot gave way. His axe flailed wildly.

The stranger circled behind him, then dove for the floor, slashing at Sallos's other foot with his blade. Ursula cringed at the audible snap of a severed a tendon.

The stranger had crippled him.

Sallos fell to his knees with a bellow of pain. He gripped his battle axe, glaring at the stranger, eyes red with rage. "Come fight me like a man," he bellowed.

Ursula knew the fight was over, even if Sallos didn't.

The stranger circled him slowly. Sallos tried to lunge for him, but the stranger merely sidestepped behind him. In a flash of steel, the stranger's blade severed the sinews in the back of the Sallos's knee. The demon howled, fear and rage tearing from his throat. He twisted his body, trying to keep the stranger in front of him, but the stranger was faster. With a lightning-fast strike, the intruder slashed through the other knee.

Sallos fell forward, crashing on his face with a boom that shook the hall.

Around Ursula, the demons in the hall sucked in a collective gasp. Sallos rolled on the ground, trying to get away—but the stranger was too fast. In one strike, he carved a gash across Sallos's chest. With another, he severed the ligaments in the demon's wrist. He worked his way around the demon, hacking through tendons, until Sallos lay immobile and trembling on the floor.

Defeated and bloody, Sallos opened his mouth and howled.

The stranger straightened, bowing to Hothgar. "I have defeated him."

Hothgar rose. "And yet he lives."

The stranger shrugged. "He is immobilized."

Bileth's nostrils flared, and angry black magic sliced the air around him. With a deafening roar, the lord leapt over the table and charged. For a moment, Ursula expected him to attack the stranger.

Instead, he snatched his son's battled axe.

Ursula watched in horror as he raised the axe above his head. He brought it down in a ferocious strike, crushing his son's skull with a sickening crunch of bone.

Chapter 19

*B*ileth lifted the axe from the brain-spattered floor, his face contorted with rage. Turning to face the stranger, he spoke through gritted teeth. "I will have my vengeance."

Lord Bileth turned, striding out of the room.

Ursula was just about ready to vomit her mushroom soup all over the table. *Maybe I'm not really cut out to be a warrior.* She didn't want to live in a world where fathers smashed in their sons' skulls.

Trying to calm herself, she rubbed the silver ring between her fingers.

After a long pause, the hall erupted with thunderous applause. The stranger bowed deeply.

And when the hall quieted again, Hothgar spoke. "Congratulations. May you fight well in the melee."

The stranger in gray nodded. Without saying another word, he turned and left. As he disappeared through the doors, the hall erupted into a chorus of chatter.

Next to her, Ursula heard Viking say, "I'd like to change my bid—"

At the table of the lords, Hothgar banged his gavel. Around him, the demon lords called for order. Hothgar stood until it was quiet enough to speak.

"I'm glad you all enjoyed the unexpected show, but we have more champions to present. Who will be the champion for the Legion of Abrax?"

Abrax rose. His icy gaze flicked to Ursula for a moment before he spoke. "I nominate Massu from my legion."

Ursula's throat went dry. *Massu. Cera's brother. The little boy with the spaceship drawings, who always wanted to be a lord.*

On the plus side, she hadn't killed him.

On the downside, one of these champions certainly would.

As the hall waited, a tiny oneiroi man entered the hall. Dressed in tight leather armor, he carried no weapon. As he walked, he drew his lips back in a snarl, revealing his razor-sharp teeth. His whole body twitched with nervous energy.

Hothgar pointed. "What in the seven hells is that?"

Abrax folded his hands behind his head. "My champion."

"He's an oneiroi," shouted Hothgar. "He cannot be a lord."

Abrax shrugged. "That is not an actual law, I think you'll find. Merely tradition. And you know how I feel about tradition." He leaned forward, his glacial gaze on the oneiroi. "Show them what you can do, Massu."

Massu leapt on Sallos's body. With a quick flip of his head, he ripped the skin from the Sallos's chest.

Around Ursula, the women gasped.

"Oh my," said Goth Princess.

Massu held the flesh between his teeth, bowing deeply.

Bile climbed up Ursula's throat. *So much for the sweet little boy.*

"So be it," said Hothgar. He stared at the oneiroi soldier. "Congratulations, Massu. May Nyxobas grant you strength."

Hothgar had begun to lift his gavel when Bael rose.

"I would like to present a champion," said Bael, his voice booming off the ceiling.

Ursula took in his massive form, his perfect, chiseled features. He was powerful. She knew that. But she didn't want him anywhere near these maniacs.

"Right, I almost forgot." Contempt laced Hothgar's voice. "Who will fight for the house of Albelda?"

Bael looked out at the crowd. "I will be defend Albelda myself. And I will win."

"Congratulations, Bael." Hothgar waved a dismissive hand. "May Nyxobas grant you the strength of a warrior." He mumbled the last part.

"He already has." Bael returned to his seat.

Ursula sipped her champagne, and Hothgar called upon one lord after another to nominate their second set of champions. By the time the lords had moved on to the fifth round of selections, Ursula had a pretty good buzz going.

Finally, Hothgar banged his gavel to signal the end of the ceremony. His voice boomed, "The champions have been chosen. There will be three trials: a melee, a race, and the duels. The melee begins when the sun sets at the Lacus Mortis, in nine hours. The challengers will fight until half remain."

Bloody hell.

Around Ursula, the women clapped, and cheers filled the hall. The lords rose, smiling and clapping one another on the back. Except for Bael, who stood to the side, his expression grim. Ursula shivered. *My fate is now truly in his hands.*

She rubbed her arms. Even with a buzz from the champagne, the hall was freezing—shadow demons didn't seem to care for heat.

Just as she was about to rise, she noticed that the hall had quieted again, and the air around her thinned. She glanced at the women, who all stared straight at the dais. At Nyxobas. Suddenly, she felt completely sober.

The chill in the room deepened. Shadow magic whorled from the god, and a hollow ache rose in Ursula's chest.

Slowly, the god opened his eyes. They shone a bright silver now. As Ursula stared at him, she could feel the void calling to her. She felt as if she was standing at the edge of a precipice, gazing into a dark abyss.

She closed her eyes for a moment, and a vision rose in her mind. She stood at the edge of the void, her body trembling with fear. But what scared her wasn't that she was going to fall in.

What scared her was that she wanted to jump.

Her eyes snapped open again, and she stared into the icy silver of Nyxobas's eyes. She'd seen those eyes in her dreams, even before she'd met him. *Why?*

"I will also be nominating a champion," he intoned. His voice sent a shudder of dread up her spine.

Hothgar bowed deeply. "Of course."

Nyxobas's eyes locked on Ursula, and cold dread spread through her chest. That piercing gaze, the face of her nightmares. And suddenly, she knew what was coming. *Nyxobas will be my death.* As he stared at her, terror stole her breath.

"No," she whispered.

His pale gaze locked on her, and he boomed, "The hound will be my champion."

"What will be her reward?" asked Hothgar. "A hound of Emerazel cannot be a lord."

"If she wins, I will release her from my service."

"And if she loses?" asked Hothgar.

"She will share the same fate as all defeated. She will join me in the void."

Chapter 20

Ursula traced her fingertips over the ring in her cloak pocket, staring out the carriage window. They flew over the barren landscape—small oneiroi houses mixed with the remains of meteor impacts. Asta's glow cast them in violet light, while above, clouds of moths swirled and danced. If she looked carefully, she could occasionally see the black form of a bat winging among them.

A bat among the moths.

On the other side of the carriage, Bael sat mute, his face fixed with a stony expression. She couldn't tell what he was thinking, but she could guess. Since he was a gentleman—despite what the other women said—he was probably considering the most painless way to kill her in the melee. A quick slash of his sword through her neck, perhaps.

Her chest tightened. *What I need is a plan. An escape route. A way to survive.*

And if not, I need to know exactly what I'm up against.

"So how did you win it?" she asked.

Bael's sapphire gaze slid to her. "Win what?"

"The tournament. When you became a lord, how did you do it?" *Give me a bloody clue, at least.*

A perplexed line appeared between his eyebrows. "I won by being the best fighter. And the strongest."

Well, that's unhelpful. "Can you, you know, provide some specifics? How did you survive the melee?"

"I killed any man who came near me." His eyes were cold as glacier water. "The same way I will survive this one."

"So you think you can kill him?"

"Him?"

"The man in gray. The one who killed Sallos."

"Sallos was weak, and a fool. The stranger will be no match for me."

She arched an eyebrow. "Even with your injuries?"

A muscle worked in his jaw. Even obliquely mentioning his lost wings seemed to set him off.

Time to change the subject. "Has anyone else ever survived? I mean, has there been more than one left alive at the end of a tournament?"

"You ask me if anyone has violated Nyxobas's edict? No, the penalty of defying the god's orders is death."

"Hothgar set the rules."

"Hothgar speaks for Nyxobas. It is the same punishment." He turned back to the window, lost in his own thoughts.

She bit her lip. Hadn't the wives said that Bael could use mind control on humans? And if so—did she count as a human? She didn't have her demon magic here. If that were the case, he could just compel her to stab herself. The fight would be over.

"I guess the other women know I'm not here as your harlot now," she muttered.

"What?" he snapped, suddenly alert.

"The lords' wives believed that's why I was here. A consolation prize for you. Apparently their husbands have some kinky desire to mind control human women. They were certain you were the same."

He stared at her, his expression unreadable.

"Could you, if you wanted? Use mind control on me?"

"I won't."

She let out a long breath. "Okay, so that's one of my fears allayed. But there's the matter of me not having a weapon."

Bael leaned forward in his chair and looked her straight in the face.

"I won't control your mind. But it won't matter. You are not going to survive this tournament, whether or not you have a sword." His words slid through her bones. "If one of the other champions doesn't kill you, I will." He looked out the window again, his jaw clenched tight.

Descending in the elevator should have come as a relief as Ursula neared the comfort of her quarters. But instead, with each passing level, it was as if an increasingly heavy weight pressed on her chest.

The full implications of her new role as Nyxobas's champion were awful to contemplate. A fight to the death—one she had no chance of winning. In order to survive, she'd have to slaughter Cera's brother, the stranger in gray, and a horde of lethal demons. If, by some miracle, none of them killed her, she'd have to face Bael, a twenty-two thousand-year-old demon.

Panic tightened its grip on her heart. *I'm going to die in this barren place, my soul sent to the crushing isolation of Nyxobas's void. For the rest of eternity.* A painful ache gnawed at her chest.

When the elevator finally opened, she turned, heading away from her quarters. Clutching the silver ring in her pocket, she strode toward the water portal, where she'd first arrived. *It's time I get the fuck out of here.* If Nyxobas wanted to kill her, he could do it in New York.

She pushed through the black door into the semicircular portal room, hurrying over to the portal. Starlight reflected off the water's surface. She pulled off her cloak, dropping it on the floor. In the next second, she'd pulled off the dress and slipped off her knickers. The cold air in the portal room raised goosebumps on her skin, and her teeth chattered.

She kicked off her shoes. In a few moments, she'd be back in her flat. She'd call Zee and tell her the whole story over a bottle of wine. Then she'd call up Emerazel and explain the situation. The goddess would quickly realize that Nyxobas had been breaking their terms, and all would be settled. Emerazel hadn't sent her here to die.

She dipped a toe into the frigid water, hugging herself for warmth. *I just need the spell that Cera used...*

Her stomach swooped. *The Forgotten Arsholes ripped all the magical knowledge from my brain.*

She clamped her eyes shut, trying to remember a single Angelic word.

Nothing.

She kicked the water in frustration, splashing the marble.

Behind her, a deep voice echoed off the ceiling. "What are you doing?"

Dread coiled around her. *So much for my plan.*

She looked over her shoulder. Bael stood in the doorway, completely avoiding looking at her.

"I was trying to escape. I'm sure you understand why, what with the certain death you promised me."

"It won't work."

"I know. Those stupid Forgotten Twats stole all my magical knowledge."

"It wouldn't matter if you remembered the spell. The spell requires Nyxobas's permission. No one enters or leaves the Shadow Realm without his approval."

She took a deep breath, teeth chattering. *Bollocks. No escape.* Grief welled in her chest, and she choked down a sob. Maybe all the lords' wives thought she was a whore, but she had some dignity. She wasn't going stand here naked and sobbing in front of Bael.

She would stand there naked and sniffling though, apparently. "Why has everything been forgiven with Abrax? He tried to overthrow the entire Shadow Realm. He's the whole reason you're in this predicament."

"He is Nyxobas's son. And the god respects brutality. Abrax demonstrated plenty of that when he tried to overthrow the kingdom."

"So that's it? It was violent enough that Nyxobas isn't mad anymore?"

She heard a long exhale from Bael. "That, and I think Nyxobas feels guilty for what he did to his son."

A shiver made its way up her spine. "What did he do?"

"It's not important right now. I can hear your teeth chattering."

"I'm going to put on my dress."

"That's for the best."

She leaned over, snatching the dress from the ground. "I suppose you still won't tell me anything about the opponents we must face, because my death is certain anyway."

"The man in gray," he said. "He may be someone known as the Gray Ghost."

"Gray Ghost?"

"No one knows who he is. Only that he rides a white bat."

Still shivering, she turned to face Bael. "The man who broke the window. He was riding a white bat." She bit her lip. "Pretty sure he was wearing gray, too."

He stared at her. "Why didn't you say so?"

"I didn't know it was important."

"Every detail is important."

She glanced down at her dress, torn at the hem by the Gray Ghost. She'd ruined every dress Cera had given her.

At the thought of Cera, a lump rose in her throat. "We need to tell Cera about Massu."

"I was on my way to tell her when I saw you."

"Sorry about the...the nudity." She had no idea why she felt the need to apologize.

Bael slipped back into the shadows. "Return to your quarters at once. You'll be warm and safe there. At least, until the melee."

Chapter 21

$\mathscr{B}$ack in her quarters, Ursula curled up in her usual spot on the sofa. With the slowly rising sun staining the sky a bright purple, fear tightened its grip on her heart. She had about five hours until someone bashed her skull in.

She'd spent her last five hours staring at Asta, the palace of nightmares. The view of the crater no longer seemed so starkly beautiful. Now Asta's shimmering spire and the clouds of moths only reminded her of the danger the day held for her. In eight hours, when red tinged the sky, she would be in a fight for her life, thousands of miles from home.

She curled up, pulling her blanket tightly around her shoulder. And when she slept, she dreamt of Bael, standing over her with a silver sword, ready to strike.

It must have been only a few hours when Cera tapped her on the shoulder. "Ursula?"

"Mmmmghh." Ursula started her morning eye rubbing routine, but stopped when she saw Cera's face. The oneiroi's eyes were raw, her hair looked like a bird's nest.

"I guess Bael spoke to you."

"The lord told me about Massu. And you. I couldn't sleep."

Ursula sat up, the memories of the ceremony crashing down

on her. Tears stung her eyes. "There must be some way for us to get through this.

Cera shook her head. "No one violates Nyxobas's edicts." She lifted a shopping bag from the floor, her jaw fixed with resolve. "Still. I won't have you appear in front of the melee looking a mess."

Ursula frowned. "This hardly seems like the time to bring me a dress."

"It's not a dress. I'm tired of you destroying my outfits. Besides, a dress wouldn't be appropriate for the melee." She tossed the bag to Ursula. "Try it on."

Ursula peered inside at the folded pile of midnight-black leather.

"What did you make me?" Ursula stood, pulling out a pair of black leather trousers, a leather corset—reinforced with steel. A leather jacket—also reinforced. And to top it off, thigh-high boots, stitched with a dozen knife-sheaths.

Despite everything she was about to face, a smile curled Ursula's lips. "This is amazing."

"I thought you'd like it."

It took only a few minutes for Ursula to zip up in the figure-hugging black leather. It fit her like a glove, and had pockets—where she could store her new lucky charm. That little ring she'd pilfered from Bael.And more importantly, she felt like she could fight in this. "You're amazing, Cera." She leaned down, hugging the oneiroi.

"You'd better not hurt Massu," Cera cautioned. "Or I'm taking it all back." Cera wrung her hands. Confusion clouded her features. "I mean, I know both of you can't live, and the lord... I just don't want to see you all hurt each other. And maybe you're right. Maybe if you live long enough, there will be some way out of this. Just make it through the melee alive, okay?"

Ursula clamped a hand on her shoulder. "I will. And we will figure something out. Maybe a loophole…" Her voice trailed off. Nyxobas probably didn't give a fuck about loopholes. "Anyway, thank you so much for making this outfit. I'll try really hard not to trash it."

Cera folded her arms. "Even you couldn't trash it. The leather stitching is triply reinforced, and the leather lined with a thin sheet of steel. And that reminds me." She snatched the bag off the floor, plucking out a knife. "It's not much, but I wanted to give you this."

Ursula took it from her, a smile brightening her face. "Finally. A real weapon."

"I believe it's what you call a shiv," added Cera.

Ursula held it up to the light. The blade, black as the void, had been carved from stone. She let out a low whistle. *Gorgeous.*

She examined the lethal tip. "What's it made of?"

"Obsidian. Be careful with it. It's very sharp."

Ursula rubbed her thumb over the hilt. It was perfectly weighted. "Did you make it?"

Cera shook her head. "No. It's been in the family for generations. When Nyxobas and his henchmen first arrived one hundred millennia ago, his demons confiscated all the onerois' metal weapons. Fortunately, their spells can't distinguish between your average moon rock and a knapped blade."

Ursula slid the dagger into one of the sheaths in her boots. Straightening, she felt a certain confidence return. *At least I have a weapon, tiny as it might be.*

Already, her nerves were buzzing with adrenaline. She shot a panicked glance at the window. When the sun began to rise here, it would be setting on the other side of the moon. "Is it time?"

"Yes. I'll be taking you to Lacus Mortis."

"I'm not going in the carriage?"

"No. The lord is taking the carriage. We will be traveling by bat. Sotz is waiting outside. It is time."

"Right." Her stomach fluttering, she glanced at the sky again, certain it was brightening.

Never before had the concept of sunrise seemed so soul-crushingly terrifying.

Sotz was waiting for them on the bridge, his feet clutching the railing. His beady eyes blinked as they approached.

"Turn around," Cera commanded.

Slowly, Sotz rotated his body until his rear faced them. As she had in New York, Cera mounted his saddle at the shoulders, and Ursula clambered on the back.

Cera turned to face her. "Take this," she said, passing Ursula a black ribbon. "Tie it around your mane of hair to keep it out of your face."

"Thanks." *What I wouldn't do for a helmet right now.* As instructed, she fastened her hair in a ponytail behind her head.

"Are you ready?" Cera asked.

Ursula swallowed hard, trying to steel her nerves. This was it. Once in the air, there would be no turning back. They were heading right for the *Lacus Mortis*. And while her Latin knowledge wasn't spectacular, she had a feeling that name translated to, "the place where you're about to die."

"I guess I'm ready."

Cera whispered in Sotz's ear, and the bat climbed over the railing. "Hold on tight," Cera shouted.

An instant later, the cold lunar wind whipped over Ursula's skin, and they were diving toward the valley floor. With her hair fastened behind her head, the improved view proved so terrifying that she shut her eyes anyway. She opened them only when Sotz leveled off.

"Are you okay?" Cera shouted above the wind.

"Yeah." *And by "yeah," I mean I'm so terrified I might puke into the wind.* "Is it strictly necessary for Sotz to dive like a maniac every time we take off?"

"It's the easiest way for him to build up enough speed to sustain flight. A bat's not really built to take two riders."

Her stomach twisted. *Brilliant. Perfectly reassuring.*

Sotz flew in a lazy curve until they faced the wall of the crater. The frigid air bit at her skin, even through her leather. Still, now that they weren't hurtling at the ground, her muscles began to relax.

Sotz slowly beat the air with his wings a few times. Then he dove toward the side of the crater. They were heading for a sheer cliff of lunar rock at a terrifying speed.

Ursula gripped onto the saddle so tightly she was about to rip the handles off. "What are you doing?" she shouted. "We're about to crash into the side of the crater!"

A moment later, in conjunction with Ursula's terrified screams, they plunged into a narrow crack in the side of the cliff. Sotz had taken them into complete darkness.

Ursula strained to see anything, total darkness enshrouded them. Unlike the subway, no lights hung to illuminate their flight. If she'd had the nerve to release her grip for a second, she wouldn't have been able to see her own hand in front of her face.

"Where are we going?" she shouted.

"Can you be quiet?" Cera barked. "All your shouting will interfere with Sotz's echolocation."

Right. Best not deafen the bat. Ursula tried to peer into the darkness for a few more moments, but she kept imagining stalactites dangling from the ceiling and smacking her in the face. So she shut her eyes and buried her face in Cera's back.

The air rushed around her, but the sensation of Cera's soft sweater against her cheek made her feel secure. After a while, the air around her seemed to warm.

Ursula lifted her head, opening her eyes. A dim, indigo light shone through the crack. Sotz's wings beat steadily. The light slowly grew brighter.

Suddenly, the tunnel widened and they burst into an enormous cavern. A tremendous cacophony of chirping and squeaking assaulted her ears, echoing off the cavern walls. It sounded like a tropical rainforest amplified through a speaker. Down here, the humid air warmed her skin. She breathed in, taking in the sharp, almost chemical scent. It took her a moment to identify it—ammonia.

A luminous glow rose from beneath them. Ursula leaned just far enough to the side to peer over Sotz's side. She gasped. They were flying over a great forest of glowing mushrooms. Enormous fungi, the size of trees, grew from the surface. Each glowed with a blinding cornflower-blue light. And between the fungi, something slithered.

Her stomach fluttered as she realized what they were. Monstrous caterpillars, the size of buses.

"What is this place?" she whispered.

"This is the rookery, for the bats." Cera pointed above. "Look. You can see them up there."

Ursula craned her neck, peering into the darkness. On the ceiling hundreds of feet above, furry bat bodies squirmed like a brown fungus.

Suddenly, Sotz jerked to the side. Out of the corner of her eye, Ursula saw a blur of brown plunge from the ceiling. It struck a mushroom with an audible splat.

"What was that?"

"Guano," said Cera. "The bats aren't exactly polite."

Ursula's stomach turned. *Lovely.*

As they continued through the cavern, Sotz continued to dodge falling guano.

"This is gross," Ursula muttered.

"The guano feeds the mushrooms," said Cera. "It's a well-functioning ecosystem."

Eventually the walls narrowed, and the ceiling sloped lower. As the sounds of the bats faded, the cavern grew dark again.

Sotz flew through the darkness for what seemed like hours. Ursula rested her head against Cera's back, breathing in the smell of garlic and bread that still hung on her clothes from the last time she'd cooked. Apart from the flapping of wings and the rush of air around them, the only sound Ursula could hear was Cera's drumming heart through her back.

Without warning, they burst free of the crevice. Ursula blinked, trying to focus her eyes. When she tried to ask Cera what was going on, her breath caught in her throat. There was no air, the sun hadn't yet risen on this part of the moon. Brutal cold bit at her skin. They were floating in the vacuum of space.

Cera pulled a purple crystal from her sweater. Her mouth moved but there was no sound. Suddenly, dark magic flashed around them. This time, when Ursula gasped, air filled her lungs.

"I'm so sorry, milady," said Cera. "I forgot that you wouldn't be able to breathe." Ursula coughed uncontrollably, wiping frozen tears from her eyes. Dark magic swirled around them, keeping the vacuum at bay.

"You don't need air to breathe?" asked Ursula.

"Some air. But oneiroi can hold our breath for a long time. It's one of the ways we are able to live on the moon." Cera pointed up. "Have you seen the Earth yet?"

Suspended above them, the earth filled the sky, a crescent of emerald and blue. Gleaming like a shadowed gem. She hadn't realized until now that from the moon, the Earth had phases, too—waxing and waning. She blinked, trying to process the rich colors.

"It's beautiful, isn't it?" said Cera. "Before Nyxobas came, the oneiroi worshiped the Earth as a god."

"I'd seen the pictures from NASA, but in person—" She spotted the outline of Europe, and felt a lump rise in her throat. "I didn't realize quite how far away it was."

Cera whispered in Sotz's ear. The bat adjusted his course, bringing them lower—closer to the barren lunar surface. They streaked over a great field of stones and boulders. Only the intermittent pockmarks of ancient meteor strikes interrupted the flat landscape.

She glanced at the sun over the horizon. *Not long, now.* "Where are we?" Ursula asked.

"The Lacus Mortis."

"What does that mean, anyway?"

Cera cleared her throat. "Just... Just *Lake of Death.*"

Yep. Just like I thought.

Ursula studied the barren plain. "This is it?" Why had Hothgar ordered the melee be held here? "There's bugger-all here!"

"The Lacus Mortis is what remains of an old lava flow," said Cera. "It's where Nyxobas built his great amphitheater."

Here, on the opposite side of the moon, the sun still hung in the sky. But it didn't look like daylight on Earth. The sun hung in a black sky, bathing the moon in pure, white light.

Ursula scanned the landscape, but she could see nothing. Not a single hovel, much less an amphitheater. She was about to ask what was going on, when she spotted the rim of a particularly large crater. A dome of silver covered the crater, so thin it was hardly visible. Sunlight streamed through the dome.

Sotz carved a tight turn as they soared through the dome of silver magic, and Ursula let out a low whistle. Just below the dome, demons filled the crater, and they sat in seats carved from the inner walls of the caldera. White sunlight shone over an enormous circular pit in the center, flat and sandy on the bottom. It looked exactly like the interior of a Roman Coliseum.

Panic raked its claws into her chest. *They've all come to watch me die. And I have nothing but a stone dagger to defend myself.*

Chapter 22

A cold fear gripped Ursula as Sotz skidded to a stop in the center of the arena. She could feel the eyes on her. *The hellhound harlot, here to perform for your enjoyment.*

She climbed out of the saddle, wincing. Fatigue burned through her thighs from the flight. *Haven't even started yet, and I'm already knackered.*

From Sotz's saddle, Cera gripped her hand. "Good luck."

"Thank you." She glanced around at the empty arena. She was the only one here. "You're not leaving now, are you? There's no one else here."

"They'll be here, Ursula," said Cera. "I must go."

Before Ursula could say another word, Sotz and the oneiroi launched into the air, the wind whipping through Cera's hair as she flew away.

Okay. So I'll just stand here in the center of the arena, with an entire planet's eyes on me. Her heart squeezed in her chest as she stood below the black dome of sky, washed in milky light.

As she stood on the dusty floor, a wave of terror washed over her. Great walls of stone, at least twenty feet high, surrounded her. Every few yards, grated doors interrupted them. And above the doors, Nyxobas's brethren sat in rows, studying her with a mixture of excitement and fear.

A great clash reverberated through the stadium, and she turned with a start. On a platform at the edge of the arena stood Hothgar, dressed in furs and a silver breastplate. A great silver gong hung beside him, and his Viking wife sat behind him, wearing a shimmering gown the color of starlight. Twelve oneiroi stood before him, each bearing a torch. The torch flames danced in the wind.

And at the back of the platform, a giant stone statue of Nyxobas loomed over the arena. Starlight seemed to shine from the statue's eyes. Ursula shuddered.

She turned, surveying the crowd again. She squinted in the setting sun.

A pig-faced man pointed at her. "Ready to die, whore?"

She swallowed hard. *Now I'll survive just to spite you.*

Glass shattered a few feet behind her, and she whirled. Someone had thrown a glass wine bottle at her. Lucky for her, the tosser had terrible aim.

She moved further into the center of the arena, out of range, inwardly cursing Cera's punctuality. *Why did she need to get us here early?*

Hothgar's enormous form cast a long shadow over the center of the crater. *When the shadows grow long...*

He slammed his wooden mallet into the center of the gong. A silence fell over the crowd, and he stared at Ursula. "I'm so glad you could finally join us, dog. You weren't too busy rutting in the streets like a bitch in heat?"

The crowd laughed, and Ursula felt a flush rise in her cheeks. Anger simmered. "I'm sorry." Her tone dripped with sarcasm. "If you want me to call you 'Nyxobas' and worship your lunar staff, you'll have to control my mind, like you do the other human women who won't have you otherwise."

Hothgar paled, but she caught sight of the slight smile that ghosted across Viking's lips.

Hothgar's nostrils flared. "Are you prepared to join the melee?"

Definitely not. "I am." She projected her voice with as much confidence as she could.

"Good," said Hothgar. "I will enjoy watching you get torn apart."

A pit opened in her stomach. She couldn't come up with much of a comeback to that particular jab. She *was* probably going to die here, and the terror of that thought ripped her mind apart. The Sword of Nyxobas lifted his large wooden mallet. With a brutal strike, he sounded the gong again. Around the arena, the doors opened with a rumbling groan.

Ursula's blood ran cold as she beheld the champions, striding through the doors. Silver tridents, lethal spears, full suits of armor. All manner of nasty-looking swords, battle-axes, and spears. Their weapons' shadows crept over the dirt like long fingers.

Most of the men were probably triple her weight. *Not feeling too stellar about my rock-knife and my fancy boots right now.*

Her heart pounded like a war drum. She searched the champions' faces, but couldn't find Bael among them. She shot a frantic look at the setting sun, drifting dangerously close to the horizon.

Hothgar raised his hands. "Champions! Welcome to the melee." He paused for effect, then boomed, "Are you ready to fight?"

Around her, the champions shouted, lifting their weapons into the air and roaring with cheers. *Didn't they realize they were about to die?*

Ursula half-heartedly raised her knife to the darkening sky, forcing herself to emit a sad cheer. "Wahey!" The sun had begun to slip below the crater's rim.

"Excellent," said Hothgar. "Now, while I am sure most of you know the rules of the melee, we have some outsiders here." He looked at Ursula pointedly. "Fortunately, they are very simple, so even a dog could understand. There are fifty-six of you. When twenty-three of you are dead, the melee ends. Only blades may be used. No magic or ranged weapons, or you will be executed. Begin when I next sound the gong."

Ursula clutched her knife, a cold sweat breaking out on her forehead. As she surveyed her opponents, panic tightened her lungs. Frantically, she searched the crowd for Bael. Rays of sunlight blinded her as the last of the sun dipped below the crater's rim. She didn't know why she was even looking for the lord. Clearly, he wasn't her protector anymore. In fact, he'd said flat out that he would kill her. Maybe she just needed to see a familiar face.

Darkness fell over the crater. Now, only the starlight, the gleaming Earth, and the amber light of the torches lit the arena.

Before she had a chance to find Bael, Hothgar raised his mallet again. He slammed it into the gong.

The sound reverberated through Ursula's gut, and adrenaline blazed through her nerve endings. Her legs started to shake, and everything seemed to move in slow motion.

The crowd rose to cheer, the champions dropped into fighting stances.

She widened her stance, circling to search the throng for danger.

She didn't have to look long.

A champion charged for her, starlight glinting off his silver helm, carved with the face of a lion.

She had no question that behind the visor, she'd find Bael's beautiful face, eyes blazing with wrath.

My angel of death, come for my soul at last.

Chapter 23

She gripped the dagger and dove out of his swing. When she looked up, Bael stood over her, his eyes flashing in his helmet.

She slashed for one of his ankles, but he deftly stepped aside.

She leapt to her feet. *I really don't want to hurt him. But if I don't, he'll kill me.*

Still, she couldn't bring herself to stab him yet. Despite what he'd said—the part about how he'd kill her—she sort of *liked* the guy.

She wouldn't be able to draw blood until he'd made the first strike. Then, self-preservation would kick in. Instead of stabbing him, she wound up for a hard left hook. But as she swung for him, Bael caught her fist in a powerful hand.

Hungry for blood, the crowd chanted: "Bael! Bael! Bael!"

"You can't fight me, Ursula," he growled.

What's he doing? Drawing it out to please the crowd?

Her heart hammered against her ribs. Of course he'd gone for the easy target first. The girl with the rock for protection.

"I can fight you," she shot back. "Maybe I can't win. But I can fight." Without waiting for a response, she kicked him in the chin.

His neck snapped back, his helmet flying from his head. When he looked back at her, his pale eyes had turned into black voids, sending ice through her veins.

Her victory didn't last long. In a blur of dark magic, he gripped her arms, pulling her to him. He towered over her, all muscle.

He leaned in close, his body warm against hers. He was pure power, and terror ran up her spine.

Bael whispered, "What are you doing?"

"Trying to fight."

"You don't have a real weapon." He dropped her wrists, and in the next second, he drew his katana.

Brilliant. A sword against a rock. This is bloody pointless.

At the sight of his icy eyes that had seen millennia of combat, her blood roared in her ears.

Run. Maybe I need to run. From his platform, she could hear Hothgar announcing *first blood,* but her eyes were locked on Bael.

Her mind raced. If she was going to get away, she'd need a diversion. The obsidian blade glinted in her hand, and she threw it at his shoulder. Effortlessly, he snatched it from the air.

Bollocks. She'd just thrown away her only weapon, but it had bought her time. She turned, scanning the arena for an escape route. Carnage assaulted her eyes—demons tearing into each other, hacking through limbs, half of them using their teeth. Two giant twins, dressed in wolf furs and metal armor, swung claymores at their opponents. *Where the fuck do I run to? Romulus and Remus over there don't look like a good bet.*

Before she could pick an escape route, Bael slid a powerful arm around her waist, pulling her close to him.

"You're unarmed," he said. "If you run, you're going to die."

He pointed to a demon with blood-red eyes stalking toward them. The creature held a nasty looking broadsword. In a moment, the only possible escape path would put her within range of him.

The rabid-eyed demon grinned. He had replaced his teeth with steel spikes. Already, blood dripped from them into the sand.

Fear coiled around Ursula's heart. It was Steel Jaws or Bael. She swallowed hard, her nails digging into Bael's arm. She had nothing left to fight with.

From behind her, the sound of metal against metal pierced her ears. *He's drawing another weapon.* She braced herself for the final blow.

Instead, Bael stabbed a katana into the sand by her feet.

Hope sparked in her chest. "What are you doing?"

"Take the blade," he said. "I was trying to give it to you."

"I thought you were trying to kill me."

"Do you think I have no honor?" he growled.

"When we were in the carriage, you literally said, 'I'm going to kill you.'"

"You deserve a fair fight. Take the blade." He loosened his grip on her, and Ursula pulled the blade from the dirt.

With the katana in her hand, she felt like herself again, like the metal was an extension of her body.

Bael pointed to the right. "That half of the arena is yours," he commanded. "If anyone gets close, kill them."

He turned his back to her, facing his side of the arena. They stood, back-to-back, so close she could feel the warmth coming off his body, could smell the faint scent of sea air that wafted from his skin.

Apparently, Bael wanted her to fight defensively. It made sense. Might as well let the others take the risk while trying to go unnoticed.

Except she wasn't really going unnoticed. Jaws raised his broadsword, grinning at her. Katana or not, she still looked like easy prey.

A few meters away, just out of range of his steel, the Gray Ghost slipped over the dirt like a phantom. As before, he'd concealed his face with a head scarf, and he gripped a dagger in each hand.

Her mouth went dry. She couldn't tell if he was heading for Jaws, or for her.

Either way, I need to be ready. She took a step away from Bael, gripping the katana's hilt. A part of her wanted to throw herself into the fray, to feel her blade cut through the air. Maybe that was Emerazel.

Jaws was coming right for her, raising his broadsword now. But before he could get to her, the Gray Ghost leapt for him, daggers flashing like a serpent's fangs. The blades cut into Jaws's back, soaking his clothes in blood.

Jaws's scream curdled her stomach. He fell to the ground, and Gray Ghost ended his torment with a quick slash to his throat.

Her eyes scanned for the next threat, and she stared at a trident-wielding demon, his skin elephant-gray. In a blur of black leather and teeth, Massu launched himself into the air. Screaming like a banshee, he attached himself to the demon's head. Ursula could distinctly hear the crunch of bone as he began to chew through the demon's face. *Fuck me sideways. I do not want to fight an oneiroi.*

She took a step closer to Bael.

Bael touched her arm, and she jumped. "Come with me."

She turned, keeping her back to the wall as they moved.

They moved back-to-back, swords drawn, but they might as well have kept them sheathed. The other demons ignored them. Instead, like sharks scenting blood, they charged toward the skirmish in the center of the arena.

"Five, six, seven deaths," Hothgar's voice boomed, his glee audible. "Only nineteen more will die today."

The demons swarmed the center of the arena like piranhas fighting over a corpse. Between shouts of pain, blood sprayed in the sand. From the melee, the sound of clashing steel rung through the air. Around them, the bodies of the fallen champions twitched.

"Eight... nine deaths," Hothgar shouted. "Prepare to light bitumen sands." His voice boomed over the arena like a death knell.

Cold fear washed over Ursula. *The bitumen sands?* The oneiroi, holding torches, ran to the edges of the arena.

"On my command," boomed Hothgar.

"Get your blade ready," Bael growled. "We need to move." He stalked toward the bloodbath in the center of the arena.

As she hurried after Bael, her eyes flicked to the oneiroi, who stood at the arena's edges with their torches.

"Now," said Bael.

There wasn't time to ask what was going on—she just had to decide to trust him. At least for now. Ursula's heart thundered in her chest, and she broke into an all-out sprint, heading for the melee. She no longer had any choice but to fight.

Around the perimeter, they dropped their torches. A ring of fire burst to life, encircling the entire arena. From the edges, the flames spread inward, searing the darkness. Hothgar was forcing them into the melee. As she entered the fray, she tried not to stare at the carnage—at the demon slicing through another's neck with a scimitar, at the blood spurting from his stump like a geyser. If she stared too long, she'd completely shut down mentally.

Still sticking by Bael's side, she looked to the right, at a demon who loomed over her with a broadsword. Blood dripped down his black beard, and he glared at her through milky eyes. "Are you ready to die, hound?"

"Can you handle him?" asked Bael.

Before she could actually answer Bael's question, Blackbeard lunged, swinging for her head. She parried, grunting as his sword slammed against hers. She dodged out of reach.

He swung again, but this time she was able to duck the blow entirely. With a savage thrust, she stabbed at his chest. Growling, he jumped back. The tip of her blade sliced the skin over his ribs. Blood sprayed her face.

"Bitch," he said through gritted teeth. "I will rape you to death."

A hot flood of anger blazed through her nerves. If she'd had Emerazel's power in her veins, she would have immolated him. Instead, raw fury burned away her fear, and she narrowed her eyes. "I'm going to enjoy killing you."

She lunged, thrusting. This time, the blade slid deep between his ribs. With a twisting motion, she directed it upward to where his heart should be. The demon's milky eyes widened with shock. A fat drop of blood rolled from his chin. Groaning, he slumped to the ground, and she pulled out her sword.

"Fifteen deaths!" roared Hothgar to the cheers of the crowd. Their cries had grown increasingly bloodthirsty as the last of the sunlight seeped from the sky.

Behind her, she heard the clash of steel. She stole a glance over her shoulder. Bael was locked in combat with the two enormous demons—Romulus and Remus.

"Can you handle them?" she shouted.

Bael swung for Romulus, grunting.

Was that a yes or a no?

Bael's sword was parried in a clash of steel. Romulus twisted his wrist, catching Bael's blade. He drove Bael's katana into the earth with a *thud*.

Instantly, Remus lunged for Bael's chest, but Bael slipped away, moving like the wind.

He'd dodged the strike, but a third opponent came up behind him—a winged man who slashed at Bael with his talons.

Ursula gritted her teeth. *Time to jump in.*

The three demons boxed Bael in. He fought in a blur of clashing steel, whirling and ducking with astounding grace. *No wonder he's so confident.* He parried the blows that assaulted him from both sides. So fast—she could hardly see what was happening—he sliced through the neck of the winged man.

"Sixteen deaths!" Hothgar boomed.

Still, Romulus and Remus pressed their assault. *Two against one isn't exactly a fair fight.* "Hey!" she shouted. "Wolf-boy. Right here."

Remus turned, snarling. "You disgust me, dog. I will eat your flesh off your bones."

She tried to ignore her body's trembling. He was maybe four times her size. Speed was her greatest asset here.

He swung for her, and she ducked. They circled each other, swords glinting in the starlight. Remus lunged for her, and she dodged back, but not fast enough. His blade ripped through her shoulder. The blazing pain threw her off balance, and she faltered.

Fight, Ursula.

As Remus prepared to strike again, she steadied herself, blocking his attack. Somehow, the surge of adrenaline flooding her system washed the pain away. The air filled with the sound of her sword clashing against Remus's. The bastard had the advantage of a much longer reach, and her muscles burned as she struggled to keep up with the fight.

And yet, as she fought him, a strange surety filled her. It was almost as though liquid shadow flowed through her muscles, making her movements fluid. Time seemed to slow down. And if she concentrated, she could predict what his next moves would be, could easily block them. *Strike from the left. Dodge. Thrust.*

If she moved in closer to him, he wouldn't be able to strike her with accuracy—not with his giant arms. In fact, he wasn't used to fighting someone her size.

He swung for her in a giant arc, and she ducked. He'd been pressing her and would expect her to dodge back. Instead, she leapt in closer. Unable to strike her with his sword, he slammed a meaty fist into her head. Her vision went dark.

Only the darkness will save you.

Yet even as her vision darkened, some ancient part of her brain took over, fighting for survival. She swung her sword, somehow certain of her mark.

And when her vision cleared again, she stared at her blade, plunged clean through Remus's neck. She gripped her sword, kicking him in the chest to pull her blade out.

Hothgar shouted, "Nineteen!"

Three kills left.

Before she could catch a glimpse of Bael, a sharp blast of pain ripped through her shoulders, knocking her off balance. She landed hard on the arena floor, bits of gravel biting into her palms. If Cera hadn't made her the reinforced leather jacket, she'd be dead by now. Even so, if they kept striking at her shoulders, she wouldn't be able to hold a weapon.

Her heart thundering, she grasped for her sword. Her fingers gripped the hilt, and she immediately swung from the ground at her attacker. Her sword found its mark in a leg, cutting into flesh and bone. Her opponent, wielding a giant scythe, screamed.

He swung for her with his blade, she rolled out of range, but not before the tip of his blade carved a furrow in her back.

In an instant, she was on her feet, staring at the reaper. *I have you.* She swung her katana in a wide arc, her steel cutting through the flesh and bone in his neck. The reaper's head rolled over the crater's floor, and his body toppled to the ground. A strange thrill rippled through her body. *Victory.*

"Twenty-one!" boomed Hothgar.

Her eyes flicked to Bael. He was still fighting. In hand-to-hand combat with Romulus.

The giant roared, "My brother has been slain!" Bael had dropped his sword. In its stead, he used the obsidian blade. *My blade.* Bael's movements were so fast, she could hardly track them. Starlight shone off the black rock, flashing in his hand. Even without the use of his magic, Bael's skill was breathtaking.

With a vicious strike, he ducked and stabbed Romulus in the groin. The demon shrieked. When Romulus doubled over, Bael slashed open his throat with a casual flick of his wrist, then rose.

"Twenty-two deaths!" shouted Hothgar.

Ursula's heart raced. *One more.*

She turned slowly, gripping her blood-stained sword, ready to slay. A bestial shriek curdled her stomach, and she turned to find Massu, burying his teeth into the back of a demon's neck. With an audible crunch, he snapped the demon's spine.

Hothgar's voice sounded like a thunderclap. "Twenty-three. The melee has ended!"

Ursula's entire body shook, and she let out a long, slow breath. Nausea welled in her stomach, and she hunched over, trying not to vomit. *I can't believe I made it.* Her body shrieked in agony where the blades had ripped her shoulders.

Soaked in blood, Bael crossed to her, his expression grim. He held the blood-soaked dagger before him. "Where did you get this?" he asked.

She tightened her lips. She was pretty sure a demon like him could tell when you were lying, but she wasn't about to get Cera in trouble, either. "I'm not answering that. I'm pleading the sixth... eighth...whatever Americans call it."

He rolled the hilt in his hands, inspecting it, before fixing her with one of his piercing glares. "The oneiroi are not your friends." A hint of steel laced his voice. "I hope, after what you just saw, you understand that."

Chapter 24

Ursula stood in the middle of the arena, next to the remaining demons. Strewn with gore, the dirt floor looked like a butcher shop. She shoved her hand in her pocket, gripping on to the reassuringly solid contours of the silver ring.

She wasn't going to argue with Bael about Cera—not now. In fact, she couldn't get her mind off the carnage she'd just witnessed, the images replaying in her skull. She clamped her eyes shut, willing her mind to fill with darkness.

It didn't work.

She turned to Bael, letting her eyes run over his battle-stained clothes. "Are you injured?"

He sheathed his katana. "No. But you are."

Not a question, but she answered anyway. "It hurts like hell."

From his platform, Hothgar raised his arms to the dark sky. "Let us congratulate the champions for a well-fought battle."

Around them, the crowd stood and roared their approval from their seats.

For just a moment, a thrill flickered through Ursula. And then, the images burned in her mind again: the severed tendons, the sprays of blood. The reaper's head. Her own blade, buried in the giant's chest.

They'd fought each other like rabid beasts. And Ursula had been right there, in the thick of it, slashing away to the dark cheers of the onlookers. Something had taken over her body, and she'd joined in the grim symphony of slaughter.

She closed her eyes again, trying to cleanse her mind of the blood. A part of her yearned for the cleanliness of the void. The words of the Forgotten Ones whispered in the back of her skull. *Only the darkness will save you.*

Maybe this was Nyxobas's plan, to give her the choice between turning into a monster and joining him in the void. Or if not, surely this was his punishment for stabbing him with the dagger.

She glanced at the statue of Nyxobas that loomed over the amphitheater, its eyes blazing. She couldn't understand any of his actions. Why did he summon her here in the first place? Why did his own son, Abrax, hate him so deeply that he had tried to overthrow the kingdom? And above all, what made him think Abrax was no longer a threat?

Maybe the will of gods wasn't really meant to be understood. In all likelihood, they were completely mental from all the time they spent in hell.

By her side, Bael stood perfectly still, his eyes closed. His chest rose and fell in an even rhythm. Entirely unperturbed by everything he'd just seen. *Just another day in the Shadow Realm.*

Hothgar banged the gong, and the noise of the crowd died.

"Of the fifty-six champions who joined the melee, twenty-three remain in his mortal realm. In glorious battle, twenty-three more have joined the void to live for eternity."

As Hothgar spoke, black-cloaked oneiroi jogged silently into the arena. Remembering Massu's ferocity, she shuddered. But these oneiroi weren't here to fight. They were here to clean up the corpses. Silently, the oneiroi dragged them from the arena. The bodies left red smears over the dirt.

Hothgar thrust his hand into the air. "Massu, can you step forward?"

Cera's brother stepped forward, his mouth dripping with fresh blood.

Ursula heard the pause, the sharp intake of breath before Hothgar spoke again. And when he did, he spoke through clenched teeth. "This has been the first melee to include an oneiroi," said Hothgar. "Despite his inferior status, he killed five demons, the most of any champion. As ordained in the warrior code, this accomplishment grants him pole position for the race."

Massu bowed deeply.

Hothgar continued, "The race will be held at Asta. We will commence when the sun reaches its peak above the spire."

Lifting his hammer, the Sword Of Nyxobas smashed the gong a final time.

The demons around her turned to leave, and Ursula bit her lip to stop the tears welling in her eyes. She turned away from Bael so he couldn't see her face.

Sure, she could use a sword. She could fight if she had to. But this had been a complete nightmare. A savage display of bloodlust, for absolutely no purpose.

And the scariest part was that she'd fit right in.

Blinking away the tears, she searched the sky for a sign of Cera. Maybe Bael thought they couldn't be friends, but whether he liked it or not, Cera was her ride home.

"Ursula?" Bael touched her arm, and she turned back to him.

He leveled his intense gaze on her. Apart from the blood spattering his cheeks, he looked perfect. Like a god himself— golden skin, thick lashes framing violet eyes, and full lips.

"You should come with me," he said quietly. "I'll heal you, but not here."

"Where's Cera?"

"She had to return to my manor." He turned to walk for one of the open archways, expecting her to follow.

She quickened her pace to catch up with him. "You didn't let her stay to see her brother fight?"

"No."

"Why? I'm sure she wanted to be here." Ursula's stomach clenched. *She must be out of her mind with worry.*

"What if he'd died? Do you think she'd have wanted to be there for that? Do you think she'd want it to plague her nightmares for the rest of her life?"

Ursula shook her head. "I'm sure she could decide for herself, if you hadn't decided for her."

"She doesn't yet know what it's like to watch..." He cut his own sentence short. "Don't question me."

Clearly, there was a story there. But she already knew if she probed further, he'd rebuff her.

Bael led her through the archway into a stone tunnel, their footsteps echoing off the ceiling. She tried to block out the pain lancing her shoulders—every step was an agony, and she could hardly keep pace with Bael.

He turned to look at her, then spoke a few words in Angelic. A glowing orb appeared in front of them, casting a dull light on the rough stone walls.

She swallowed hard. "I'm confused why you'd care about protecting Cera's feelings. You said the oneiroi are not our friends."

Pearly light shone at the end of the tunnel.

"No. They're not, but that doesn't mean we must be cruel to them." He stole a glance at her. "You fought well today."

"I don't feel great about everything I saw today."

"It's not your first battle. You fought the oneiroi in the fae realm."

She bit her lip. "Yes, but they seemed so vicious then. So inhuman. Now that I know Massu drew spaceships as a little boy, it will be hard to cut his head off. Plus, this battle served no purpose except to entertain people I hate. They could have just given you your manor back and saved us all the carnage. But where would the fun be in that, for people like Hothgar?"

At the end of the tunnel, they stepped out into the cold night air. On the barren, gray land, lines of carriages wound over the landscape. Bael turned, walking a few paces to his black and silver carriage.

He pulled open the door, motioning for her to enter.

She sat, laying the sword across her lap, and he climbed in next to her, closing the door.

"Take off your jacket," he said.

She did as instructed, peeling off the black leather jacket. Blood poured from her shoulder, and she tried not to look at the deep gash that had ripped through tendons and muscle.

Bael's jaw tightened at the sight of it. Remus's blade had found its way past her jacket's collar, straight into her flesh.

He touched her skin, just on the edges of her wound, and closed his eyes. Shadow magic swirled from his body, rushing over her injury in a soothing wave. She could feel the pain leaving her shoulder, replaced by a soft tingling sensation, a powerful caress.

Warmth radiated from his fingertips. Were these gentle hands the same ones that had just slaughtered four demons?

She gazed into his eyes, and her pulse raced. Maybe it was the trauma of the fight, but with him so close to her, with his powerful hands on her body, she couldn't think straight.

173

"Where else are you injured?" he asked softly.

It took her a moment to remember how to speak. "My back."

He glanced away. "You'll need to take off the corset, and face the other way."

Her pulse raced faster, and she turned away from him. She slowly began unbuttoning the front of her corset, then pulled it off. Her nipples hardened in the cold air.

She felt Bael's warm fingertips trace just over the wound. "You were protected by two layers of Cera's armor, I see. What weapon cut through to your flesh?"

"A scythe."

"Did you kill the reaper?"

"Yes."

She felt his magic washing over her skin, soothing the pain and warming her body at the same time. When she could no longer feel the pain from the cut, Bael's fingertips grazed lower over her back, and heat shot through her body. Despite the cold, a blush rose on her chest.

She tensed. *Ursula, you sick bastard.* Why was she thinking about sex now? She'd just taken part in a massacre.

Bael pulled his hand away. "You can dress again.

She pulled the corset around herself, buttoning it up again. She was certain her cheeks were flushed, and that Bael would notice the blush on her body, the dilated pupils. What would he think of her getting turned on by his touch after everything that had just happened?

Then again, she was pretty sure she'd read once that sex and death went hand-in-hand. During the bubonic plague, people reacted one of two ways: they walked through the streets, whipping themselves in penitence. Or they shagged strangers in the woods.

Apparently, she was the stranger-shagging type. If she had to guess, Bael was probably more likely the self-flagellating kind.

She fastened the button on the top of her corset. "Are we going?"

"You must return to the manor, but I'm not joining you."

"Why not?"

"I must attend to business with the lords." She glanced at him, certain her cheeks still glowed from the intense pleasure of his touch. "I forgot to thank you for the sword."

"You deserved a fair fight. But don't forget that in the end, only one of us can live."

His words sent a chill through her. "I know." *And there's not much of a chance it will be me.*

He started to shut the door, but turned back to her. With a furrowed brow, he leaned in to the carriage and met her eyes. "When you get back, pour a lavender bath. It will help with the nightmares."

He leaned out again, closing the door with a final click.

Chapter 25

Cera jumped to her feet the moment Ursula opened the door to her quarters. The oneiroi's eyes were frantic, her question unspoken. Faint sunlight streamed through the darkened windows.

Ursula held up a hand. "He's fine. Massu is fine. And so is Bael. We all made it."

Cera dropped to her knees, clasping her hands together. "Thank the gods. I knew it would be okay, just for today." She rose, her eyes wide. "Massu is entirely unharmed?"

"Not only unharmed, but he won the tournament. He killed five demons."

Cera's hand flew to her mouth. "Don't lie to me."

"I would never lie to you. He slew five with his bare hands." *With his teeth, really.*

"Oh my gods. Oh my gods," said Cera softly, kneading her hands. She paused, her eyes widening even further. "Bael fought well, too?"

"Yes, he's fine," said Ursula with a sigh. "Not a scratch on him. He moves like the wind."

Cera dropped her face into her hands. With her face hidden, she could easily be mistaken for a child.

"What's the matter?"

"I didn't know who was going to open the door: you, milord, or someone else. If it had been another—"

Ursula's throat tightened. *Any other demon would have killed you, wouldn't he?* Despite Bael's warning, she couldn't reconcile this sweet woman with the savagery she'd seen from Massu. Could Cera fight that way? It was hard to believe this little seamstress with her cardigans could eat a man's flesh off his skull.

"Cera?" she asked tentatively. "Do all oneiroi fight with their teeth instead of weapons?"

"What?" Cera wiped a tear from her eye.

"Do oneiroi ever use swords or daggers?"

Cera's brow furrowed. "Of course oneiroi use swords. Why would you ask that?"

"Your brother—" *And frankly, all the other oneiroi I've ever battled.* "Massu didn't use his a sword. He used his teeth."

"No." Cera shook her head. "No. Don't tell me that."

Ursula's blood chilled. "What's wrong?"

"That way of fighting is forbidden. Those who taste the forbidden flesh turn into beasts. They become the Corrupted!"

Ursula's mouth went dry. *Abrax has apparently screwed up a whole lot of oneiroi.*

Frantic, Cera gripped her hair. "Once an oneiroi starts, he can't stop. The call of blood is too strong. Before Nyxobas arrived, the Corrupted were ostracized—sent to wander the wastes, where they fed upon each other like wild beasts."

"What is the forbidden flesh?"

"Any raw meat. It only applies to oneiroi. It's something in our nature. Eat too much meat, it changes us. Stokes a different kind of hunger. We become stronger, faster, and angrier, but at the cost of our minds." Her lip curled back from her teeth. "I would murder Massu if he weren't certain to die in the melee. He should have never allowed himself to become Corrupted."

Given the ferocious look on Cera's face, Ursula didn't fancy Massu's chances in a fight against his sister. Even if he'd won the tournament.

A knocking at the door interrupted them, and Cera hurried over to it. "Who is it?"

"Bael." His voice boomed through the door.

Cera flung it open. Bael stood in the doorway in clean clothes that fit his muscular body perfectly. The lunar wind blew a tendril of hair in front of his eyes.

"Milord." Cera bowed. "I'm so relieved you are unharmed."

He nodded at her. "Thank you. I wish to speak to Ursula. Alone."

"Yes, of course, milord." Cera hurried from her quarters, and Bael shut the door behind her. He narrowed his eyes, studying her as he walked closer. "How does your shoulder feel?"

"Fine." She crossed her arms. She couldn't stop thinking about the feel of his fingertips on her bare skin. Just looking at him, she could feel a blush creeping into her cheeks. Bael hadn't actually shown any interest in her, and anyway they were supposed to kill each other. So what the hell was she thinking about his hands for?

She needed to change the subject. "Did you know that Abrax has been feeding oneiroi raw meat?" she blurted.

"Yes. It turns them into savage fighters—brings out the beast within them."

"Right." She swallowed hard. "Thank you for healing me."

His brow furrowed, and he looked at the ground. She had the impression he wanted to ask her something, but he couldn't quite get the words out.

"Did you want something?" she prompted.

"I thought perhaps you wouldn't like to eat alone. I was hoping you might join me for dinner."

Now that was unexpected. She glanced down at her leather outfit covered in sand and dried blood. "I'll need time to change."

"Of course. I'll return in an hour." He turned, departing as suddenly as he'd come.

As she filled the bath, Ursula peeled off the blood-stained leather trousers and corset.

Cera had been right about the strength of the material. A few slashes had pierced through the reinforced leather, but it still hung together. Still, something would have to be done about the grit that seemed to permeate every crease and fold. If she wore it again, she'd get a rash.

She stepped into the bath, letting the warm water soothe her burning muscles.

She closed her eyes, but the images from the fight flooded her mind: Remus, impaled on her sword. The reaper's head, detaching from his body, the hot spray of crimson blood. Her eyes snapped open again.

She reached for the soap—lavender-scented. Bael had said it would chase the nightmares away. She rubbed it over her skin, working up a pale blue lather, washing away the blood and grit. When she inhaled deeply, some of the images faded from her mind.

Still, a voice nagged in the back of her mind. Fighting—viciously—had come so easily to her. So who was F.U.? What had she done that slicing through a man's neck came as naturally as breathing? Ursula swallowed hard. She couldn't help but wonder if F.U. had been something of a monster.

And she had the strange feeling that Nyxobas knew all about F.U.'s monstrosity. Still, Ursula couldn't remember a damn thing.

She stepped out of the bath, toweling off. As she examined her skin in the mirror, she could find not a single scar marring her pale skin. Bael's magic had worked remarkably well. In fact, as she gazed at herself in the mirror, she couldn't stop thinking about the feel of his powerful magic, kissing her body. What would his lips feel like on her bare skin? The lords' wives had said he was an amazing lover.

She gritted her teeth. *Stop it, Ursula.* It was ridiculous. He was going to kill her—he had no *choice* but to kill her. Unless, by some miracle, she managed to slaughter him first. And here she was, wondering what his lips would feel like on her bare skin.

"There is something really wrong with you, you know that?" she said to her reflection.

Wrapped in a towel, she climbed the stairs to the bedroom she never used. Cera had left some dresses in there.

She opened a drawer, plucking out a pair of purple knickers. She slid them on over her hips, then crossed to the closet. She pulled out a dress—a stunning indigo. She stepped into it, pulling it up over her shoulders. Her milky-white legs shone through the sheer fabric. Delicate, glimmering stitching wound up the front of the dress. *Cera is an absolute genius.*

She slipped into a pair of deep-blue heels.

Cera had left a makeup kit on the dresser, and she rubbed blush into her cheeks.

She felt like she was preparing for a date, which was completely insane. She was meeting another warrior, for a post-slaughter feast, before they jumped into the fray again.

Still, after everything she'd seen, it was a relief to do something normal. The mundane tasks of lining her eyes with black, slicking lip-gloss over her lips—a rich red, the color of—

She slammed the lipstick on the top of her dresser. *That's enough of that.* She wasn't going to think about death right now. She pulled a soft, white cloak from the closet, and wrapped it around her shoulders. Before leaving the bedroom, she shoved the silver ring into her pocket.

A knock sounded from downstairs. *He's already here.*

She hurried down the stairs and pulled open the door.

Bael stood in the doorway, dressed in a midnight-blue cloak, with a deep gray suit underneath. "Ursula. Thank you for joining me. Cera arranged dinner in my hall."

Her stomach rumbled as she stepped outside. "I'm actually starving."

They walked across the bridge, the lunar wind nipping at her skin.

"I thought you might be hungry," he said. "Battle either turns your stomach or leaves you ravenous."

She frowned as they hurried over the bridge. "F.U. seems to have a brutal side."

"F.U.?"

"Former Ursula. Me, before I lost my memory."

He arched an eyebrow. "Right. Her brutal side may have saved your life."

He led her into the lion atrium, where milky sunlight streamed through the shattered wall. On the dark side of the room, candlelight danced over the smashed tile, and her heels crushed the fragments of the floor. "Why don't you repair this place? It didn't seem to take you long to repair the broken window in my quarters."

"I want to remember." He pulled open an onyx door, revealing the tunnel illuminated by glowing mushrooms.

She rubbed the ring between her fingers. "And how long will you leave it that way as a reminder?"

"Until I make things right again."

She took a deep breath. Making things right again meant reclaiming his manor. And that meant she had to die. Dread coiled around her heart. "Will you make sure I have a quick death, if it comes to it?"

His icy gaze slid to her, and his jaw tightened. "Of course. And I'd ask that you do the same for me."

"Do you really think I'd stand a chance against you?"

"Like you said, F.U. knew how to fight. You move like a phantom."

"Too bad I have no idea why."

"That's a mercy."

Surprise flickered through her. "You think severe retrograde amnesia is a mercy?"

"Believe me. There are far worse things than forgetting." Ice laced his tone.

Okay. So that's an awkward topic.

As they walked, Ursula ran her fingers along the rough walls. "Did the oneiroi carve this?"

"No, it was here when I won the manor."

She frowned. "So the previous lord made it?"

Bael paused, reaching out to touch one of the glyphs in the stone, his powerful body just inches from hers. She could feel the heat coming off him, and his delicious smell distracted her. Maybe her attraction to Bael wasn't totally crazy after all. If she was going to die soon, at least she could enjoy her final days.

"No one knows what the symbols mean," he said. "Not even the oneiroi. These tunnels have been here for as long as anyone can remember—even before Nyxobas arrived."

He turned, walking again, his heels echoing off the tunnel ceiling.

Ursula picked up her pace to keep up with him. "I don't understand. Why would anyone take the trouble to burrow through one hundred feet of solid rock?" *And more importantly, is there a way I can use this as an escape route?* Though it was pretty difficult to escape an entire moon. *Perhaps I can hide down here for decades like a mole person, living on mushrooms.*

"I'm not entirely sure why it's here," said Bael as he reached the end of the passage. "But I think it's on account of those." He pointed to the giant indigo crystals on the cavern's ceiling. Together with the luminescent mushrooms that clustered around them, they bathed the cavern in a pale violet light.

Ursula stiffened as a subtle vibration began to hum inside her belly, tugging her closer to the source of the magic, as if on an invisible thread. "What are they?"

"The light of the crystals amplifies magic," Bael continued. "I think whoever carved the tunnel wanted to be closer to them."

They crossed to the narrow stone bridge that hung between the stalactites. Following Bael, she took a tentative step onto the bridge. Her stomach swooped. On either side of the stone strip, the cavern floor dropped away. She shuddered. "It looks like Nyxobas's void."

He turned, violet light sparking in his eyes. "You've seen the void?"

Her heart raced. "Can we have this conversation on the other side of the bridge?"

"Of course."

He moved swiftly to the other side of the bridge, turning to offer his hand. "Is everything okay?"

"Just a little vertigo."

"As long as you don't try to stab me with a corkscrew again."

"Was that supposed to be a joke?"

"I have been known to tell a joke in my twenty-two thousand years."

"And are they the best jokes the world has ever known?"

He shot her a sharp look. Apparently, her jokes weren't funny.

When they reached the central platform, Ursula saw a small, black marble table standing in the center, with two chairs on either side. Two silver domed trays lay on the table, along with a bottle of chilled champagne and glasses. Bael gestured for her to sit.

She pulled off her cloak, wrapping it over the back of her chair. Bael's eyes slowly slid up and down her body, and he took a deep breath.

She sat across from Bael. His gaze locked on hers. "The clothing you wear distracts me."

A blush warmed her chest. "Is that a bad thing?"

"No. Yes. It's hard for me to think straight when I can see your skin through your dresses. Or when I see you standing naked in the portal room. Or that corset—"

"Is this why you asked me to dinner? To lecture me about nudity?"

"No."

"I thought you were supposed to be a legendary lover, not a major prude."

A smile curled his lips. "Is that what you've heard?"

Blushing, she drummed her fingernails on the tablecloth. "That's what the lords' wives say."

Suddenly serious, he frowned. "But you understand that we're not lovers, nor will we ever be. One of us will die soon, and I could never be with a hound of Emerazel in that way."

Angry heat warmed her cheeks. *Well, now I feel like a total idiot.* "Of course I know that. That's not what I meant. And anyway, I'd never want to be with a...an ancient shadow warrior..." she spluttered. She was pretty sure her cheeks were a fetching shade of crimson right now.

"Of course."

"Are we going to eat?" Avoiding eye contact, she pulled the dome off her tray. She wasn't sure what had just happened, but it stung like hell.

Neatly arranged on a plate lay a roast chicken and a watercress salad. *Most awkward non-date in the history of non-dates.* Why had he asked her here?

I'll just eat in silence. She picked up her knife and fork, cutting into the chicken.

Bael pulled the dome off his tray, and steam curled into the air. "The next trial is a race. You will need training."

"I'll be fine. I'm good at running."

"We won't be running. We'll be riding bats. You will need to learn how to fly one."

"Great. And you're going to train me?"

"Yes."

She swallowed a bite of her salad. "Why, exactly, are you so eager to help a hound of Emerazel?"

"I told Nyxobas I would protect you."

"That was before he threw me into the melee," she pointed out.

He took a deep breath. "I don't know why I want to help you." He frowned. "I suppose it's an unfair disadvantage that you're not native to the Shadow Realm. Like I said, you deserve a fair chance."

She cut into her chicken. "So you're just big on fairness?"

His gaze roamed down her body, then up again. "If someone is offering you help to save your life, you'd do best not to question it."

"Fair enough." She sipped her champagne. "I'd just like to note your inconsistencies."

"Noted."

"Is that all you wanted to talk to me about? I mean, that and how we're not going to be lovers?" *Whoops. That sounded bitter.*

"I wanted to talk to you about Cera," he said.

Oh. So that's why I'm here. "You already told me. The oneiroi are not my friends." She obviously wasn't going to change his mind. No point in arguing.

"It's more than that." He reached into his pocket, pulling out the obsidian knife. "This weapon. It could have cost Cera her life if anyone had learned where it had come from. Her desire to protect you puts her in danger."

Guilt pressed on her chest. "I hadn't thought of that." She frowned. "Really though, if you'd given me the katana before the melee, it wouldn't have been an issue."

His jaw tightened. "That was a last-minute decision."

She swallowed a bite of chicken. "So a part of you thought, 'maybe I'll just kill the hound.'"

His eyes pierced her. "A part of me thought a quick death at my hands would serve you best."

"What made you change your mind?"

He shrugged. "What if I'd been wrong? What if you're stronger than I'd thought? I don't know you. You don't even know you. You deserved a chance." He speared his chicken.

She took a swig of her champagne. "Thank you for the chance."

Her mind flooded again with a vision of the gore-strewn crater. Anger simmered, and the sting of Bael's rejection only worsened her mood. "I just—I don't understand this world. It's savage. Nyxobas is savage. He'll kill an oneiroi just for having a rock-knife. He forces his subjects to slaughter each other to prove themselves. Father and son hate each other. No one is actually happy here."

Dark magic whorled off his body, angrily slashing the air. "As if your goddess is any better."

Ursula slammed a hand on the table. "How many times do I have to tell you? She is not my goddess. I don't remember what F.U. did."

"That's right." His voice dripped with sarcasm. "She's F.U.'s goddess."

"Exactly."

"And F.U. was perfectly innocent, I'm sure. A pure follower of Emerazel, who knew how to wield a sword like the most savage assassin. Who Nyxobas has chosen as his champion. Who can't seem to control her fire, and who felt the need to wipe her memories clean to wash away the horror of what she'd done. A coward's way out."

His words slid through her bones, and an image of a burning house rose in her mind. What *had* she done? "You don't know that F.U. was a monster."

His powerful magic slashed the air around him. "When you threw the dagger at Nyxobas, what exactly was going through your head?"

She shook her head. *I don't want to get into that.*

Bael leaned in closer, his eyes piercing. "I can see that you're hiding something. Tell me what you were thinking?"

Tears moistened her eyes. She swallowed hard. "The voice said, *kill the king*."

He leaned back. "And yet, you're not a savage at all. Not like the shadow demons."

"I don't know where the voice came from."

"Easy to be blameless when you have no memories though, isn't it? When you divorce yourself so thoroughly from your former life that you think of yourself as two people. You're not a killer... F.U. is. How convenient for you."

"It's a little hard for me to defend these accusations when I have no memory. Forget the katana. *This* isn't a fair fight."

"Don't you get it, Ursula?" Venom laced his voice. "Having no memory is a blessing. Stop feeling sorry for yourself and count yourself lucky."

She gripped her knife, tears stinging her eyes. "And what did you do, Bael, to end up here in this wasteland below your manor?" She gestured at the empty cavern. "What guilt eats at you, that you've created your own little void? No messy emotions. No one close, no one to hurt you. Pretty safe here, among the mushrooms and the rocks, isn't it? Tell me, Bael. When was the last time you loved anyone but yourself?"

His eyes shaded to a deep black. "That is none of your concern, hound."

"The lords' wives told me you were an amazing lover. But it doesn't seem you kept any women around for long. No wonder you adore Nyxobas. You're just like him. Lost in the void. Talk about a coward's way out."

She stood, her legs shaking, and crossed back to the stone bridge. As she crossed, she peered over at the sheer drop into darkness.

And the darkness called to her.

Chapter 26

Ursula stopped when she reached the atrium. When she'd come through here with Bael, the candles in the sconces had been lit, and sunlight had streamed through the hole in the wall. Now, darkness shrouded the entire space, as if it were night. The hair rose on the back of her neck. Something was wrong.

"Cera?" she called out, her voice echoing off the ceiling.

Maybe I'd do best not to call attention to myself.

She edged back to the tunnel, and then a cloaked figure stepped from the shadows. A cold chill struck her like a slap in the face.

"Ursula," he cooed. Abrax's voice was unmistakable. A soft rasp, simultaneously terrifying and hypnotic. "I was hoping I might run into you."

He pushed back his hood, revealing his perfect porcelain skin and glacial gray eyes. Black magic twisted around him. Not angry and savage like Bael's, but cautious—almost tentative. Little tendrils that searched the darkness, probing for answers. One snaked by her throat, cold as a corpse's fingers.

He stepped toward her and she shrunk back toward the tunnel. That was her only chance of escape, even if it meant a humiliating retreat to Bael after their argument.

But Abrax wasn't a demon she could fight. He wasn't even a demon. He was a demigod. And without Emerazel's magic flowing in her veins, she didn't stand a chance.

If she let him get too close, he'd lure her in with his seductive spell. He'd drain her soul and send it to Nyxobas's void. She took another step back toward the tunnel. A few more steps and she'd be within the relative safety of its walls.

"Ursula," he purred. "Don't be afraid. I'm not here to hurt you."

You must think I'm a total mug.

Just as she began to turn, Bael appeared in a blur of night magic. "What are you doing in my manor, incubus?"

"Oh, did I interrupt something? A lover's quarrel?" Abrax smirked, his magic retreating. "You know that Nyxobas strictly forbids liaisons between hounds and his demons. But, of course, I'll overlook it. I am sympathetic to perverted urges, secret passions... a bit of unnatural fornication between the godlike and the beasts."

Ursula gagged. *Did he just say unnatural fornication?*

Bael's eyes burned with black fury. "What are you doing here?"

"I wanted to congratulate you two on your performance in the melee. Fighting side by side as you did. It was like watching a ballet performed by trained serpents."

"That's not why you're here," said Bael, his voice cold as ice.

Abrax flashed a brilliant, white smile. Everything about him was repulsive—apart from how he looked. "Correct. I wish to parley."

From what Ursula knew, "parley" was some kind of medieval English way of saying, "I'm going to talk a lot and then screw you over."

Abrax took a step closer to the pair. "You saw how well Massu performed today."

From the shadows behind Abrax, a pair of oneiroi stepped into the light. Ursula hadn't even noticed them before—truly, the oneiroi were creatures of shadow.

They stood to Abrax's right—one tall and one short. An iron muzzle covered the shorter man's mouth, and when he lifted his face to the light, she recognized Massu's eyes.

The larger oneiroi held an iron chain leashed around Massu's neck. Massu glared at Ursula and started for her, but the other oneiroi yanked him back.

"I brought him along to say hello," said Abrax.

Massu growled, jerking at his chain like an enraged pit bull.

"I hope you understand that I will win the tournament with Massu as my champion." He glared at Bael. "Do you still have your wife's portrait hanging in that room? I hope you'll leave it up. I'd like to gaze at her face while I fuck my courtesans in your manor. Sorry, *my* manor."

Bael's magic whipped the air around him. She could feel the fury rolling off his body. He was exercising all of his strength not to rip Abrax's head right off his body.

On a balcony two levels above, a flicker of movement caught her eye. A small figure peered over the rail.

"Massu will not win," Bael growled. "And when my wings are returned to me, I will take my place as Nyxobas's Sword once again. You may be his son. But he will never deem you worthy."

The night magic began to swirl around Abrax again, and the temperature dropped. Ursula's breath clouded around her head.

Cloaked in shadows, Abrax disappeared—only to appear again directly behind her. With a single, powerful hand, he pinned both of her arms behind her back.

"She's very interesting, don't you think?" Slowly, he ran a cold finger along her cheek, sending an icy shiver through her body. "I should have been her guardian. I don't know what she is. Not a normal human. Not a normal demon. She repulses and attracts me at the same time, and that is an intoxicating combination."

With her arms pinned behind her back, she struggled to free herself. Abrax's grip was ironclad.

Slowly, Bael stepped closer. "Get away from her, incubus."

Abrax gripped her by the back of her hair, pulling back her neck. The timbre of his voice changed becoming stronger. "Give her to me, and I will see that you keep your manor."

"No." Bael's razor-sharp voice cut through the air.

"You'll give up your manor for this dog? What is she to you?"

Snarling, Bael began to charge for Abrax—but a burst of magic from Abrax sent dark filaments of night magic racing across the room, wrapping around Bael's chest and mouth.

Abrax's grip on Ursula's arms was surely crushing her bones. "Abrax," she spat. "Do you think your daddy will be pleased that you're assaulting his champion?"

"Shut your filthy mouth, you abomination," said Abrax. "If I can't have you, no one will."

Ursula's heart skipped a beat. *Think, Ursula. Think.*

She slid her leg between Abrax's, and he pressed against her, moaning into her ear. "Have you changed your mind, little dog?" Gritting her teeth, she kicked upward, into his groin.

Abrax grunted, releasing her arms. Then, he pushed her onto the floor.

"Massu. Get your dinner."

The taller oneiroi ripped the mask off Massu's face. With a shrill scream, Cera's brother leapt for her throat. She rolled to the side, and Massu landed softly on the tile, like a cat. She clambered to her feet, as Massu leapt again.

She blocked his attack with her arm. A white-hot jolt of pain seared through her as Massu buried his teeth in her forearm. She screamed.

He clawed at her, pulling her hair, exposing the soft skin of her throat.

"Massu!" Cera's clear voice pierced the darkness. "Stop this right now, or I will give you a hiding!"

Massu loosened his grip on Ursula's arm, his silver eyes wide.

"Destroy her," said Abrax.

Massu's gaze turned back to Ursula. Hungrily, he licked his teeth. Ursula's gaze flicked to Bael. Out of the corner of her eye, she glimpsed him slowly working his way out of the bonds. *Come on, Bael.*

"Massu!" Cera shouted. "What did I tell you? Don't make me come down there."

Massu's head swiveled between Abrax and his sister. His arms trembled with indecision.

Cera called out again. "Massu, you let her go. You are not meant to be the Corrupted." "What is wrong with you?" Abrax roared. "I gave you a command."

Massu's turned back to her, baring his teeth, and she glanced at Bael again. In the shadows, he'd ripped away the filaments.

He roared, a sound of pure masculinity, a primal challenge.

His eyes wild, Massu leapt for Bael's throat, a blur of black and silver. A ravenous missile bent on the destruction of Bael's perfect face.

But he never made it that far. A sleek black blade glinted in Bael's hands, and Ursula watched as Bael plunged it into Massu's chest.

Cera's agonized wails echoed off the atrium walls, and bile rose in Ursula's throat.

Bael lifted his knife to Abrax. "You may be the son of Nyxobas, but I will kill you to protect my manor."

Night magic gathered around Abrax once again. The inky tendrils waved furiously about his head. "You killed my champion."

Starlight glistened in Bael's darkened eyes. "You violated the rules of the tournament."

Ursula took a step closer to Abrax. "Your father must be pretty cross about that whole army you raised against him. And here you are, breaking his rules again. How does he punish you? I imagine it's unpleasant."

Abrax's eyes blazed like starlight and his jaw dropped, like he'd been slapped in the face. Slowly, he turned and began to stride toward the hole in the wall at the far side of the atrium.

When Abrax reached the gap in the wall, he turned to face them, the tall oneiroi at his side. His gaze slid to Ursula. "When I capture you and force you into submission, the memories of today will only intensify my pleasure."

A shiver inched up her spine.

Shadows curled around Abrax and his oneiroi, completely enveloping them until they disappeared. Cera's cries still echoed through the atrium.

Bael turned to her, his face stony. "I must go to Cera. Show me your arm, first."

She lifted her arm, wincing at the vicious teeth-marks puncturing her skin. Bael let his powerful magic caress her skin, but this time, she took no pleasure in it. Her eyes slid to Massu's lifeless corpse, and nausea welled in her gut.

She hardly noticed Bael leaving.

She stood alone in the atrium, listening to the sound of Cera's cries. A deep, gnawing loneliness pressed on her chest.

Suddenly, it hit her. She was going to die here in the Shadow Realm, among a legion of demons who hated her.

Chapter 27

Ursula hurried into her quarters, pulling open her door. Once inside, she shut the it behind her listening for the familiar click of the lock. For the first time in her visit to the Shadow Realm, she actually appreciated the sound.

She ran for the bathroom, kneeling in front of the toilet, then heaved up her dinner. As she wiped a shaking hand across her mouth, she tried not to think about Abrax.

He'd corrupted the oneiroi. And she didn't know what he wanted to do to her—only that everything about him horrified her. What did he mean—she's not a normal demon, nor a normal human?

She peeled off her blood-soaked dress, letting it drop to the floor. He sensed something about her, something that stoked his perverse desires. What sort of an abomination *was* she?

She grabbed a cloth, running warm water over it, and washed herself off. In a daze, she snatched a fresh nightgown from upstairs, and slipped into it. Half of her wanted to go to Cera, but Bael was already with her. He'd slaughtered her brother, yes. But he still viewed himself as her protector.

Sunlight streamed in through the window, but tired as she was, she'd be able to sleep through it. She curled up onto the sofa and let her eyes drift shut.

She slept fitfully, dreaming of the reaper she'd slaughtered today. Remus chased her through a forest of bones, and Massu waited for her in a desolate wasteland. Each dream ended as they pulled her down and into the unending abyss of Nyxobas's void.

"Ursula?" A female voice jolted her from her sleep.

Ursula rubbed her eyes, blinking at Cera, her eyes red-rimmed.

An image flashed in her mind—Bael's knife slashing through Massu's throat.

"Cera?" She sat up, throwing her arms around Cera. "I'm so sorry about Massu."

"Abrax killed him," said Cera softly.

"What do you mean?" she loosened her grasp.

"The lord… Abrax killed his soul when he fed him raw meat."

Ursula nodded. "I hope to kill Abrax some day."

"Another thing we have in common," said Cera grimly.

The rich scent of food wafted past Ursula's nostrils.

Ursula frowned. "Please tell me you didn't cook. You should be mourning, not making me breakfast."

"I didn't cook. The lord instructed another of his servants to cook for us."

Ursula arched an eyebrow. "He's okay with us eating together? He said it was dangerous for us to be friends."

Cera shrugged. "I think he figures we're in danger no matter what. Might as well not be alone for it." Cera beckoned her to the bar. "Come. Join me."

Ursula stood, crossing to the bar. Since she'd puked up her dinner last night, her stomach was completely empty. Her mouth watered at the sight of orange juice, fresh fruit, toast, eggs, and a carafe of coffee. Cera had already set out two plates.

Ursula took a seat next to Cera and scooped eggs and fruit

onto a plate. Ravenous, she dug in, working her way through the eggs and toast. She took a sip of coffee, then glanced at Cera.

The oneiroi pushed her food around on her plate.

"Not hungry?" asked Ursula.

"Not today."

"It will take time, I imagine," said Ursula.

"I hadn't seen him in decades. I guess in some ways, I'd mourned him already. But I didn't need to watch him die."

Ursula nodded. "Bael said to use lavender for the nightmares."

Cera grinned. "He is wise. And what does he have planned for you today?"

"I'm not entirely sure. He said he was going to train me to ride one of the bats, but then we had a big argument, and he said I was a monster, and I said he lived a void like Nyxobas because he was scared of emotions."

Cera stared at her.

Ursula sipped her coffee. "So anyway, I'm not sure if he's still going to help me."

"Well, if he does plan to train you, the main thing is to hold on tight. It's really not that difficult if you remember to respect the bat."

"How do you do that?" Ursula asked.

"You talk to them. They'll respond to your instructions."

"They know English?"

"No, but they understand tone and inflection."

A knock sounded on the door, and Ursula jumped up. *Guess we're still on, then.* "I'll get it." She hurried across the floor, flinging open the front door.

With the sunlight streaming behind him, Bael stood in the doorway, dressed in black riding leathers. His gaze trailed over her nightgown.

Of course, she hadn't bothered to get dressed before she flung open the door. But then—after their conversation yesterday—she had the strongest urge to distract him out of spite.

"Hello, Bael. Come on in." She turned, knowing that he'd get a full view of the nightgown's plunging backline.

"Do you plan to wear clothes to this training?"

"Thinking about it," she said, turning back to him. She let the sleeve of her nightgown fall down, exposing her shoulder, but not so far that he could see her breast.

His gray eyes pierced right through her. "Are you doing this on purpose?"

Cera cleared her throat. "I feel it's time for me to leave."

"Not yet," said Bael, his eyes still locked on Ursula. "Please help Ursula find some clothes."

Cera let out an exasperated sigh. "Honestly, I don't know what's going on with you two."

As Cera hurried toward the stairwell, Ursula called out, "Make sure it's not too distracting for Bael! He gets distracted easily."

His jaw tightened.

She crossed her arms. "Wouldn't want you falling off your bat."

Bael's features softened, and he glanced away. "Is Cera okay?"

"As good as can be expected. She wants to murder Abrax, but that is perfectly reasonable."

Bael stared at the floor. "I had to kill Massu. Abrax had driven him insane. Once corrupted, there is no returning from the madness."

Ursula nodded. "I know. Plus, he was about to mess up your pretty face."

Bael glared at her. "Pretty?" He spat the word like an insult.

Cera's footsteps thundered down the stairs, and she bustled into the room with a bundle of clothes in her arms.

"That was fast," said Bael.

Cera nodded at the pile. "These should be appropriate for training."

"Thank you, Cera."

Bael nodded, his gaze landing on the top of the pile—on the lacy black knickers and bra.

He turned to walk for the door. "I'll meet you on the roof." When he was halfway to the door, he turned to face Cera, nodding so deeply it was almost a bow. "I'm sorry for your loss."

Chapter 28

*U*rsula stepped out of the elevator and onto the roof, shielding her eyes from the bright sunlight. On the sleek black roof, Bael crouched next to the bulk of an enormous black bat. As she approached, her heels clacking over the marble, Bael turned to look at her.

She wore thick woolen leggings, a leather jacket with a fur collar, and black riding boots that almost reached her knees. To complete the getup, she wore a large leather-covered helmet. She'd asked Cera if the helmet was strictly necessary, but the oneiroi had insisted.

Bael's lips curled in a smile. "Nice helmet."

She frowned. *I knew the helmet was a bad idea.* "Cera said it would protect my head."

Snorting, the bat shifted. It was monstrous, at least twice the size of Sotz.

She pointed. "Am I riding that?"

Bael patted the bat's back. "Vesperella? No, she's *my* baby girl." He put his fingers to his lips and whistled. A flapping of wings beat the air, and a moment later, Sotz landed next to her.

"I think you'll find it's easier to learn on a bat you're already familiar with."

She nodded at Sotz. "We've been getting to know each other."

"Can you steer?" he asked.

"Not really." *Not at all.*

Bael nodded. "You'll need to learn how to do if yourself if you want to have any hope of surviving the race."

"So how does it work? There was a harness that I held onto before." Ursula tried to remember how she'd seen Cera steer, but her vision had been blocked by Cera's back.

"You need to learn to ride bareback." Bael climbed onto Vesperella, demonstrating as he spoke. "You can hold onto the loose skin just behind the ears. Then just direct the bat's head the way you want it to fly." He tugged Vesperella's head to the right.

Ursula took a deep breath, glancing at Sotz. He narrowed his eyes. As she moved in closer, a low rumble rose in his chest and he bared his teeth.

"Easy, Sotz," said Bael. "Just step over his shoulders. You'll need to crouch a little bit."

"His shoulders?"

"Where the bat's wings connect to his chest," said Bael. "You'll want to sit right up against them. When he's flying, grip onto his chest with your calves." His gaze slid down to her legs. "You'll need to use your thigh muscles to hold on."

Ursula stepped over Sotz's neck and eased herself down. The moment her bum touched his back, he clambered forward toward the edge of the roof.

"Slow down," she shouted, tightening her thighs around his body. She gripped the loose skin behind his ears.

An instant later they were streaking down the roof and into the air. She glanced down at the crater, hundreds of feet below, and her breath caught. When Sotz curved wildly to the right, she lost her grip on his skin. Her heart thrummed wildly.

Panic blazed through her body, and she reached again for a grip, but Sotz twisted away from her. The motion sent her sliding to the side and she grabbed blindly, her fingers wrapping around the soft skin of one of his ears.

Sotz let out an ear-piercing shriek, bucking and jerking his body. She tried to hold on, but he threw her into the air.

Her heart stopped, and everything seemed to slow down. For a brief moment, her momentum keep her on an upward trajectory, and the whole valley of the crater spread out before her. She could see the houses of the oneiroi, Asta's purple spire, even the faint shimmer of magic along the rim of the crater, magic that—unfortunately for her—created gravity. She hurtled toward the ground, terror screaming through her mind. A scream tore from her throat.

As the wind ripped through her hair, something jerked the back of her jacket, halting her descent. In the next moment, Bael was pulling her on to Vesperella.

"Hang on to me!" he shouted over the wind.

Instinctually, she wrapped her arms around his neck, her face pressing into his chest. The bat was too large for her to get a grip on with her legs. Instead, she wrapped them around Bael's waist. He leaned in, steering the bat through the air. His heart pounded hard through his shirt.

She clung to him as he guided Vesperella out of a deep dive. The g-forces pressed her against his warm body, and she breathed in the scent of sandalwood by the sea. His sweet breath warmed the side of her face.

"Don't worry," he said. "The first time you fall from a bat is always the scariest."

The first time?

She could feel his muscles shifting as he expertly controlled the bat. With the wind rushing over their bodies, Bael directed Vesperella back to the rooftop in a great lazy arc.

"When you fly again," he said, "don't grip too tightly. It will spook him. You must be gentle with the bat. As I'm steering her now, even a slight twitch of my fingers is enough to make her respond the way I want."

Ursula swallowed hard. *Talk about distracting.*

Bael guided Vesperella into a soft landing on the roof, and Ursula unclenched her legs from Bael's waist. She stepped off, fighting dizziness.

He smirked. "Given the grip you had on me, I know you're strong enough to hang on."

"Thank you for not letting me die."

"I had a feeling you might need some assistance on your first flight. I almost smashed into those rocks over there on my race to get you." He pointed to a particularly sharp looking crag. "But, the main thing is to never grab a bat by its ears. They're very sensitive. I'll call Sotz and you can try again. "

Before Ursula could protest, Bael was whistling for the bat. This time, Sotz landed next to Bael, his beady eyes trained on her. Ursula was relieved to see that his ear appeared undamaged.

Bael reached down and scratched Sotz's head. "It's okay, little guy. She's just a little clumsy."

"Well, there's no need to rub it in."

"Let's try it again," said Bael.

This time when she sat on Sotz's shoulders, she didn't lower her full weight. Instead she crouched down and whispered into the bat's ear.

"I'm sorry, Sotz. I didn't mean to hurt you."

She nuzzled her head against his. Sotz's fur was soft as velvet, and while he didn't pure like a cat, he didn't growl either.

"You're a good bat. A *good* bat," she repeated. She scratched behind his ears as she had seen Bael do with Vesperella. Then she gingerly lowered her full weight.

This time when Sotz launched, she already had a firm but gentle grip on the skin behind his ears. They hurtled toward the ground, and her stomach dropped. Gently, she pulled back on Sotz's neck and he leveled off. They flew above the crater's floor, barely one hundred feet above the ground, racing over the little stone houses and narrow alleys of the Shadow Kingdom.

"Good boy," she whispered in his ear.

The sound of beating wings made her turn her head. Bael flew twenty feet away, the lunar wind ruffling his dark hair.

"That's better," he shouted over the wind.

"Thanks."

"Lean forward, and allow your weight to shift with each beat of his wings."

Ursula leaned forward until her chest was inches from Sotz's neck. The position felt a bit more unstable. But when she began to shift her weight with each beat of Sotz's wings, she saw that Bael was right. The ride smoothed out into a smooth glide.

"That's it," said Bael. He and Vesperella swooped under her and Sotz. With two great beats of Vesperella's wings, he took the lead. "Follow me!"

Ursula marveled at his change in demeanor. He seemed so comfortable on the bat, like he actually enjoyed life. It was hard to believe this was the same man who'd slit Massu's throat just hours ago.

Bael led her and Sotz in a great curving turn back toward the rooftop. When they were a hundred feet away, Bael and

Vesperella dove for the roof at a terrifying speed. At the last instant, Vesperella spread her wings, landing gracefully on the marble.

Now he's just showing off. She leaned forward to whisper in Sotz's ear. "We got this, big guy." She tried to bring the bat in slowly, but as the roof rose to meet them, she instinctively leaned back. Sotz tensed as he tried to decide whether to land or to pull back up into the air. He chose landing, but they hit the roof with a jerk that knocked her straight from his back. She slammed against the marble, rolling a few times before coming to rest on her back.

When she opened her eyes, Bael stood over her, a look of concern on his face. "Are you all right?"

"I'm fine." Still lying flat on her back, Ursula brushed the dust from her jacket.

"Good, because you must be in one piece for this evening. We have been invited to dinner at Asta with the lords and their wives."

Chapter 29

$\mathcal{A}$ few hours later, Ursula and Bael stepped down from his carriage and onto the marble, on the very top level of the crystal spire. The sun burned bright in a black sky—thankfully, not at its zenith, yet.

She wore a gown of shimmering white silk, with a plunging backline, now covered by a pale blue cloak.

She stole a quick glance at Bael. "Remind me again why we're here?"

"As lord, I'm required to attend dinners at the spire."

She arched an eyebrow. "And remind me why I needed to come?"

"Because your presence will distract everyone enough that I won't need to speak to anyone."

She cocked her head, the wind whipping through her hair. "I'm not sure that I distract everyone. I think that's just you."

He shook his head slowly. "Everyone watches you."

That's disturbing. Steeling her nerves, she glanced out at the dancing swarms of lunar moths. Asta's purple light shone through their wings, as they wove and dodged silently around the spire. For some bizarre reason, she felt strangely at home here. At peace.

She reached into her cloak pocket, rolling the silver ring around in the palm of her hand.

"We should enter," said Bael.

She turned to see him pulling open a black door that led into a dark hall. She stepped inside, walking at Bael's side. Some insane impulse overtook her, and she slid her arm through his.

She felt his muscle tense as she touched his elbow, but he kept silent.

The hallway opened into an enormous rectangular hall, the walls painted silver. A spray of ravens had been painted over one of the walls. Black chandeliers, lit with candles, hung from ceiling above two long, onyx tables.

The lords sat in silver chairs around the table—apart from Hothgar, who sat in an enormous, throne-like chair at the head. The wives sat at the other table.

A small oneiroi servant bustled up to Ursula, beckoning her forward. "This way, milady."

The servant led her to an open seat at the wives' table, then held out her hand for Ursula's cloak.

Ursula pulled it off. "I'll keep it with me, thank you." She wanted to keep the silver ring as close as possible. She'd need her little good luck charm to get through tonight.

As she draped her cloak over the chair, a hush fell over the group. Eleven pairs of eyes locked directly on her, taking in her pearly gown. And as before, she was seated near Viking, Goth Princess, and Talons.

She glanced at Viking, dressed in a sea-green gown. A deep purple bruise discolored her chin. She nodded to Ursula.

The other women weren't quite so friendly. Goth Princess turned away, showing Ursula her pale back, clad in black lace.

Talons scowled at Ursula, tapping a long red claw on her

silver goblet. Talons's silver hair tumbled over a violet gown. "Who invited the dog?"

Ursula narrowed her eyes. "The name is Ursula."

Viking twirled her champagne flute, shooting a sharp look to Talons. "Easy, Budsturga. We're not supposed to make a scene."

So that was Talons's name—*Budsturga*.

Goth Princess shot her a dark look. "It upsets the balance to have a human in here. And the smell is unbearable."

Ursula cocked her head. *You want to do catty? I know how to do catty.* "That's funny. Your husband Abrax doesn't think I'm human. Apparently, that's what he likes about me."

Princess glared. "He has a perverse fascination with freaks."

Ursula plucked her glass from the table. "Doesn't speak well of you, does it?"

Viking slapped the table. "I said, we're not to make a scene. Honestly, ladies. Who is the real enemy, here?"

Budsturga's face was incredulous. "What in the heavens are you talking about? The oneiroi?"

Viking leaned in, whispering, "When was the last time you saw a woman fight? Our husbands say we must do as they say because women are weak." She gazed right at Ursula. "But Ursula is proving them wrong. If they are wrong about Ursula, maybe they're wrong about all of us."

Goth Princess crossed her arms, practically pouting. "What makes you hate your husband so much, anyway?"

Viking shrugged. "I hate yours, too. He is a monster. But Hothgar is the one I have to live with. You see this?" She pointed to the purple bruise on her chin. "That was because I lost a bet on the melee."

Budsturga stabbed her talon into a canapé. "Men are brutal, yes. Best avoided."

Viking turned to Ursula. "Surely Bael is different. He's unmarried. But I'm told he does like women. Is it true what they say about him as a lover?"

Ursula cleared her throat. "I wouldn't know. We train together. That's it."

The furrow in Viking's brow suggested she didn't believe this. "Of course, ladies of the Shadow Realm would never bed a man before marriage. But I assumed a woman such as yourself..." Her sentence trailed off.

Ursula's eyebrows shot up. "I didn't realize demons had rules about sex before marriage."

"Not all demons," said Goth Princess. "Only the nobles of the Shadow Realm."

Ursula nodded. "And let me guess. It only applies to female nobles."

"Of course," said Budsturga.

Viking leaned in close. "It really doesn't seem fair. We should get to try them out before committing. The first time I kissed Hothgar was at our claiming ceremony. It was a horrific disappointment, but by then it was too late."

Ursula took a sip of wine, nearly too engrossed in the conversation to notice the waiters bringing bowls of steaming mushroom soup. "What's a claiming ceremony?"

Viking slurped her soup. "It's the ceremony when a husband claims his wife. It is the one tradition the warriors of Nyxobas adopted from the oneiroi. And because it comes from the beasts, it's positively savage."

Ursula shook her head. "But what is it?"

Budsturga stabbed another crudite with her talons. She'd have a hell of a time eating soup. "When a warrior claims a woman, they exchange rings. Then, the contract is sealed with a public display of lust. Nothing too far, Nyxobas wouldn't allow that. But the warrior must show sexual domination over his woman."

"As you can imagine," the Princess sighed, "Abrax took things a bit far."

"It's a marriage ceremony?" asked Ursula.

"More like an engagement," said Budsturga.

Viking's cheeks reddened. "Hothgar proposed in Asta's spire, then forced his tongue down my throat in front of the other lords. He ripped off my top. Frankly, that was the last time he showed any interest in me, and that was over a thousand years ago."

Goth Princess shrugged. "Men only want what they can't have." Her dark eyes slid to Ursula. "The forbidden flesh. And yet you're telling us Bael has no interest in you?"

Ursula's cheeks warmed. "Apparently not."

Viking wiped the soup off her chin, staring at Goth Princess. "Asharoth. Why does your husband hate Bael so much?"

Asharoth—apparently, that was her name—cocked her head. "He is the son of a god. He demands worship. And Bael has never been sufficiently submissive. His role as Sword of Nyxobas always rankled Abrax."

Viking threw back a long gulp of wine. "Hothgar isn't even a demigod, and he demands worship. You should see the inside of his temple."

Ursula ate a spoonful of her soup. *This sounds good.* "And what would I find in the inside of his temple?"

Viking giggled. "We can't always get humans here in the Shadow Realm. They simply die so easily. But when we run low on human slaves, Hothgar has his dolls."

Ursula leaned in over her soup. "What does he do with his dolls?"

Viking held her hand to her face, whispering. "He gets drunk on vodka, and uses his magic to animate them. He has them bend down to worship him, calling him Nyxobas. One or two he declares to be heathens, and he crushes them beneath his feet."

"And the whole time," added Budsturga with a wicked smile. "He has his lunar staff out."

"And I thought my husband was perverse," said Asharoth.

Ursula's lip curled. "And you're not allowed to have any fun with other men while your husbands do whatever they want?"

Asharoth's jaw dropped. "Of course not."

Ursula sipped her wine. "You ladies are getting a raw deal."

Asharoth shrugged. "It's not all horrible. As soon as a man claims you, you are protected. No man may touch another man's wife. No one may harm us. And men are forbidden from killing the women they've claimed."

Ursula stared. "That's it? They can't kill you? Like I said, you're getting a raw deal."

Before anyone could respond, a commotion erupted at the lord's table.

Bael stood. His dark magic whipped the air around him. "Abrax attacked me in my manor. He crossed my threshold uninvited."

Hothgar held out his hands, a placating gesture. "I know you're angry—"

"I'm not angry." And yet, icy wrath laced his voice. "But I want the fealty to which I am entitled."

Hothgar waved a dismissive hand. "As I said already, you killed his champion."

"His champion attacked me like a wild animal. If Abrax hadn't invaded my house, his champion would still be alive. I'm owed a fealty."

Hothgar rose. "And as I said, your killing of his champion is fealty enough."

"I know you two are colluding. A lord's manor is sacrosanct. A real Sword of Nyxobas would never allow this transgression."

Abrax leaned back in his chair, studying his nails. "Maybe you should have been more careful and not lost your wings." His gaze flicked to Bael.

"If you weren't Nyxobas's son, I would have slaughtered you months ago," Bael snarled. He turned, walking from the table and out of the hall.

Abrax's gaze slid to hers, and Ursula's stomach turned. *Time to get out of here.*

Budsturga leaned in to her, whispering, "I think you should follow him."

Ursula rose, yanking her cloak off the back of the chair. *You don't have to tell me twice.*

Chapter 30

*B*ael waited for her in the carriage, and she ran across the onyx platform. She yanked open the door, clambering inside.

She took her seat across from Bael, trying to catch his eye. As the team of bats pulled the carriage into the air, he studied the window intently.

She shoved her hand in her pocket, toying with the silver ring. "The lords' wives really aren't that bad."

He cut her a sharp look before fixing his gaze out the window again. Clearly, he wasn't in the mood for conversation.

She closed her eyes, trying to rid her mind of the image of Hothgar parading before a congregation of animated dolls, stroking his lunar staff. Despite herself, laughter escaped, and she covered her mouth.

"What in the gods' name is funny at this moment?" asked Bael.

"Did you know that Hothgar animates dolls to worship his knob?"

Bael's eyes widened. Slowly, a smile curled his lips. "I did not. Perhaps I could have lived without that knowledge." He kept his eyes on her, studying her intently. All traces of tension had left his face. "Would you like to go riding when we return to the manor?" he asked quietly.

"On bats, I assume?"

Bael nodded.

"I'm not really dressed for it." Ursula glanced down at her evening gown. "I suppose, with the enormous slits Cera cut up the front, I could get my legs around a bat."

Bael cleared his throat. "The cloak will keep you warm. It's beautiful, hunting in the daylight, the way the sun catches the moths' wings."

How could she say no to that? "I suppose I could really use the practice."

"Good." He leaned back in his seat.

Pale sunlight streamed through the window, sparking off his icy eyes and illuminating the perfect contours of his face. She had the strongest impulse to reach out and touch him, but he'd already told her how he felt about "hounds." And if she thought about it, the rebuke still stung. Obviously, he didn't like hellhounds. So what kind of women *did* he like?

She bit her lip. There was no reason she should care. They were going to fight to the death in less than a week, if she even made it that far. Clearly, the wine and the altitude had already gone to her head, muddling her thoughts.

What she needed was to focus on the race that lay ahead of her.

She drummed her fingertips on the seat. "For this race coming up, is there anything else I need to know besides flying?"

He shook his head. "You'll only need to follow behind me, and try to stay on the bat."

"Where does the race take place?"

"Around Asta's spire. We race in three loops."

She nodded slowly. "And the winners are the fastest?" She frowned. "I really do need the extra practice. I can't imagine anyone there will be slower than me."

"Just try to keep up with me."

She felt the carriage touch down on the roof, sliding over the marble, and she grasped a handle to steady herself.

Bael opened the door, and she stepped out onto the gleaming roof. Bael stared up at the black sky, and he put his fingers in his mouth to whistle for the two bats.

As the carriage lifted into the air, she hugged her cloak tightly around herself. "Did you say something about hunting?"

"Yes. Hunting for moths."

She scrunched her nose. "Do we have to kill them?"

His brow rose. "Are you suddenly wary of drawing blood? That's not the warrior I saw slaughtering demons twice her size in the melee."

She shrugged. "I have a strange affinity for the moths." *Because they're prey, and so am I.*

"We needn't kill them, if you don't want to."

She shielded her eyes, catching a flicker of movement in the dark sky.

Gracefully, the two bats glided onto the roof, just a few feet away.

Bael mounted Vesperella, gripping his neck while Ursula climbed onto Sotz's shoulders. She wrapped her legs around Sotz, and the fabric of her dress fell away from her thighs. *I'm going to have a bit of wind burn by the end of this journey.* Bael stared at her for a moment longer than necessary before lifting into the air.

By the time she and Sotz found their way to the roof's edge, Bael was already circling in a wide arc above her.

She tightened her thighs around Sotz, leaning forward to whisper into his ear. "Follow Vesperella."

Sotz beat his wings, taking flight off the roof's edge. He climbed higher, until he flew just beside Bael and Vesperalla.

"Nice work!" Bael shouted over the wind.

"Soon, it'll be second nature."

Bael's flight climbed higher in the sky, rising above the crater's rim, and Ursula followed a few yards behind, moving in time with the beating of Sotz's wings.

"See if you can keep up," Bael yelled. He leaned down, increasing his speed.

Ursula leaned low over Sotz's neck. Simply adjusting her weight was all the encouragement he needed. His wings beat more strongly as they raced around the crater's edge in the pearly sunlight. Ursula's hair blew wildly about her head, but she could still see a stunning view of the crater.

Ahead of her, Bael and Vesperella charged forward, extending their lead and climbing higher into the sky.

Ursula crouched even closer to Sotz. "Can you catch them?"

Sotz's wings whooshed thorough the air and they sped up. Ursula's pulse raced as the wind whipped over her skin.

Despite the icy cold that bit into her exposed knees, a strange feeling rippled over her body, almost as if she *belonged* here, up in the air under a clean, black sky.

She pulled alongside Bael, thrilling at the speed of the flight. They'd climbed higher than she'd ever flown in the carriage, swooping up above Asta's spire. A frothing sea of moths rose up before them.

With a whoop, Bael directed Vesperella straight at the moths. Sotz plunged after them so fast, Ursula almost lost her grip. She tightened her grasp on the bat just as they hit the edge of the cloud.

The moths parted as they entered, both encircling them at a safe distance. Sotz's ears perked up, and a low growl rose from his chest. A rich sound vibrated through her gut—the deep thrumming of the moths' beating wings.

Sotz winged forward, deeper into the cloud.

Ursula leaned into him. "We're not killing today, Sotz. Just riding."

Another growl rose from his throat. She had the feeling he wasn't thrilled about that idea.

Beating his enormous wings, Sotz rose again, climbing out of the cloud of moths until she could see the black sky once again.

From here, Bael led her and Sotz around the edge of the cloud. The writhing mass extended high into the dark sky. Form there, the light of Asta reflected off of the moth's wings, washing them in flashes of purple and violet. There was something almost hypnotic in the way they undulated around the spire.

One hundred feet above her, a bat burst from the cloud, a bleeding moth in its jaws. Another followed. She could hear the beating of their wings as they passed over her. Sunlight highlighted their forms in the dark sky, beautiful and terrifying at the same time.

Far above her, another bat burst from the cloud. Ursula gasped. The pale form was unmistakable—the white bat of the Gray Ghost.

"Bael!" she shouted.

He turned to look at her, but when she tried to point, the white bat had disappeared.

"What was it?" he asked, circling back.

She followed his path, the wind whipping through her hair. "The bat of the Gray Ghost."

"Did you see where it went?"

"No!" *Bloody thing disappeared. Much like a ghost.*

Leaning down close to Vesperella, Bael began curving back to the manor. Ursula leaned closer to Sotz, picking up speed to keep pace with Bael. Her pulse raced with a sharp thrill as they swooped lower over the city. *I actually think I can do this. I can keep pace with Bael just as well as anyone.*

She might have frostbite on her legs at this point, but the clean feel of the lunar air called to her. Somehow, she felt she was meant to fly.

And clearly, so was Bael.

Vesperella dove sharply for the roof of Abelda, and Ursula followed close behind. As the black marble drew nearer, Sotz beat his wings, slowing his descent. He glided gracefully to a landing by Vesperella's side. Bael was already dismounting.

She stepped off Sotz. The inside of her thighs burned from exhaustion, and the outside from the freezing wind.

She straightened, glancing at him. "I take it you miss your wings."

"It's hard to get used to being grounded after twenty-two millennia of flight."

She smiled. "The lords' wives said you were worshipped as a god in the old days."

"The lords' wives have a lot to say about me."

"And yet you're still a total mystery."

He eyed her cautiously. "What do you need to know?"

A chilly lunar wind toyed with her hair. "You said you were from Canaan. Where's the rest of your family?"

"Dead," he said flatly.

Shit. She shouldn't have brought that up. She already knew his wife had died. She swallowed hard. "I meant your parents."

"Dead. A long time ago." He climbed back on to Vesperella's back. "You should get inside. You're going to freeze."

Before she could respond, Bael leaned forward on Vesperalla's shoulders and whispered in her ear. Vesperella's wings stroked the air, and Bael surged upward into the black sky.

Chapter 31

$\mathcal{U}$rsula sat on the sofa, rubbing a salve into her palms. She eyed the sun, edging dangerously close to its zenith, and her pulse sped up. *Not long now.*

She'd been practicing on Sotz for several days, building up her speed and control. And now, the day before the race, her muscles burned with a deep fatigue.

She pulled up her dress, wincing at the sight of her inner thighs, rubbed raw from spending hours each day winging around the crater with Sotz.

She dabbed the salve onto her thighs, working it into her skin until some of the red faded to a pale pink.

F.U. may not have ridden a bat before, but she seemed to understand the principles of controlling a beast, making it conform to her will with subtle shifts in muscle, little twitches of her hands. Feeling every movement of Sotz's muscles and sinews. Directing him as though he were an extension of herself. She wasn't as skilled as Bael, of course, but she was getting there.

At Cera's insistence, she'd even dipped her toe into the art of clasping her arms around Sotz's neck to ride upside down, her hair dangling toward the moon's surface. That particular move still made her heart leap into her throat, but she'd attempted it, nonetheless.

She slid her hand into her pocket, glancing at the door. The one thing that had been conspicuously absent over the past few days was Bael. He'd completely disappeared after their conversation about his dead family. *Nice one, Ursula.*

Instead of training her, like he'd said he would, he'd just disappeared into his manor. She wasn't even sure anymore if he still planned to help her in the race, or if he planned to knock her out of the sky. Apparently, stabbing someone with a corkscrew was a forgivable offense. But ask someone a personal question, and you've taken things too far.

She rose, crossing to the bar. Cera had left a neatly folded pile of riding clothes—her racing outfit for tomorrow. Cera had fashioned a leather outfit of a shimmering black—so she could blend into the sky. Ursula ran her fingers over the soft leather, frowning.

Why, in particular, was it important that she blend in to the sky? If they were only racing, she didn't need to disguise herself.

Unless, of course, there was more to it.

A little knock sounded at her door—Cera's knock, and she hurried across the room. Her stomach rumbled. All this riding had given her an uncontrollable appetite, and with any luck, Cera had brought her dinner.

But when she opened the door, she found Cera standing with a bag of clothing instead of a tray of food. Clear sunlight streamed through her hair, and she lifted the bag. "A new dress."

Ursula pulled open the door, motioning for her to enter. "And why, exactly, do I need a new dress right now?"

"The lord has requested your presence at dinner." She thrust the bag at Ursula. "I've made the dress distracting. I have a feeling the lord needs a bit of distraction."

"Where has he been for the past several days?"

Cera shrugged. "How should I know? He doesn't run his schedule by me."

Ursula frowned. "Cera, can you give me more specifics about this race? Why, exactly, would I need to be camouflaged."

Cera's silver eyes widened. "I'm not supposed to tell you."

Ursula's stomach dropped. "Tell me, Cera."

"I believe the lord is going to fill you in over dinner. Now get dressed, and go meet him in his quarters."

Ursula stared at her reflection in the mirror. She'd piled her hair on her head in a messy up-do, and she wore a silk-wrap dress—with an appropriately plunging neckline. She ran her hands over the smooth silk, the same pale gray as the clouds of moths. The skirts seemed to float around her legs.

A black-jeweled necklace completed the ensemble—the same color as her knickers. Not that Bael would ever know that.

As she put on her eyeliner, she hummed to herself—David Bowie's "Major Tom." A terrible dance remix of that song had always played in District 5, but suddenly the lyrics seemed much more meaningful to her.

What she wouldn't give right now for a normal night. Cheap wine from the Crobar, loud music, maybe a greasy burger before a night bus home. Granted, her life before Kester burst into her kitchen had been pretty shit. Unemployed, single, and completely broke. But at least she hadn't been surrounded by psychotic demons hell-bent on destroying her.

As she stood back to admire her reflection, a loud bang came from her door. *Bael's knock.*

On her way to the door, she pulled on a black cloak, shoving her hand into her pocket to feel the reassuring smoothness of the silver ring. She pulled open the front door to find Bael standing in the gleaming sunlight in a fitted gray suit.

"Ursula."

She crossed her arms. "There you are. I was beginning to wonder if you'd fallen into the chasm."

"I had matters to attend to over the past few days." He turned to cross the bridge, clearly expecting her to follow.

Outside, an icy breeze rippled over her skin. "So you weren't avoiding me?"

"Why would I do that?"

They crossed into the atrium, and she shrugged. "I don't know. It's just that you said you'd train me to ride, and then you disappeared into your man cave for days. Coincidentally, it was directly after I asked you a personal question."

He turned to her just long enough to arch an eyebrow. "As I said, I had matters to attend to. And I understand Cera was able to train you. She tells me you've been improving remarkably well."

In the narrow tunnel, her heels echoed off the ceiling. "Speaking of the race. Can you tell me why Cera made me a black suit for the competition?"

"I would imagine she thought it contrasted rather fetchingly with your fiery hair."

"Is that another one of your jokes?" She nudged him with her elbow. "I meant, why did she mention it was important for me to blend into the dark sky? Why would I need to go unnoticed, if we're only racing?"

Bael cleared his throat as they crossed into the cavern. "She should not have mentioned that."

Hot anger ignited. "I knew you were hiding something from me!"

"We will discuss it over dinner." He pointed to the narrow stone bridge. "I don't want you losing your footing again as we cross the bridge. There are only so many times I can catch you mid-air."

"Right," she said through clenched teeth.

She trod carefully over the stone bridge, trying not to stare too deeply into the abysses on either side. If she lost this race, she'd find herself permanently trapped in the void, in complete isolation for the rest of eternity. Just the thought of it made her stomach tighten with dread.

She stared at Bael's back as he gracefully crossed over the bridge, his movements fluid. *At least one of us is going to end up in the void.* A lump rose in her throat.

Bael crossed to a black marble table laid out with a domed platter and two glasses of wine. She pulled off her cloak, then took a seat across from him.

His gaze flitted over her neckline, and she heard the sharp intake of breath.

His brow creased. "I thought we'd talked about your dresses distracting me."

"We did. I decided that I definitely do not care. Now will you tell me what's going on with the race?"

Sighing, he pulled the lid off the platter, revealing a roast ham with glazed carrots on the sides. Her mouth watered. Apparently, Bael knew exactly how to distract her, too.

Greedily, she pulled two slices of ham onto her plate and cut into them.

"During the race, you must stay as close to me as possible." He served himself a slice of ham.

"You said to follow you. I don't really understand why. I can't exactly beat you if I'm stuck behind you."

"If you're going to survive, you'll need to stay near me."

She stopped eating, her stomach clenching. "Why?"

"So no one slaughters you while you're riding."

She stared at him. "You told me it was just a race. You never said I needed to practice with a sword. This is a major disadvantage."

"Learning to ride a bat is complicated enough. If we'd added a sword into the mix, you wouldn't have survived the training."

Her fingers tightened around her fork. "You didn't even give me a chance," she spluttered. "Tell me everything I need to know. Now. Don't spare any more details."

He sipped his wine. "Like I said, the race is around Asta's spire. There are two groups. We start at the same place, but fly in opposite directions."

"The groups pass each other at the opposite side of the spire?"

"Exactly. The goal is to make three passes between the points. Or we stop when twelve have died."

"Three passes?"

He shrugged. "They've never gone further than two."

Her mouth went dry. "What kind of weapons are used?"

"The same as the melee. Nothing ranged or magically enhanced. The best riders always win. A good rider can evade even those armed with lances."

"Right. Sounds wonderful. I'm bringing my katana."

"You have a better chance of survival if you stick near me."

She nodded slowly. "And I'm just supposed to trust your judgment. You've withheld crucial information about the race until I no longer had the chance to practice. Plus, every now and then you point out that you will kill me."

Gold candlelight danced over the fine planes of his face. "I *will* have to kill you. Just not tomorrow."

Something cold gnawed at her chest. "And you're okay with that?"

His jaw tightened. "It doesn't matter if I'm okay with that. We don't choose the rules. The gods do, and they do not care for our lives. You must choose if you are predator or prey. There is no in-between. And while I'm pretty sure that F.U. was a predator, I'm not sure you're quite the same." He leaned in closer. "If you don't even have the stomach to kill a moth, how do you expect to survive a brutal sword fight while flying on Sotz? You're better off hiding behind me."

She shook her head, panic rising in her chest. "This whole thing is insane. I don't understand how I'm supposed to depend on you one day and then wait for you to kill me the next. And what if I don't want to play by Nyxobas's rules? There's got to be another way out of this tournament that doesn't involve us killing each other."

"There is no way out," his voice boomed, reverberating through her gut. "Just because you've found a way to forget all the horrible things that have ever happened in your life does not mean that everyone gets a happy ending. And just because I've trained you out of some misguided sense of duty does not mean that I'm your friend. I must either kill or die, and the same is true of you. You mean nothing to me, hound."

His words hit her like a punch to the gut, and she dropped her fork on the table. "You're a predator, so you say. I mean nothing to you. And you're determined to kill me." Humiliatingly, she could feel the tears welling in her eyes. "And yet here you are, asking me to trust you. Asking me to leave my sword behind while you protect me."

He leaned back in his chair, studying her. "I feel obligated to give you a fair fight."

"Before you kill me?" Angry heat flooded her cheeks. "Bollocks. If I'm destined to die—if I'm prey—then what's the point of going through all this effort? Why go through the trouble of training me at all?"

He simply stared at her, the candlelight flickering in his eyes.

She stood and grabbed a handful of ham to eat alone in her quarters. As she turned to leave, she shot him a final glare. "I'm bringing my katana tomorrow."

Chapter 32

Ursula and Cera stood on the roof of the manor, looking out over the crater. From the black sky, the pale light of the sun shimmered over Asta's spire, and warmed her skin through her clothes.

She shielded her eyes with her hand, glancing at Cera. "Thank you for teaching me to ride Sotz."

Cera shot her a stern look. "You'd better not die today."

Icy dread flooded her body. "I'll do my best."

Cera leaned closer, giving her hand a squeeze. "If you don't go now, Ursula, you'll be late."

Ursula put her fingers to her lips, whistling for Sotz. After a few moments, a shadow passed over their heads, and Sotz landed on the rooftop, just by the building's edge.

Her stomach turning, Ursula crossed to the bat. Her fingers grazed her katana's hilt. A part of her wondered if Bael had been right. Maybe she should have listened and left the katana at home. But she couldn't exactly rely on someone who kept saying he planned to kill her.

Taking a deep breath, she settled herself on Sotz's shoulders, gripping tightly with her thighs. Sotz clambered to the building's edge, then took flight over the crater.

As Sotz winged toward the spire, she rehearsed her plan: stay alive. She'd try to stay out of the fight and engage only if attacked.

She soared over the crater, thrilling at the feel of the wind in her hair. As Sotz drew closer to Asta, she tightened her grip on his fur. Around Asta's peak, workers had erected a great wooden platform that ringed around the spire. And from the platform, a long wooden dock jutted out into the lunar winds, like a wharf.

Ursula circled closer. In the center of the platform, Hothgar stood, flanked between his wife and his giant gong. The other lords mulled around, sipping from silver goblets. *How fun to drink cocktails while watching death rain down on the city with a perfect, panoramic view.*

The other riders already soared through the air, showing off by turning flips and racing around the peak. Bael flew in a lazy circle around the perimeter, apparently unconcerned with showboating.

Arcing closer, Ursula glanced down at the crater. A vast sea of Brethren swarmed around the spire's base. Unlike the arena at Lacus Mortis, this venue stood right in the center of the Shadow Realm. Anyone in the entire kingdom could get there—and it appeared the entire kingdom had, in fact, showed up to watch the champions die.

A loud crash rang through the air, reverberating through her gut. Hothgar's gong. *Things are about to get started.*

Hothgar raised his hands to the sky, his dark magic swirling around his body. As he spoke, his voice boomed over the crater. "The sun has nearly reached its zenith. The riders must approach the dock."

Ursula's heart was beating so hard, it threatened to break her ribs, but she gently guided Sotz lower, joining the line of riders on the dock. As she flew closer, she could see that the starting positions on the dock alternated directions—some facing clockwise, and some counterclockwise. Apparently, these would be the two groups.

She picked out Bael's muscled form at the end of the dock, facing clockwise. Her pulse racing, she angled Sotz lower to the dock. As she approached, her pulse racing, she was gripped by the terrifying fear that she'd overshoot the bloody thing entirely.

At the last moment, Sotz skidded to a halt, clinging on to the dock's edge. At his clumsy landing, she lurched forward, grunting, before regaining her balance. Sotz inched back, and Ursula took a deep breath, surveying her competition.

She'd landed between a lanky demon with a narrow mustache, and a noseless creature with skin the color of ice. The iceman turned to glare at her, growling.

Leaning forward, she glanced down the row again at Bael. They faced the same direction. In theory, she could follow behind him—assuming he really meant to help her.

At the end of the dock, Hothgar stalked closer, his dark eyes gleaming in the sunlight like black pearls. "Ah, Emerazel's dog. I realize a bitch like you is used to riding your way to the top, but you won't be doing it by opening your legs today."

She snarled at him. "Don't you have some unfortunate dolls you need to seduce in your temple?"

Hothgar's eyes flashed with rage. The lanky man to her right barked a laugh. Ursula shot a quick glance at Viking, who laughed behind her hand. Suddenly, she was glad she'd brought the katana. She wanted to show the city what a woman could do— that they didn't need to submit to their men because they were weak.

As her muscles tensed, ready for battle, Ursula tried to flash her bravest smile at Hothgar's wife.

Above the spire, the sun blazed bright—right above the peak. A cold sweat broke out on her brow. She swallowed hard, tightening her grip on Sotz, feeling his heart thumping through his fur. As she leaned forward, she surveyed the riders once more. Each demon dressed in muted shades of gray, blue, and black—some in furs and armor. Only one rider stood out—the Gray Ghost, draped in white, his face covered by a scarf.

At the end of the line, Bael wore his black fighting gear, his lion pendant glinting in the sun. He faced forward, his grip tight on a long lance.

In a race like this, a long weapon like a lance was a huge advantage. *Might have been nice to train with one.*

Hothgar's voice boomed, "The race will commence when I sound the gong, at the sun's zenith."

Ursula's blood roared in her ears. Her palms were sweating so much, she wasn't sure she could keep hold of Sotz's fur. Her eyes wandered to the crater's floor, hundreds of feet below. What would a body look like if it fell from this height?

The pause that followed seemed to stretch for eternity, and Ursula closed her eyes, trying to marshal control over herself, trying not to picture the explosion of guts from a person's mouth.

At last, the gong crashed, reverberating around the crater. She tightened her thighs on Sotz.

Sotz launched into the air.

Around her, the riders soared, the wings of their bat beating the air. Ursula leaned down, urging Sotz forward. As they arced around the spire, she fell slightly behind the rest of the pack, and she stared at the back of Flesh Scales. There was no shame in hanging behind the others. If this was a fight to the death, might as well let the front of the pack take the brunt of the attack.

The crowd below cheered, and her heart pumped harder. *The other half of the champions must be close.*

They burst into view, weapons glinting in the sun.

Ahead of her, Bael and the other riders spurred their bats to a faster pace, and the two camps collided in clashes of steel. From the corner of her eye, she glimpsed Bael's lance punching straight through a demon's chest.

Keeping out of weapons' range, Ursula watched two bodies fall to the crater's floor, leaving puffs of smoke just like little meteorites.

"Two kills!" the announcer shouted. "Ten remain!"

Arcing behind the main fray, she looked up.

Her stomach leapt into her throat. The Gray Ghost was flying directly for her, his face covered with his scarf. He pointed an enormous ash lance directly at her chest.

Ursula gripped Sotz's fur tighter. She couldn't fight a lance with a sword—the lance would knock her off Sotz before she got within striking distance. But hadn't Bael said a good rider could avoid a lance with the right moves?

She clung tightly to Sotz, arcing away from the attack. Then, she clung to Sotz's neck, and let her body slide down, so that her legs dangled beneath him. The lance grazed Sotz's shoulder.

As she flew hanging from Sotz, adrenaline burned through her nerve-endings. In the distance, she heard the announcer calling out two more deaths. The lunar wind whipped through her hair, and she gently urged Sotz upright again. When she righted her bat, the Gray Ghost had disappeared. The other riders surged forward, already moving on to begin another circle around the spire.

Ursula leaned down, trying to keep pace with the three riders winging ahead of her. Bael's silver lion insignia flashed in the sunlight.

She urged Sotz forward as they arced around the edge of the spire, the violet crystal gleaming in the sunlight. If she weren't moments away from possible death, it might have been exhilarating.

As soon as they slammed into the riders a second time, her hackles were raised. Three riders were already charging for Bael. She arced closer to him, watching as his lance rammed into the chest of the lead rider. The horned demon shrieked, falling from the sky.

Still, two other riders pressed on Bael—and one of them slammed a lance right into Vesperella, goring the bat. Blood sprayed in the air, and Vesperella's wings folded together.

To Ursula, it was like watching in slow motion, even though it happened in an instant. Panic ripped its claws through her heart, and she watched as Bael released Vesperella's neck. He stood on her back for a moment. Then, a thousand feet in the air, Bael leapt towards the rider who'd just killed his mount, grasping at his feet. Vesperella tumbled, blood spraying from her hide as she grew smaller in the sky. Bael's lance sparked in the sun as it fell.

Bael hung by one hand, dangling from the bat's foot, and two other riders moved closer. Vultures, waiting for their chance to finish him off. One moved a little too close, and in a gravity-defying move, Bael swung his body into the air. He landed on the rider's back. It took only an instant for him to fling the rider off.

The remaining rider began to close in on Bael. With Bael unarmed and on an unfamiliar mount, the ice-skinned demon saw a chance for easy prey. He unsheathed a cutlass.

Clenching her jaw, she raced lower toward Bael, the glacial lunar wind whipping over her skin. Saving Bael wasn't part of the plan, but she wasn't ready to watch him die. She ripped her katana from its sheath, charging for the ice-demon. Her body moved fluidly with Sotz's, as if she'd been doing this all her life, and her gaze locked intently on one thing. Her prey.

No one expected death to come from the woman. From the bitch. No one expected *her* sword to find its way clean through their neck.

Crimson blood sprayed through the air as she cut through the demon's head.

The demon's body slumped, then rolled off his bat.

"Twelve down!" Hothgar's voice boomed.

As Ursula glanced down at her blood-soaked sword, a chill spread through her veins. *Predator. It seems, the answer is predator.*

Chapter 33

*U*rsula stared at the thick blood dripping from her sword, then sheathed her weapon. Eyeing her, Bael nodded mutely, then began winging back to the dock. She swooped behind him, still catching her breath. Despite the cold lunar air, sweat matted Sotz's fur and dampened her clothes. Every one of her thigh muscles burned. She wanted to soak in a warm bath for days.

As she closed in on the dock, she maneuvered Sotz to land a little more gracefully this time. He touched down between Bael and a lanky demon in a black doublet. He turned to her, giving a little bow.

She leaned into Sotz, whispering, "That was some good flying." The bat looked up at her with his beady eyes in an expression that could have been mistaken for relief.

"Nice swordsmanship," Bael said, studying her. "A natural assassin."

"It was an easy kill." *Okay. I sound a little like a sociopath.*

An image burned in her mind—her sword slashing through the ice-demon's neck. It *had* come naturally to her.

Wherever she'd come from, F.U. had been a formidable predator. Ursula swallowed hard, eyeing Bael, the sunlight sparking in his eyes, a pale blue-gray, the color of ice floes.

If she needed to kill this man, she'd need F.U. to come out and finish the job. Ursula just wasn't quite psycho enough.

Hothgar stalked toward them, his black cape floating on the wind. "The remaining champions must now choose their opponents for the duel. Of the fifty-seven original champions, eight remain. And what an interesting lot you are." He smirked. "Bael the Fallen of Albelda, Zoth of the giant of Pleion, Inth of Alboth, Bernajoux of Zobrach, Valac of Phragol Mocaden, Chax of Azimeth, and our phantom rider, who could be absolutely anyone." His nostrils flared. "And how could I forget Emerazel's filthy bitch."

Ursula's fingers tightened on her sword's hilt. "Why do I have the disturbing feeling that you'll be animating a ginger-haired doll when you get home tonight?"

"Silence!" Hothgar roared, his cheeks reddening. When he'd regained his composure, he smoothed the front of his shirt. "You must now choose your opponents. With eleven kills, Bael is our leading Champion. He will choose first."

Ursula swallowed, as dread filled her veins. He had been promising to kill her. So did he want to get it over with or delay the inevitable? An icy wind toyed with her hair, rippling over her skin.

Bael shot her a quick glance, and for a moment, her stomach clenched. "I will fight Zonth of Pleion," he announced, his voice booming.

A giant man, dressed in furs and silver, snarled, revealing a row of jagged teeth. Apparently, that was Zonth.

Hothgar raised a hand. "After Bael's eleven kills, the second choice goes to the man all the commoners are calling the Gray Ghost."

From behind his scarf, the Gray Ghost shouted, "Chax of Azimeth."

Hothgar nodded. "Next to choose—my champion, Bernajoux." Hothgar flashed a mirthless smile. "As lord of the Pleion, I will select Bernajoux's champion for him. He leads my legion. He slaughtered twenty-seven men at the battle of Mt. Acidale."

The lanky man in the doublet bowed his head. With his delicate mustache and thin hands, he didn't look like a formidable opponent.

Of course, looks could be deceiving. Hothgar glared at her. "Bernajoux will slaughter the dog. I have so wanted to see what her insides look like."

A chill washed over Ursula's skin, and Bernajoux bowed deeply.

Urusla straightened on her mount. *Okay. That was creepy, but my opponent could have been worse. At least I'm not stuck with Zoth. Or worse—Bael.*

"That leaves Valac of Phragol Mocaden vs. Inth of Alboth," continued Hothgar. He raised his hands to the pale sun. "The duels will be held at the Lacus Mortis in two days." As he spoke, his voice seemed to boom over the entire crater, rumbling through her bones.

Below, the bloodthirsty crowd erupted with cheers.

* * *

Cera waited for her on the roof, her white skirts billowing around her.

When Ursula landed, Cera rushed over to her. "What happened?" she asked, her silver eyes frantic. "Where is the lord?"

Ursula's muscles groaned as she stepped off her mount. "He's fine. He's on his way." She stumbled as she stepped off Sotz.

Cera steadied her, squeezing her arm. "What else? Who do you have to fight at the duel?"

Ursula's muscles still shook from the adrenaline rush. "I need to fight a demon named Bernajoux. He didn't look quite as intimidating as the rest, to be honest. But Hothgar really wants his own champion to slaughter me."

She glanced out at the crater, catching a glimpse of Bael soaring through the sky.

Cera squeezed Ursula's arm again. "He really is magnificent."

"Too bad we have to slaughter each other," Ursula muttered.

Cera's eyes glistened. "The lord will give you a quick death. He is merciful."

"Wonderful."

Bael arced over their heads, then landed on the roof. He stepped off his mount. In the sunlight, blood and gore glistened off his black clothes.

Cera frowned at his mount. "Where is Vesperella?"

"Dead."

"I'm sorry, milord," said Cera. She looked him up and down, taking in the bloodstains that soaked his clothes. "I will lay out fresh clothes for you." She hurried off, leaving Ursula alone with Bael.

Suddenly cold from the damp sweat soaking her clothes, she shivered.

Bael studied Ursula. "Ursula. You will join me in my chambers in three hours."

The way he barked orders set her teeth on edge. She crossed her arms. "I guess that since you've been ordering people around for twenty millennia, you forget how to make a request," she grumbled, before realizing she'd said it out loud.

The corner of his mouth twitched in what almost looked like a smile. "Will you join me in my chambers in three hours?"

She nodded. "Why not? If we're going to fight to the death in a few days, I might as well learn everything I can about you."

"I like the way you think," he said.

246

"And is there a purpose to this visit?" When she thought of what he'd said to her before the race, his words still felt like a slap in the face. As she stared at his ruthlessly beautiful features, hollow loneliness ate at her. "You've already made it clear that we're not friends and you don't care for me at all, so I'm wondering what the point is."

"You must learn to use shadow magic." He took a step closer, his large form looming over her. "Bernajoux will cut you down if you do not allow me to train you."

She nodded. "And you want the chance to kill me yourself?"

He now stood so close she could feel the warmth emanating from his body. "I will make it painless," he said softly. For just a moment, he let his fingertips brush down her shoulder. "Bernajoux will not."

She looked up at him. He stood over a foot taller than her. "Bernajoux didn't look that scary."

"Bernajoux is powerful and sadistic. There is a reason Hothgar likes him."

Chapter 34

Balancing carefully, she walked across the stone bridge. This time, she'd come barefoot and wearing her simple black gown. She didn't need to risk plunging off the side of the bridge because she'd stumbled in her heels.

In her pocket, she gripped the silver ring, feeling its reassuring familiarity between her fingers. For just a moment, her gaze flicked to the abyss, and a shiver crawled up her spine. The darkness called to her.

"Ursula," Bael's voice rose from the shadows, smooth as velvet.

As she crossed into the main cavern, she caught the outline of Bael's enormous form, sitting in his onyx throne. Candlelight sparked in his eyes, and wisps of night magic flickered around him. Raw, dark power roiled around him.

"Come closer," he said.

She padded across the cold stone floor, gazing up at him. Seated in his throne, he towered above her. When she stood only a few feet from him, she could see his piercing eyes, so cold against the warmth of his golden skin.

Suddenly, she felt completely unsure of herself. "What do I need to do?" she asked, rolling the ring in her fingers.

"I need you to feel the magic." His cold aura snaked over her skin, caressing her body.

Powerful shadow magic thrummed along her ribs, skimming her breasts. It encircled her neck. Instinctively, her head tilted back, exposing her throat. As Bael's magic wrapped around her body, it seemed to thrill her at the same time as it filled her with dread. A chill spread over her skin, goosebumps rising on her arms. When she exhaled, her breath clouded around her face. Under her cotton dress, her nipples hardened. She hugged herself, and her teeth began to chatter.

His gaze slid down her body and up again. "You can feel the magic? That is good."

"It's freezing." She clenched her jaw to keep her teeth from chattering.

"Yes. Shadow magic comes from the void." Bael's voice sounded distant, like he was speaking from a thousand miles away. "It is the cold of the depths of space, the endless nothingness between stars. As you learn to channel it, your other senses will learn to feel it, too."

Standing before Bael, she continued to shiver. She wasn't entirely clear why she had to stand below him like one of his subjects while he loomed over her in his throne. "So how do I learn to channel it?"

"It won't be easy. But you're off to an impressive start. When I was first learning, it took me weeks before I could sense the magic. Perhaps F.U. already had some practice. "

As Bael's magic slid over her body, she was pretty sure her lips were turning blue. "I don't think I understand the concept of channeling shadow magic. What does it mean?"

His enormous hands enveloped the ends of the throne's arms. "Besides Nyxobas, only certain immortal beings can channel shadow magic directly. It's called gods-magic. Demigods can use it. Nyxobas grants his power to his Sword, so Hothgar has it, as did I before I lost my wings. Abrax has it by virtue of being his son. Now, I can no longer create night magic on my own. Neither can you. You have to learn to absorb it from another source, to take it into your body for later use. That is called channeling."

With all this shadow magic in the air, she really should have worn a cloak. "Right. And how do I channel it?"

Leaning forward, he held out a hand. "Come to me."

Her eyebrows shot up. "What now?"

"I'll act as your conduit. You will draw power from the throne. Magic flows into the onyx from the crystals that form this cave. But if you're subjected to it directly, the power might flood you."

She wasn't entirely sure she understood where he wanted her, but her cheeks were warming already. "So...you want me to sit on your lap."

He loosed a sigh, as though he were losing patience. "Yes. It's the only way you can learn."

"Okay." Her pulse began to race. Something about the thought of being so close to Bael's powerful body sent a strange thrill through her. She tugged up the hem of her skirt, climbing the three steps to Bael's throne.

Turning her face to hide the embarrassing blush in her cheeks, she sat in his lap. He slid a powerful hand around her waist.

Despite the icy magic whirling around him, his muscled body began to warm her.

"I'm going to allow the magic to flow through you, okay?" His breath warmed the side of her face.

She had the strongest impulse to reach back and touch his face, but she resisted. He had said she meant nothing to him, that he felt bound to help her out of some misguided sense of duty. It was humiliating that she even had to rely on him for help. Still, she supposed she had to take help where she could get it.

She straightened. "I'm ready."

Icy magic wrapped around her ribs, kissing the bare skin at her throat—a dizzying, electrical charge of power. As her back began to arch, her legs fell to either side of his. His arm tightened around her waist. Then, from all around her, the shadow magic flowed into her chest, freezing her from the inside out.

A painful, hollow dread bloomed in her chest, a ravenous hunger. The world around her seemed to fragment and collapse, and darkness clouded her vision. She could no longer tell where she was—couldn't feel Bael's body beneath hers, couldn't tell up from down.

From the depths of the void, an image burst into her view: Bael, pressing a dagger to her chest. In shockingly swift movement, he shoved it under her ribs, stopping her heart.

There, she saw herself lying in the dirt, her skin gray, her jaw slackened, lips blue. Red hair spread limply on the bloodstained ground. Dull green eyes, full of mute horror. And in their lifeless reflection—flames. A burning room. The fire that would eat her alive.

As quickly as it had arrived, the image was snuffed out again, and she stood at the edge of an abyss. She just needed to take one more step, to plunge into an isolation so complete it would gnaw the flesh from her bones. An uncontrollable urge pulled her into the void. *I don't exist. I never did. I never will.*

"Ursula!" A deep voice boomed through the void.

She could feel something again—a warm hand on her body. She shivered uncontrollably, her teeth chattering.

"Ursula!" Bael's voice called to her. He pulled her closer to his warm body. She'd changed position, her legs now sideways on his lap. The magic had seeped from the air, but she still shivered. The chill spread through her chest.

Bael's arms enveloped her. "I'm not sure what happened. I was modulating the power. It shouldn't have overwhelmed you like that."

She glanced up into his eyes, that icy gray...

Once more, her vision went dark, and she found herself standing on a dark cliff. There was something she needed to get to—a woman with red hair like hers, and fierce brown eyes. An old man, his hands spotted with age. A wall of darkness slammed against her.

You don't want to remember those things.

She felt a sharp tug from the center of her chest, drawing her to the edge. And when she glanced into the void, its vibrations sang her name. A dark lullaby...this was her mother, her father, her home.

"Ursula!" Bael's voice called her back.

Freezing cold, a violent convulsion overtook her body. Aching sadness pierced her chest.

Bael pulled her in closer, his powerful arms surrounding her. "Ursula. Stay with me. Remember who you are."

Her arms were around his neck, as if she was clinging to him for dear life.

"Use your own memories to warm your body. Think of your life. Use your memories to fill the void."

Hollow agony filled her ribs. "I don't have any memories."

"Right. Maybe that's the problem."

He slid his hand up her chest, pressing it onto her heart. At the touch of his hand between her breasts, her skin began to warm. A dark heat whispered up her spine, curling her back. She swallowed hard. "What are you doing with your hand?"

"I'm drawing the magic out of you." His perfect lips were mere inches from hers.

She could feel a hot blush rising to her cheeks, her body responding to his touch, whether she wanted it to or not. She was sure he could see her pupils dilating, the sheen of sweat rising on her skin.

How easy would it be to just lean in? She knew how he felt—that he didn't care for her at all. But right now, with her body curled into his, with the warmth shooting through her core, she could hardly think straight.

"Tell me what you saw?"

Her pulse raced, and she tried to clear her head. "I saw myself dead. On the dirt of the Lacus Mortis, I think. A burning room. A woman with red hair and an old man. It was like a part of me wanted to remember, but another part of me forbade it. But mostly, I saw the void. And I wanted to jump in."

She was warm now, and sweat beaded on her face. She licked her upper lip, tasting the salt.

Bael's keen gaze seemed to take in the movement, his fingers tightening on her waist nearly imperceptibly. She didn't need him to keep drawing the magic out. *So why am I not telling him to stop?*

His eyes lowered to where his hand pressed between her breasts, and he sucked in a deep breath. "I don't know why or how you pulled that much power at once, or why you're so drawn to the void. We need to find a way for your body to handle shadow magic without becoming overwhelmed. I've always done that by remembering my life. My early life. We'll have to find another way for you."

What were Bael's memories, the ones he rolled over in his mind when the void beckoned? Suddenly, she had a burning desire to know everything about him. She glanced at the black cord around his neck, and she tugged it from his shirt. A thin silver ring—the female twin of the one in her pocket, hung from the end of the cord.

Bael's hands flew to her fingers, tightening around them.

Oops.

She heard his sharp intake of breath, then he pushed the ring back under his collar.

Swallowing hard, she rose. *What the hell am I doing?* "Sorry. I really don't know why I did that."

"It's fine."

He released her fingers, and she dropped her hand. "I saw one more thing."

"What?"

"You. Shoving a blade into my heart at the arena."

A muscle tensed in his jaw, and his expression darkened. "I think that's enough for today. Get some rest."

Shadows gathered around him, and her skin grew positively frigid once more.

Chapter 35

Ursula stood by the window. In the distance, the sunlight glinted off of Asta's spire. Despite the pearly rays of sunlight, dark thoughts clouded her mind.

Sitting on the onyx throne, she'd completely lost control, flooded by shadow magic. She'd seen horrifying glimpses of her past, little fragments that lacerated her with horror. And perhaps, she'd seen a glimpse of her future.

Unable to warm herself, she pulled a blanket around her shoulders. Something about her disjointed memories filled her with a deep chill.

Bael had said she'd probably blocked her own memories to forget the horrible things she'd done. And the closer she got to remembering her past, the more she feared he was right. Whenever she thought of the burning room—the red-haired woman, the words *kill the king*—guilt pressed on her ribs like a hundred rocks.

Somewhere, deep under the fog of her forgotten memories, lurked a wild animal.

And if she didn't want to succumb to Bael's blade, maybe it was time for her to unleash the beast. After all, if she couldn't even kill a moth, how could she drive a weapon into Bael?

The odds against her were hard enough without hesitation. If she faltered, she'd be dead. Jaw slackened, red hair stamped into the dirt. The void had been trying to tell her something.

Throwing her cloak around her shoulders, she ran out the door into the sunlight. She hurried over the bridge into the atrium, where the lion's mosaic seemed to leer at her from the floor. She pulled the lever in the wall. After a moment, the lift clanked down in the middle of the room. She stepped inside the iron lift, trying to clear her mind. The elevator creaked upward past the manor's empty floors.

On the roof, the lunar wind nipped at her through the wool of her cloak, and she stepped out onto the marble. Shielding the sun from her eyes, she whistled for Sotz. It took only a few moments for his shadow to pass overhead, and he glided to a landing on the roof's edge.

Carefully, she climbed onto his back, gripping his fur. She squeezed her thighs, sending him soaring over the roof's edge. The wind whipped over her skin, pure and clean. As she leaned into Sotz, she asked, "Want to hunt?"

Immediately, Sotz swooped toward Asta, beating his wings harder. As they soared for the writhing cloud of moths, the sound of beating wings filled the air. A deep humming that vibrated her very core.

When they reached the cloud, the moths parted, fluttering around them, just out of reach. In the cocoon of moths, the sunlight dimmed, like they were walking in a deep forest.

Just as Sotz arced around the spire, an enormous moth shot in front of them—gray wings with faint purple spots. Sotz dove for it, and Ursula gripped tighter. *Time to unleash the beast.*

As Sotz neared, the moth folded its wings and dove. Sotz pursued, his wings pumping. Like a meteorite, they hurtled for the lunar floor, wind racing over her skin. Her pulse raced, a dark thrill rippling through her.

The moth burst out of the cloud, fleeing for his life. Ursula pressed herself tight against Sotz's back. The moth twisted and spun, but inch by inch, they gained on it. The ground neared, and Ursula started to direct Sotz out of the dive, but the moth was only a few feet from his nose. With a final burst of speed, he hammered his wings, snatching it from the air. Only a few hundred feet above the ground, she tugged Sotz's fur to pull him up again before they smashed into the lunar floor.

Sotz chewed happily on the moth as they carved a slow circle around the base of the spire. Now, she could feel the night magic emanating from the tower. It washed over her skin in waves, but it didn't seem to chill her as it had before. Her heart raced with the thrill of the hunt, her body energized.

After she caught her breath, they climbed back into the cloud. Sotz beat his wings, taking her higher and higher, above Asta's spire. He raced upward, until they nearly reached the edge of the magical dome.

The moths thinned, and the crater spread out before them—a great caldera, full of Nyxobas's brethren. And beyond, more craters, ancient lava fields. A great expanse of barren land.

Ursula shivered. Suddenly Sotz tensed. A flicker of movement above caught her eye. Her gaze landed on the great white bat. The Gray Ghost's steed.

"Can you follow it?" Ursula asked.

Sotz beat his wings, rising higher behind the albino bat. The creature flew with powerful beats of its wings and they raced to keep up with it. It moved swift as the night wind, its downy fur stark against the dark sky. They winged upward, skimming the edge of the dome.

But when the bat reached the shimmer of shadow magic, it simply passing into the shadow beyond.

Ursula swallowed hard. *How can it fly in a vacuum, with no air?*

Ursula directed Sotz right up to the edge, until the magic shimmered only inches from the tips of his outstretched wings.

She peered into the darkness beyond. The bat was gone.

Chapter 36

$\mathcal{U}$rsula arrived a few minutes late for their second magic training session, and she hurried across the stone floor. This time, she'd worn a soft velvet cape to keep her warm. As before, Bael sat in his onyx throne, cloaked in shadows. Bael gazed down at her, his pale eyes piercing the shadows. "You're late. Take off the cloak."

"Why?"

"I need to see how your body uses the magic."

She swallowed hard, untying the cape and letting it fall to the floor. She wore another of Cera's creations—a purple silk gown, with slits cut all the way up to her thighs.

She cocked her head. "Would you like me completely naked, or is this good enough?"

A low growl rose from his throat, and for just a moment, his eyes darkened before returning to gray. "That will be fine. We'll start with you standing there. I'm going to let the shadow magic wash over you once again. See if you can root your body to the ground. Use the basalt at your feet as an anchor. Feel it beneath your toes, and let the night magic inch slowly up your legs, up to your hips, and don't let it fill your chest until you're in control."

She nodded. She wasn't entirely sure she knew what he was talking about, but she'd give it a shot.

"Close your eyes," he said.

She did as instructed, and in the next moment, she felt a wave of powerful night magic wash over her, spilling through her body like ink. An image rose like the flames—the old man, his wrinkled hands handing her an athame. Bael, pressing a knife into her heart.

The wall of blackness slammed into her, knocking the life from her chest. Darkness threatened to consume her from the inside out.

"Ursula!" Bael called to her.

Shivering, she opened her eyes. Bael had pulled her into his lap, wrapping his arms around her. His warmth enveloped her, and she could feel his heart beating hard against her body. Once again, he pressed his hand between her breasts, drawing out some of the magic.

"That didn't go well," she said through chattering teeth.

He shook his head. "You let it happen too quickly. The magic completely overtook you, like it was drawn to you. Whatever you are, Ursula, the darkness wants you."

"Aren't I the lucky girl?"

"I'm going to try it one more time, allowing through only the smallest amount of magic. I'm going to see if I can help your body control it."

As his body warmed hers, her pulse began to speed up.

"I could see your muscles tensing when you stood there, like you were scared of it. Maybe if you don't resist so much, you'll have greater control. Are you ready?" His breath warmed the shell of her ear.

She nodded, straightening.

Bael allowed the tiniest wisps of magic to curl from him. With his arm wrapped around her back, his fingers rested on the hollows of her hip. Her back arched.

A soft, electrical buzz kissed her ankles, moving up her leg. A delicious vibration—cold, but thrilling at the same time.

"Where do you feel it?" he asked.

Without realizing what she was doing, her legs parted slightly. Her bare skin peaked out of the slit in her dress. "It's moving up my legs."

"Good." Bael's hand hovered just over her leg, not touching her, but guiding the magic. Under her dress, the magic caressed her bare skin.

"Let the magic move slowly," he said. "Take control of it."

As his hand moved in the air above her legs, silky shadows worked higher up her thigh, and she felt her knees falling away just a little more.

She turned to him, her eyes on his perfect lips. Gods, she wanted to press her mouth against his.

His thrilling magic had moved all the way up her inner thigh, and her breath came fast. *If he keeps going, I will lose my mind. If he doesn't keep going, I will also lose my mind.* She was supposed to be focused on the magic, but all she could think of was that hand hovering just over her thighs. How she wanted him to touch her skin, to slide those powerful fingers under her silky underwear. Her breath hitched.

"Do you have control?" he asked.

"Not even close," she breathed, her chest flushing. *What the hell is wrong with me?*

His gaze met hers, and he leaned in, his mouth just inches from hers.

In the next instant, his muscles tensed. "I'm sorry," he said.

Ursula's jaw dropped. She couldn't quite remember how to put a sentence together. "It's fine." Her cheeks burned. *What just happened?* She wasn't entirely clear why he'd apologized.

A look of confusion—one she'd never seen on Bael's face before—had overtaken his features. "This isn't working. Maybe me acting as a conduit is interfering with your ability to feel the magic. Maybe you should try it on your own. If I see you losing control again, I'll stop it."

She nodded. "Of course. I think I'm ready. That all...totally made sense," she blustered.

She jumped off the throne, mortified that her flushed chest gave her away. *Stupid pale skin.*

Bael rose, walking down the steps. "The second I see you losing control, I'll pull you off."

She nodded, still lost in a daze, then sat in the throne.

As soon as she sat, cold magic thrummed over her legs. As Bael had instructed, she concentrated on moving it slowly up her body, inching it up her legs. Inky shadows flickered over her skin, seeping into her pores, climbing from her calves upward. Magic thrummed up her thighs, her hips, filling her body with raw power. As it raced into her chest, filling her ribs, a wave of blackness slammed into her. For just a moment, she stood in a burning room, and an ancient hand passed her a knife. *I need to think of a happier time.* The walls of her apartment in New York came to her—a field of blue and gold wildflowers under an azure sky. *Home.*

Her eyes snapped open again. Bael had been reaching for her, but the look in her eyes seemed to stop him.

She looked out on the world through new eyes, her senses sharpened. As she gazed around the cavern, she could see shadows flickering in the crystals, could smell the warm earthy scent of the mushrooms. And the sound of Bael's beating heart filled her ears.

"Now," she commanded from the throne, her voice resonating off the rock. "Teach me to move the way you do."

Chapter 37

$\mathcal{B}$ael stood across from her in the cavern. "I can see the magic curling off your skin. It suits you. But you won't be able to move the way I do."

Her body buzzed with dark magic. She tried not to think about Bael's hand, running up her thigh. Had he seen the blush creeping up her chest? "Why not?"

"It takes months to learn."

"I want to try it anyway."

He sighed. "There's no harm in trying."

She crossed her arms. "How long does this magical charge last, anyway?"

"Until you use it up."

She cocked her head. Power charged her muscles, and she had a burning desire to use it. "So tell me. How do you move that way? If I remember from New York, you can disappear. Like smoke."

"Shadow running. It's quite useful in a fight, as you could imagine."

"And how does it work?"

"Once you're charged with night magic, you can move from place to place just by thinking." A cloud of smoke curled around Bael. He flickered out of sight, reappearing twenty feet away.

"You just think of where you want to go?"

"You concentrate, and the magic takes you there. But you must get a feel for shadow magic first. Let it become one with your body."

"I'm going to try it."

She closed her eyes, picturing Bael—his golden skin, the smell of his body—like Mediterranean air. The feel of his beating heart against her ribs.

In the next moment, she was pressed against his powerful body. He looked down at her, surprise flickering across his beautiful features.

"Sorry." She backed away from him. "I didn't mean to get that close."

His brow furrowed. "How did you do that?"

"You told me how to do it."

He shook his head slowly. "No one learns it right away. Maybe F.U. learned it, but...there aren't many lumen crystals on Earth."

"I want to keep practicing."

He drew a deep breath. "Fine. But not here. Come with me to the atrium."

"Why not here?"

"Because one misstep, and you will plunge into the abyss."

"Good point."

She plucked her cloak off the floor, but with the night magic rushing through her veins, she hardly needed it. Now she understood why a demon like Bael felt invulnerable to the cold.

She followed behind him over the narrow bridge—so like her visions of the void. But she no longer felt a strong desire to throw herself in.

As the got to the other side of the bridge, she walked by Bael's side, her arm brushing against his. Every time she thought of his magic skimming up her thigh, a dangerous heat burned through her body. But what did that even mean?

She'd become dangerously aroused, and then he'd jerked away, like he was on fire. Had he realized—was he disgusted by it? The very thought of his revulsion made her want to curl up in the void and never come out again.

You mean nothing to me, he'd said. Ursula had always been of the opinion that you should take someone at their word. Occam's razor and all that. Plus, it was impossible to guess what another person was thinking, so all you had to rely on was their words.

She stole a quick look at Bael, who faced straight ahead. He probably wasn't thinking about the feel of his hand on her thigh. And neither should she, considering they were both facing death in a few days. *Get it together, Ursula.*

The Black Death was parading through the city streets, and there she was, dreaming about shagging.

The tunnel opened up in the atrium, and Bael stopped, eyeing her. "I don't know how, but you've already worked out how to move. You concentrate on where you want to go and your body moves there. But you must use this power sparingly. If you shadow run, you use up your magical reserves. During the duel, you won't have a way to recharge. You must be judicious."

"I understand."

He pointed to a spot on the mosaic floor. "Can you shadow run from where you are now to the lion's mane?

Ursula concentrated, feeling the shadow magic ripple through her body, rushing over her skin like a night wind. In a blur of black, she reappeared on the mane. The shattered tile bit into her bare feet.

She folded her arms. "Easy peasy."

"Don't get cocky." He pointed to a place behind him, close to the wall. "Now try here."

Ursula stared at the spot, in the half of the room where the mosaic tile lay intact. She breathed in, letting the shadow magic wash through her body. As she flitted through the air, Bael reached out, letting his fingers brush over her arm.

She leaned against the wall, catching her breath. "I felt you touch me." She could still feel the warmth of his fingers on her forearm.

"Yes. I wanted you to know that just because you're shadow walking doesn't mean you're invulnerable. Someone with a blade could still do damage if you're in the wrong place."

"Noted."

"One more task." He pointed at the door of her apartment. "Shadow run to your door."

"That's it?"

Bael nodded.

Fatigue began to burn through her body, but Ursula channeled the shadow magic once more. It rippled through her chest, energizing her body. She concentrated on the sleek black door to her quarters. But when she tried to flicker to the spot, she found herself ten feet short of her destination.

Confused, she turned to Bael. "What happened?"

He stepped over the shattered tile. "Another important part of our lesson. You can only shadow run for a limited distance. About ten yards." He studied her. "How do you feel?"

Her entire body ached as though she'd run a marathon. Her hips and thighs screamed with exhaustion. "Completely knackered."

"Good. That's the final caveat—shadow magic is fatiguing. If you use it too much, you'll be too tired to fight."

She wiped a hand across her brow. "I need a nap."

"I will have some lumen crystals brought into the atrium. If you hold them close, you should be able to absorb their shadow magic, just like you did on the onyx throne. You can practice shadow running."

"I take it you don't want me to use the throne."

"Perhaps we should keep our distance until the duel." Shadows seemed to gather around him, and he wouldn't meet her eyes. She had an overwhelming sense that he was hiding something from her.

"Of course," she said.

He turned, disappearing into his hall.

Ursula swallowed. A wisp of the hollow void flickered in her chest.

Chapter 38

Ursula stood in the center of the lion mosaic, a lunem crystal in each hand. Tendrils of shadow trickled from her fingers, gathering on the floor in a black mist. Dark magic thrummed through her bones, chilling her skin. Her breath misted around her head.

Bael was most certainly hiding something from her. Something about the way he wouldn't look at her when they'd said goodbye made her muscles clench.

She waved a hand through the air, watching the shadows flicker around it. *I just need to make sure I'm strong enough to fight him when I need to.*

Magic pooled in her body, flooding her muscles with power and demanding to be used. She lowered the crystals to the floor, and focused on a spot across the room.

Shadows rushed over her skin, through her gut, and her stomach flipped as she felt herself brushing the void. She reappeared ten feet away. *I've got this. I'm a natural.*

She straightened her back, then concentrated on a place near the lion's mane. Almost instantly, she flitted across the room in a cloud of black smoke. Wisps of magic curled around her fingers, tingling along her skin.

Most of the raw power had seeped from her body, but some of the magic still buzzed up her spine. *Let's see what I can do when the power is fading.*

She glanced at a spot near the onyx door, letting the shadows carry her through the air. But this time, she appeared a few feet short. Her toes throbbed as warmth returned to them. The magic was almost gone. *A good reminder to conserve magic in the duels.*

Bael's onyx door stood only a few feet away, cold and black as the void. She crossed to it, running her fingers over the smooth, cold surface. Wisps of shadows trailed from her fingers into the stone. The onyx seemed to absorb her magic, thirsty for shadow power.

Bael had warned her away from his quarters, and that only made her more desperate to find out what he was hiding.

Her mind churning, she turned to walk back into her own quarters. As she took a step, a scraping sound echoed off the atrium walls, and she whirled.

The stone had rolled to the side.

Ursula stared at the open door. Apparently, the magic from her fingers had acted as a sort of key, unlocking Bael's chambers.

And of course, under no circumstances should she go inside. It would be an intrusion, and a dangerous one at that. She didn't need to provoke Bael's wrath *before* the duel.

Then again...

If he was hiding something from her, it was better to know what it was.

She swallowed hard, taking a tentative step into the tunnel, but the interior was too dimly lit for her to see anything.

Nothing moved in the tunnel, but distant voices echoed off the cavern walls. Male voices. Who did he have in his quarters? The man seemed to live in total isolation, and suddenly he was holding a party.

She crept further down the hallway, and the darkness gave way to the purple glow of mushroom light. She hugged the walls, trying to stay in the shadows. As she walked, the voices grew louder, but she couldn't hear what they were saying.

She pressed on, her pulse speeding up. At the end of the tunnel, she hesitated. As soon as she stepped out onto the stone bridge, Bael would see her. She crouched, straining her ears. The voices grew softer, until they faded away entirely. Slowly, she rose. Silence had fallen over the cave.

She waited another minute, then crept from the tunnel. She tiptoed over the stone bridge, cringing with each scuff of her shoe.

As she entered his cavern, she surveyed the space: his marble table, the violet crystals, and his forbidding throne overlooking it all. Nothing out of place.

Ursula shivered, looking at the yawning blackness of the abyss around her. Who, or what, had been talking in here—and where the hell had they gone?

Depleted of magic after her shadow running, her muscles ached.

Bael's throne seemed to call to her, luring her forward with its promise of thrilling power. If she sat in it, shadow magic would flood her body, filling her limbs with strength. A part of her wanted to give in to its lure entirely. Relinquishing her humanity, letting the void take her soul, becoming one with the god of night.

She brushed a fingers along the throne's arm, only to pull her hand away with a jerk when the image of an endless chasm filled her mind.

What am I thinking? An eternity of nothingness would drive her insane.

She surveyed the platform again. *I know I heard voices in here.* She took a tentative step around the throne, expecting the stony floor to continue on, but she gasped as she found herself on a cliff's edge. A deep chasm yawned behind the throne—too dark to investigate.

She ran back into the cavern and yanked out a small, glowing mushroom that grew near the wall. She held it like a candle, and it cast a cold light over the floor.

She crossed back to the cliff's edge behind the throne, and held the mushroom over the side. A pair of metal pitons jutted from the stone, with thick rope wrapped around either end. The top of a rope ladder—that's where the men had disappeared to.

Chapter 39

*I*f one thing was clear at this point, it was that she should turn around and scurry back to her quarters. She could still pretend that she hadn't snuck into Bael's chambers uninvited, when he'd explicitly told her to stay away. *We should keep our distance,* he'd said.

But she knew he was hiding something from her. She was a warrior now, and she'd do whatever it took to learn about her opponent.

Why, exactly, was she worried about protecting his feelings and his request for privacy, when in a couple of days he'd be ramming a knife into her heart, ushering her into the void with a violent death?

If she wanted any hope of walking out of that arena alive, she'd better learn everything she could about her greatest adversary.

She rested the mushroom on the stone behind the throne, and it cast a dim violet light on the rope ladder until it dwindled into darkness.

She climbed over the cliff's side, gripping tightly to the rope. Once she had both feet firmly on the rungs, she retrieved the glowing mushroom, clinging to its stem as she slowly climbed down. With each step down, the shadows seemed to close in, darkening the mushroom's light.

A cold sweat beaded on her forehead. *I can't tell if I'm brilliant or a complete moron.* That would all depend on the outcome of this particular excursion.

The ladder swung as she moved, but it seemed to be anchored at the bottom. She peered down at the heavy darkness. Her pulse began to race. Was there an end to this descent?

Her breath came faster. She closed her eyes, trying to calm herself. But as soon as her eyes were shut, a vision flashed in her mind: Bael piercing her chest with a dagger.

Bollocks. The vision was becoming so clear, it felt like a premonition more than a nightmare.

Focus on the task at hand, Ursula. She stepped down another rung. *Release foot. Move free hand down a rung. Carefully unclasp the hand with the mushroom. Repeat the entire process again.*

Just when she was certain she'd be climbing for the rest of eternity, her foot brushed against a gravel floor. She tentatively released the rope, shocked to find the solid ground beneath her. Fatigue burned through her muscles, shaking her legs.

The fungus illuminated rocky walls and a rocky room, covered in antiques. *What the hell?*

At one end, the walls narrowed into a tunnel—perhaps where Bael and his friend had gone. And the rest of the space was covered in curiosities: an old ship's clock propped on a dusty table, a stuffed raven in a cage, a horned demon's skull in a bell jar, furniture covered in draped sheets. And propped on a wooden stand, the corkscrew she'd used to stab Bael.

Apparently, this was Bael's storage space.

As she scanned the room, her gaze landed on an overturned picture frame next to the ship's clock. When she flipped it over, her stomach swooped. Bael's beautiful wife stared back at her, her brown eyes sad and serious.

Ursula ran her finger over the hole in the painting. *Why did he put you down here?*

She turned it over on the table again exactly where she'd found it. She could try to work out the Freudian complexities of Bael's psyche another time. Perhaps, if she managed to survive the duel.

Further down the tunnel, a shout echoed off the rock, and her heart began to thump. If she was going to follow the sound of the voices, she needed a weapon.

Her pulse speeding up, she crouched, pulling out a box from below the table. She rummaged through old compasses and tools until she found the obsidian blade—the one Cera had given her. *I do believe this belongs to me.*

Her feet crunched over the gravel as she crossed to the tunnel, gripping the knife in one hand and the mushroom in the other.

As she made her way through the tunnel, the fungus glowed over runes and twisting symbols carved into the walls—the same ones she'd seen in the passage above.

At the end of the tunnel, a pale light glowed. And as she drew nearer to the light, she pressed against the tunnel wall, hoping to remain unnoticed. Here, the air grew thick with humidity. A high-pitched squawk echoed off the walls.

She peered around the corner. Much like the passage to Bael's throne room, this passage also opened into a larger chamber. Among a sea of darkness, luminescent mushrooms lit the air. The warm air had an earthy, fungal aroma, and her skin dampened. She wiped a hand across the back of her forehead.

This must be the rookery she had flown through with Cera on her way to the melee.

A gravel path wound through the forest of mushrooms. She dropped her little toadstool by the entrance to the passage and followed the path.

Chapter 40

Up close, the mushrooms were even bigger than she'd realized—the size of elms. They glowed a faint cornflower blue.

Her feet crunched on the gravel path that wove between them until the gravel gave way to a loamy soil. She caught a flicker of movement a hundred feet to her left—a large, furry body that slowly undulated around a mushroom stalk.

Her stomach clenched. One of the caterpillars she had seen from Sotz's back.

Another giant insect slithered to her right, its green body curling up a mushroom. She stared in horrified fasciation as it tore out a chunk of fungal flesh with an enormous pair of incisors.

But as she pressed forward, something else caught her attention—the resonant sound of Bael's voice, chanting in Angelic. *Time to hide.* She slipped off the path, moving from stalk to stalk until she got a clear view of the action. She peered out from behind a mushroom, sweat dampening her clothes.

Turned away from her, Bael stood in the center of a clearing, surrounded by mushroom stumps. He wore his black riding cloak. Around him stood a cluster of demons dressed in gray cloaks, their hoods pulled over their heads. Even without seeing their faces, she could tell by their short stature they were oneiroi.

Bael finished his spell, and the oneiroi began to chant in another language—one she'd never heard before.

A chill deepened around her. Whatever spell they were casting, it channeled shadow magic. The oneiroi hunched closer together, and the temperature plummeted. Their voices rose into the air, and a sharp burst of shadow magic ripped through mushrooms. A silent detonation that slammed Ursula in the chest like a fist. Hollowness pierced her, and she fell to her knees, her body shaking from the blast of power.

The darkness threatened to pull her under, and for just a moment, she saw a flash of Bael, holding the knife to her chest.

Stay grounded, Ursula. She sucked in a breath, feeling the damp earth beneath her knees and hands. The air felt thick and warm again. She opened her eyes, her gaze landing on Bael. He still stood before the oneiroi, completely unperturbed, as if a massive blast of magic hadn't just ripped through the mushroom forest.

Thick shadows coalesced around her, and magic simmered in her chest. The blast had completely recharged her body.

"Did the necromancy work?" asked Bael.

"I don't know," said a hooded oneiroi. "It hasn't moved."

She shifted position, trying to get a glimpse of what they were looking at. They seemed to be staring down at something in the center of the circle, but she couldn't tell what.

"Again," said Bael. "We must chant the channeling spell once more." He pulled his hood over his head, chanting again in Angelic. Shadow magic flickered over Ursula's skin.

Did he say necromancy? What the hell is he up to?

She needed a better vantage point. Her gaze flicked to a short mushroom about fifteen feet away. If she could get to the top of the mushroom, she'd have a clear view. *Good thing I'm charged up with magic, now.* She could shadow run there without a problem.

She stared at the mushroom's cap, then let her body fill with shadow magic. She flitted through the air, reappearing on the mushroom's cap. For a moment, she began to slide, then she dug her fingers into the mushroom's flesh, its luminescent juices staining her hands.

She glanced up at Bael and the oneiroi, and her mouth went dry. They surrounded a prostrate form. Long and lean, he lay stretched out on the ground, his skin gray as a corpse. Had they killed him?

As Bael and the oneiroi chanted, the creature lay still as a grave. A chill of shadow magic raised goosebumps on her arms. Any second now, they were going to blast the air with magic again.

She crawled to the edge of the cap, then let herself drop down to the soft earth. She hurried behind a stalk, just managing to find cover when a second blast rocked the forest. Shadow magic blasted through her bones, and she fell to the ground. Ice seized heart, and the void spread through her veins like poison.

It called to her. *Accept the darkness.*

So easy to fall into the void...

Her fists tightened, and a fire roared in the hollows of her mind, a room in flames. The scent of burning flesh, agonized screams piercing the air. *The best way to fight ice is with fire.*

The ice in her chest thawed, and she crawled to her knees. She felt the warm dirt beneath her hands, pressing into her knees. *I'm here,* she told herself.

She glanced up at the strange coven. In the center of the circle, the corpse now stood.

"What are you?" said Bael.

"You know me as the Gray Ghost," it said in a hollow voice.

Chapter 41

$\mathcal{S}$omething slithered in the corner of Ursula's vision. A shudder crawled up her spine, and she slowly turned. One of the enormous caterpillars was descending the trunk of mushroom just above her head. Thick as an anaconda, with a head the size of a bowling ball, its mandibles snapped audibly. Fear slithered over her skin.

Bael's voice rumbled through the forest. "Did you hear something?" He sniffed the air. "I smell something, too."

Ursula's stomach clenched. *He can't smell me?*

"I'll go check," said one of the oneiroi.

Fuck. They're coming right for me.

She pressed her back to the stalk, trying to avoid being spotted. Unfortunately, she was now trapped between the giant caterpillar and the approaching oneiroi. Adrenaline burned through her veins.

Frantically, she looked around. A smaller mushroom stood a dozen yards away—further than she'd ever shadow run.

She couldn't see the cap, but she needed to find a way to get there before the sodding caterpillar ripped its fangs into her head.

Swallowing hard, she envisioned the top of the mushroom cap. Shadow magic rushed through her bones, carrying her through the air. An instant later, she smacked into the top of mushroom.

Even with the relatively forgiving softness of the mushroom's surface, the landing took the wind out of her.

She dug her fingers into its flesh with her nails.

Still, from here, the oneiroi—or Bael—would be able to spot her if they looked up. She needed to get to the canopy's next level.

She narrowed her eyes, focusing on the mushroom caps that towered over her. In the next instant, her body whispered through the air, and the shadows slammed her onto another mushroom top. She dug in her fingers, anchoring herself to the mushroom.

Below her, she could hear the oneiroi mutter to himself, "I could have told him it was just a caterpillar."

Clinging to the mushroom, Ursula lay perfectly still, listening to footsteps moving closer to her. A cold sweat beaded on her skin. She inched forward, spying the tops of the men's heads. The Gray Ghost walked by Bael's side, his hands cuffed behind his back.

She waited until the footsteps faded before dropping down the lower mushroom, then sliding off to the damp ground.

Her jaw ached from where she'd smacked into the mushroom's flesh, but the caterpillar at least appeared to have retreated. As quietly as she could, she followed the path back to Bael's manor. The last of his oneiroi disappear into his storage space.

What were her options? She could wait, then try to sneak back when they'd all climbed up the ladder.

But in all likelihood, they'd be mulling around his cavern, blocking her exit. In fact, they could be mulling around the old storage space. The Gray Ghost's hands were secured behind his back—he was unlikely to climb anywhere.

Right now, the oneiroi were probably guarding him by the old furniture and compasses.

A lump rose in her throat. *In the brilliant/moron stakes, the needle is swinging wildly toward fuckwit.*

She'd just have to find another way out—one that didn't involve revealing herself to Bael. She turned, walking in the opposite direction from the way she'd come. The forest had succumbed to an eerie silence, and a chill spread through the air. She hugged herself.

As she drew closer to the clearing where Bael's coven had conducted the spell, the soil crunched below her feet—frozen solid from the stunning blast of Bael's shadow magic. She had no idea how Bael and the oneiroi had remained standing for that, when the blast had nearly ripped her skin off.

She peered into the clearing. Where the coven had stood, nothing covered the soil but a layer of ice.

She turned back to the bath, walking on, her teeth chattering. Honestly, she had no idea if this direction led to a way out, but it was worth a shot.

The air grew warmer as she moved away from the clearing, following the path deeper into the mushroom forest.

Along the path's edges, the mushroom stalks clustered. The path twisted and wound like a serpent between them. Up ahead, she caught a glimpse of a slithering movement, and goosebumps rose on her skin. She drew Cera's blade from her belt.

In this part of the forest, the mushrooms towered as high as sequoias, and just above their enormous caps, she could hear the echoing shouts of the bats.

Her skin grew cold as she took in the landscape. Here, among the larger mushrooms, the caterpillars were everywhere. A giant insect slithered over every stalk, crunching through fungal flesh.

A scream pierced the silence, and she whirled to find two caterpillars fighting over the carcass of a third.

Her skin crawled, and her fingers tightened around the blade. *Isn't that charming?*

Her throat went dry, and she hurried further along the path. But instead of continuing on through the forest, the path ended abruptly with the edge of a cliff.

She gasped. Spread out below her, a second mushroom forest extended into the distance. Hundreds of feet below, mushroom gaps glowed—sea-green, periwinkle, and cornflower blue. Stunningly beautiful, like the surface of a luminescent sea.

A grunting noise behind her made her turn her head. Two caterpillars crawled toward her, saliva dripping from their mandibles.

Her heart sped up. *Okay. Now, I'm trapped between giant flesh-hungry insects and a cliff.*

A third caterpillar inched down a mushroom stalk to her right, and a fourth flanked her from the left. Her throat tightened. *I'm definitely a fuckwit. Good to know.* They closed in on her, and she clenched her fingers on the hilt of the obsidian blade.

On the path, one of the caterpillars reared up before her, like a snake ready to strike its prey. Her blood roaring, Ursula slashed at the caterpillar's body. Cera's blade sliced deeply into its flesh.

The caterpillar fell back with a shriek. The other insects stared at it, as if in horror. Then they lunged for it, tearing into its flesh.

She loosed a breath. *Better him than me.*

She scanned the horizon, searching for a place she could shadow run. But the entire path now crawled with caterpillars, a sea of writhing fur. Running was not an option. As soon as they were done feasting on their fallen comrade, they'd come for her. She slashed at another insect, cutting into the flesh below its head. Shrieking, it writhed on the ground. She kicked it backward, toward the oncoming crowd of hungry predators.

Like sharks scenting blood, the caterpillars descended on it ravenously. *How long can I keep this up?* She gasped for breath.

Her muscles burned. Something brushed her foot and she looked down to see a caterpillar only inches from her. Instinctively she kicked it over the edge of the cliff. The creature cartwheeled down in a whirl of fur, bouncing off the sides before splattering on a mushroom cap.

If she didn't find a way out of here, she'd be joining the caterpillar corpse on that mushroom cap, her guts splattered over the lower forest.

The sound of bats shrieking echoed off the walls, and a spark of hope lit in her chest. *Is there a chance that Sotz is out there somewhere?*

She whistled sharply, just as a caterpillar lunged for her. She dove to the side, dodging its attack, and her face smacked hard into a rock. Pain shot through her skull. Still, it had worked. The caterpillar's momentum carried it over the side of the cliff.

Around her, the other caterpillars edged closer, ready to finish her off. Panic ripped her mind apart. *How the fuck do I get out of this?*

She gripped the knife, pointing it at the giant larvae. "Back off, you furry fuck-maggots!" she bellowed.

Instantly, the larvae stilled their movements.

She frowned. *Why the hell did that work?*

Behind her, the distant flapping of wings beat the air, and relief washed through her. *Sotz.*

The caterpillars weren't scared of her, but apparently, they were scared of bats. She glanced behind her, thrilling at the sight of Sotz's dark shape descending. She whistled again. *Hurry.*

With nowhere to land, he flew along the edge of the cliff. As he passed under her, she jumped.

Chapter 42

She clung to Sotz, breathing in the familiar smell of his fur, feeling the comforting beating of his heart. She sucked in a shaky breath, her legs trembling. She'd survived, by the skin of her teeth.

All around them, bats shrieked, their voices echoing off the walls. Still, a sense of calm warmed her body. If she could survive an attack by a legion of caterpillars, maybe she had a chance against Bournajoux.

She leaned down, whispering, "Take me home."

Sotz soared through the darkness. As the light dimmed, the cacophony of the rookery dampened. After a few minutes of peaceful darkness, they burst into the light of the crater. Asta's now-familiar spire towered over the ground—an oddly welcome sight at this point.

Sotz curved in a slow arc toward the manor.

Ursula took a deep breath, reveling in the clean air, the feel of the wind and the milky sunlight on her skin. She belonged in the air—not buried in a dark tunnel.

Sotz swooped low toward the manor's roof, then landed gracefully on its slick surface. Ursula caught her breath, her heart still pounding hard.

"Thank you for coming for me, big guy." She rose, her muscles aching. *Not super bright to get into a fight before my actual fight, but too late to fix it now.*

For a moment, Sotz brushed against her leg like a cat, then launched himself off the roof.

As she walked to the lift, she touched her heart, feeling it pounding hard through her shirt. She stepped into the lift, and a stiff lunar breeze rushed over her skin.

The elevator slowly creaked down, past one shattered floor after another, and she wrapped her fingers around the metal bars. She still had no clue what Bael had been doing with the oneiroi. She had no idea he interacted with them at all. How exactly had he ended up with the Gray Ghost in a mushroom forest?

As the lift lowered into the atrium, she glanced at the door to Bael's chambers. She'd left it open, but someone had since closed it. She glanced around furtively, taking care that no one caught her sneaking back into her quarters.

She hurried over the bridge into her living room, then made a beeline for the bath. Blood, mushroom juice, caterpillar fluid, and mud coated every inch of her body, and she stank like the bottom of a grave. She glanced at herself in the mirror. A deep purple bruise had bloomed just below her eye.

As she filled the bath with warm water, she ripped off her clothes. She shoved them under the bathroom sink. *I'll find a better hiding place later.*

She stepped into the bath, relishing the feel of the warm water against her burning muscles. She lowered herself down, letting the water soothe away the aches in her thighs. Still, her face throbbed where she'd smacked it against the rock.

She dunked her hair under the water, then rose again, reveling in the warmth of the bath. It was nearly time for her real battle—

the battle against Bernajoux, and whoever else. And she'd need to be clean and rested for the fight.

She grabbed the lavender-scented soap, rubbing it over her skin and working up a frothy lather before washing her hair. When she'd finished soaping up, she dunked under the water again, rinsing off the suds.

From the living room, a heavy pounding punctuated the silence. Her heart sped up. *Definitely Bael's knock.*

As she stepped from the bath, water dripping from her skin, he knocked louder. *And he seems a little cranky.*

He continued to pound on her door, and she yanked a towel off the rack, quickly drying off.

Bael slammed his fist into the door. "Ursula!"

Fucking hell. She wrapped the towel around herself.

"I need to speak to you." His voice boomed through the door, an edge to it that made her spine stiffen.

Why do I have the feeling he knows what I did? "Coming!"

She pulled open the door to find Bael standing in the doorway, his hands clamped tightly on either side of the door frame.

He gazed down at her, a cold fury flashed in his eyes. "Where have you been?"

Ursula's mind raced. How much did he suspect? She could lie completely and say she'd been in her flat all evening, but he must know something.

"I took Sotz for a ride." The best lies always have a hint of truth.

"Did you open the door to my quarters?"

Once you start a lie you cannot budge. "No."

His gaze trailed over her bare shoulders. "I smelled you."

Her cheeks warmed. "What? I don't smell that strongly. And anyway, I wasn't anywhere near you."

Bael studied her for a long moment, then his fingers lifted to her face, cupping her chin. "What happened?"

Ursula brushed her fingertips over her cheek. "I hit a moth when I was flying."

He stared at her for a long moment before grazing his fingertips over the bruise. A rush of shadow magic kissed her cheek, soothing the dull pain below her skin.

He dropped his hand. "Are you hurt anywhere else?"

A million dirty jokes raced through her mind, but she didn't think Bael would react well to them. Instead, she mutely shook her head.

"I believe someone broke into my quarters."

She bit her lip. "That's terrible," she blustered. "Do you think whoever it was is a threat?"

His icy gaze rooted her in place. "No. But when I find the intruder, I will deliver a painful death."

As Bael turned to leave, ice shot through Ursula's veins.

Absolute, complete fuckwit.

Chapter 43

Ursula woke on the sofa in her silky nightgown, tangled in the soft blanket. She rose, stretching her arms above her head, and glanced at the clock. She could hardly make sense of the damn thing, but she was pretty sure she only had twelve hours left before the duel began. Her stomach fluttered.

Despite the soothing bath she'd taken after her adventure, her legs still felt like dead weights. The shadow running had sucked the life out of her.

Bael's anger still roiled in her mind. She'd gone from the promise of a swift death to the threat of a painful one, having learned nothing at all from her intrusion into her quarters.

A knock sounded at the door—softer this time. *Cera.*

Barefoot, she padded downstairs and pulled open the door. Cera stood in the doorway holding a silver tray, a bag draped over her arm. "Lunch?"

Ursula nodded. "Is it lunchtime already? I've nearly lost the ability to keep track of time, since the sun never sets."

"Mushroom sandwiches." Cera bustled into the room, heading for the bar. She dropped the bag on the floor. "I let you sleep in. Bael told me you had a late night."

Ursula's stomach rumbled audibly. Even mushroom sandwiches sounded good. "Thank you, Cera."

"The lord said you hurt yourself flying, but I see he healed you."

As she crossed to the bar, Ursula forced a smile. "All better." *Until he severs my head from my body.* No. He wouldn't do that. He'd said a *painful* death, and that wasn't painful enough.

Ursula took a seat at the bar beside Cera and pulled a plate in front of her. She bit into the fresh bread, and the lightly salted mushroom flesh. Her fight against the caterpillars had certainly given her an appetite.

Cera chewed thoughtfully, her eyes glistening. She seemed subdued today. After a few moments, she turned to Ursula. "I don't like the thought of you dueling against the lord. There is no way for this to end well."

A sharp pang pierced Ursula's chest. Cera was right. She shrugged. "At least he said he'd kill me swiftly, if it came down to it."

Unless he figures out I'm his intruder.

Cera nodded.

"Would you describe him as a merciful sort?" asked Ursula. *Like, is he likely to go back on his swift death promise if he gets mad enough? Will he be stabbing me to death with my own ribs.*

Cera tilted her head. "To his enemies? Not particularly."

Wonderful. She took another bite of her sandwich.

Cera frowned at her. "You seem awfully relaxed."

"Why wouldn't I be?"

"The duel is in two hours."

Panic clenched Ursula's heart, and she jumped up. "What? The fight is in two hours?" she practically shouted. "I thought I had twelve hours or something. I can't read the bloody lunar clock."

"Relax," said Cera, nodding at the bag on the floor. "I cleaned and re-stitched your fighting gear."

Ursula's pulse began to race, and she stripped out of her nightgown. It took her only a few minutes to slip into the reinforced leather.

Her hands trembled as she buttoned up the corset. "Thanks, Cera."

Sadness shone in Cera's eyes. "Will you kill the lord?"

A lump rose in Ursula's throat. "If I have to. I know you care for him."

"It's not just that." Cera bit her lip, one of her sharp teeth piercing the skin. "If you kill him. Will you keep me as your servant?"

"Of course!" She touched Cera's shoulder. "Or at least, I'll make sure you're safe. I'll take you with me back to New York."

Cera wrapped her arms around Ursula, squeezing her. "Thank you. Otherwise, the other lords would probably kill me."

Ursula pulled away from Cera, looking her in the eye. "There will always be a home for you in New York. You've seen where I live. If both Bael and I die, take Sotz and fly there. Tell Zee you were my friend. She'll look out for you."

"Thank you." Cera squeezed her hand. "But I'd like you to find a way for neither of you to die."

Ursula's heart ached. She couldn't help but feel that she'd already witnessed her fate—Bael, shoving a blade into her heart. The life leaving her eyes, her jaw slackening, lips turning blue. Red hair stamped into the dirt. Dread coiled around her heart.

Her gaze flicked to the door where she kept her katana, but the sword wasn't there. Her pulse began to race. "Where's my sword?"

"I saw the lord take it," Cera said softly.

A hot tendril of rage coiled through Ursula's body. "I'm going to be in a fight to the death in less than two hours, and Bael has taken my only weapon?" Angry heat warmed her cheeks. "I thought he was trying to help me. He helped me in the melee. He trained me to shadow run."

"Don't get too upset. You'll have to think clearly in the fight."

"What fight?" she shouted. "He just left me without a weapon? What was the point of everything he's done? Why not just kill me in the melee instead of giving me two weeks of false hope? What kind of person does that?"

Of course, he wasn't a person. He was a demon—a predator. He'd told her as much.

Was he even capable of human-like emotions? Love or empathy? Or was he like all the other demon lords deep down— driven by a dark impulse to conquer and dominate? To screw with people's heads for sport?

Surely, if he kept his wife's wedding ring around his neck, he must have loved her. Ursula pointed at the spot on the wall where his wife's portrait had hung. "Cera, you know the portrait of that woman that used to hang there?"

"Elissa, yes. The lord's wife."

"What happened to her?"

Cera's face blanched, and she looked at the floor. "He wouldn't want me to tell you."

"Tell me." Ursula's stomach turned. "I need to know."

Cera's eyes glistened. "She died."

"I know that. But how?"

"Stabbed, I think. With a sword."

A growing sense of dread crept up Ursula's throat. "Who stabbed her?"

Cera spoke so softly, Ursula nearly didn't hear. "The lord."

"Bael?"

Cera nodded mutely, and Ursula's world tilted. Her heart thumped hard, and she ran upstairs, snatching the silver ring from its spot on the dresser. Frantically, she rubbed it between her fingers.

But this time, it brought her no relief.

As Cera called for her, she ran out the door.

Chapter 44

Ursula gripped Sotz tightly with her thighs, guiding her toward the arena. The icy lunar wind whipped over her skin as she arced lower. Here, on the other side of the moon, no sun burned in the sky. Only the silver glimmer of stars lit her way, and the bright glow of the Earth, hanging in the sky like a vibrant gemstone.

As before, torches burned before the platform, held by oneiroi. The crater's seats crawled with demons and oneiroi. Oneiroi with great hunks of meat walked the aisles, shouting the price of a slice of roast. Oneiroi maidservants held trays laden with steins of beer.

All along the benches, demons waved banners with the insignia of the houses they supported—a lion for Bael, a scorpion for Abrax, a satyr for Bileth...

As she descended over the arena's floor, a great whoop rose from the crowd. To her shock, the crowd began chanting her name. *Apparently, they don't hate the hellhound harlot as much as they once did.*

In fact, maybe someone from the crowd had a weapon they could lend her...

Sotz touched down on the ground and she stepped off, surveying the space. As before, she stood alone in the center. She still wasn't clear where they were supposed to go before the start of the duel, so she might as well start here.

Hothgar stood on the platform, a silver cape billowing in the wind. He stared at her, his eyes completely black.

And by his side, Abrax sat in a dark throne, just below the statue of his father. Abrax's eyes had that same eerie, silver sheen as his father's.

Ursula turned, scanning the crowd, searching for a weapon. Didn't any spectators bring swords to death matches? She couldn't find a single sheathed weapon—not even a dagger. Panic stole her breath.

Before she had the chance to give in to her fears completely, Hothgar sounded the gong. The knell reverberated through her bones, and her pulse began to speed up.

Hothgar's voice boomed across Lacus Mortis. "The dueling commences soon, a fight to the death. Only one man will remain standing."

He didn't even bother to correct himself, to add in the possibility of a woman remaining standing. Anyone watching at this point would realize she didn't have a weapon—that she was basically here to be slaughtered.

Hothgar raised his hands to the night sky. "I call upon Zoth of the giant of Pleion, Inth of Alboth."

As Hothgar called out the names, the fighters strode from a dark tunnel on the side of the arena.

"Bernajoux of Zobrach," Hothgar continued. Ursula glanced at her opponent—her lanky, and apparently sadistic opponent—dressed in a starry doublet. As he took his place, he bowed to Ursula.

"Valac of Phragol Mocaden," Hothgar boomed. "Chax of Azimeth, our Phantom Rider, now known as the Gray Ghost."

Ursula's stomach clenched. *Bael hadn't taken him out of the running? What the hell was his game?*

Hothgar smirked. "Ursula, the Harlot of Hellfire.

"And, our last champion, is the reason we're all here to today. The lord of Abelda, formerly the Sword of Nyxobas, will be fighting to retain his manor. Bael the Fallen." Hothgar solemnly intoned.

Ursula turned, her heart squeezing, and she watched Bael charge from the tunnel like an ox entering a bull-fighting ring. He wore a silver lion helm and a pair of thick leather trousers. No such protection guarded his tattooed chest, however. He strode into the arena shirtless, his godlike physique on full display. He'd left the bandages at home, and she got a full view of his lethal-looking tattoos: stars, lightning, a razor-sharp thunderbolt.

How could someone blessed with such beauty and physical grace be so dead inside? Too much time in the void, obviously. The betrayal felt like a punch to her gut.

But as he moved into the center of the arena, she studied him closer. In one hand, he clasped a silver broadsword, the same color as his helm. But in the other, the katana.

He stopped just by her side, a thin sheen of sweat on his tawny skin, and she looked up at him, her heart slamming against her ribs. Beautiful and terrifying at the same time. A man who looked like a god, but had murdered his own wife.

He held out the sword by the hilt. "Here."

Hope bloomed in her chest. For just a moment, she had the strongest impulse to throw her arms around him, but she remembered what Cera had said about his wife.

She took the sword from him, her eyes moistening with tears of relief. "Why did you take it? I thought you were trying to get me killed."

He shook his head. "You still think I have no honor? I had it cleaned and sharpened."

She stroked her fingers over the hilt. "Thank you. You could have told me, I guess."

"I thought you'd have understood me better by now," he said softly.

"I don't understand you at all." A tear rolled down her cheek, and she turned away to wipe it off her cheek. She did not want the other fighters to see her crying, but her emotions were churning out of control.

Ursula held up the sword, watching it flash wickedly in the starlight. She studied the steel for a moment—it *did* look sharper. She turned back to Bael, but he'd already taken his place at the end of the line of champions, just on the other side of Bernajoux.

Hothgar held out his hands once more. "The eight that remain have proven their skill in battle and air. Today, the duels will test their prowess in single combat."

All around her, the crowd roared, baying for blood.

"The contest begins with Bael and Zoth." Hothgar nodded at the two demons. "Proceed to the field of blood."

Ursula's mouth went dry. *Not big on euphemisms here, are they?*

Along with the rest of the champions, Ursula stepped away from the center of the arena. She glanced at Zoth—a massive demon, his arms as thick as tree trunks. Furs and metal breastplates encased his gargantuan chest. In one hand, he held an iron buckler. In the other, a short bastard sword.

He grinned, revealing a ragged row of teeth.

Bael stepped forward, drawing his sword. Although Bael

stood at least six and a half feet tall, the behemoth had a good foot on him. Still, Bael didn't appear in the least bothered, despite the monster looming over him.

"When I sound the gong," Hothgar bellowed, "the duel begins."

An icy wind whipped over the arena, and a deathly silence fell. Even though she'd learned that Bael had slaughtered his own wife, she wanted him to survive this. Maybe he wasn't a sociopath. Maybe there was some valid reason, like his wife was a monster who needed to be put down.

But then, why would he keep her painting on his wall? And the wedding ring around his neck?

What possible reason could someone have for slaughtering someone he loved?

So that was the memory he was so desperate to run from, the one that tormented him.

She watched as Hothgar lifted his mallet and slammed it into the brass gong. The crowd roared.

Zoth slammed the flat edge of his sword against his own shield, in an apparent attempt to intimidate Bael. Zoth shifted his weight from one foot to another.

His tactic didn't appear to be working. Bael stood perfectly still. He held his sword loosely, his body perfectly relaxed. Only his eyes betrayed any tension as they carefully tracked the demon's movements. Watching that penetrating alertness in his gray eyes, she began to understand the true meaning of *predator*.

The air seemed too thin around her and then suddenly Zoth charged. Propelled forward by shadow magic, he aimed his sword straight at Bael's heart. At the last possible moment, Bael swiftly stepped aside, like a toreador dodging a charging bull. But his sword remained steady.

In a beautifully savage motion, he ripped it through Zoth's torso. The demon slumped forward, and Bael pulled his sword from the creature. Blood and gore pooled in the dirt.

Zoth mutely opened his mouth to scream, but in a swirl of shadows, Bael was standing over him. His silver sword flashed in the starlight, and he slammed the blade through Zoth's neck.

Ursula's blood ran cold. The whole fight had taken maybe two seconds. Bael displayed a level of skill she wouldn't be able to match if she practiced for a thousand years.

Her knees began to shake. She could only hope her own death would be just as quick.

For a few pregnant moments, the crowd fell completely silent. Then, a chorus of boos filled the air, and a team of oneiroi ran out to clear the body. Zoth's blood left a thick streak of crimson across the crater floor.

The crowd was not happy. They'd wanted a duel. This had been an execution.

Hotghar approached at the front of his stage. "That was—" He paused to think. "Very efficient."

Bael nodded silently, his face perfectly still. For just a moment, his icy glaze flicked to her as he took his place at the end of the line.

Definitely a sociopath. Ursula reached into her pocket, her fingers coiling around the silver ring. She rolled it between her fingers. *What would he do to me if he learned I'd crept into his quarters?*

Hothgar banged his gong again, silencing the crowd.

Of course, no one had bothered to tell them the order of duels, so she had no idea when she'd have to fight Bernajoux. Nervously, she glanced down the line at him. Something about the smug grin he wore infuriated her.

Hothgar's booming voice summoned Valac of Phragol Mocaden and Inth of Alboth to the field of blood. Inth stepped forward, wearing a full suit of armor and carrying a long pole arm. Valac—a muscular demon whose skin had a bluish hue—stood across from him, gripping a battle axe.

The crowd fell silent as the two demons faced each other. Slowly, Inth wove the end of his spear in the air, and a magical charge crackled form the point. Valac growled, a deep sound that seemed to rumble over the dirt.

Deep in her pocket, Ursula rolled the silver ring in the palm of her hand. Even though both men were large, the match was clearly unbalanced—a knight in armor versus an unprotected barbarian. Her fingers tightened around the ring.

A magical charge erupted from the pole arm with a loud crack. Just as the bolt of magic was ready to strike Valac, he twisted sideways, dodging the attack.

Snarling, Inth began recharging the pole arm by swinging it in the air. But before he could strike again, Valac closed the gap between them, stepping safely past the tip of the pole arm. He slammed his axe through the pike, hacking off the tip. The crowd roared.

Inth had just been thoroughly emasculated.

Inth's armor creaked as he drew a sword from its sheath. But Valac slammed his axe into Inth's shoulder, denting the metal. Inth bellowed in pain, but his armor had saved him from losing his arm.

Inth lifted his sword to swing, but his armor slowed him and he was unable to land a blow. Valac's ax slammed against his armor again and again. *Thunk. Thunk. Thunk.*

Inth spun, trying to keep Valac in sight, but he seemed unstable on his feet. Now, Ursula understood the strategy. Less armor meant greater agility.

Just as she thought all was lost for poor Inth, he whirled in a one-eighty. He slammed his metal-encased fist into Valac's head. The crack of skull reverberated across the crater.

How did he manage a blow like that?

A burst of cold air struck Ursula's face. *Ah. He used shadow magic.*

Valac fell to his knees, blood pouring between his fingers. Inth raised his sword and Ursula closed her eyes.

Bile rose in her throat. *I can't say I was ever overcome by the desire to watch someone's head split open.* By the full-throated roar of the crowd, they did not share her sentiment.

When she opened her eyes again, she stared at Valac's limp, blue body on the dirt. The sword had cleaved through his skull.

The field of blood was aptly named.

Hothgar's announced, "Well fought, Inth."

The knight pulled off his helm. Sweat slicked his platinum hair, and blood oozed from the joints of his armor.

"Thank you," he said gruffly. Limping slightly, he returned to his spot at the end of the line.

Ursula's stomach dropped as she stared at Hothgar. The Sword of Nyxobas seemed to stare right at her, his eyes dark as onyx. And above him, Nyxobas's statue stared into the void, eyes gleaming like cold starlight.

Any moment now, it will be my turn.

Hothgar slammed his mallet into his gong. "And now, a fight that should prove extremely satisfying for us all." The wind toyed with his silver cape. "Bernajoux the Unvanquished and Ursula the Whore. Can you please step into the field of blood?"

The crowd's screams pierced her to the bone.

Instead of a suit of armor, Bernajoux wore a velvet doublet. He neither looked like a medieval knight, nor an unhinged barbarian giant. He'd slicked back his dark hair, and straightened his thin mustache into a perfect line. He carried a narrow sword at his hip.

Ursula's body hummed with raw nerves. He didn't look like much of a match, but Bael had described him as a sadist. She took her spot, about six feet from him.

As the sound of her heart pounded in her ears, the gong reverberated through the crater.

Bernajoux drew his blade—a rapier. The thing looked flimsy—a long piece of narrow steel, no thicker than a ruler.

Ursula pulled her katana from its sheath, feeling its comforting weight in her hand.

Turning his body sideways, he pointed the blade at her. He arched an eyebrow. "Are you ready?"

"Of course."

Bernajoux's licked his lips. The sight of his long, pointed tongue distracted her.

Bernajoux took the opportunity to strike, springing forward like a venomous serpent. Reflexively, Ursula parried, her sword clanking against his.

"Very nice," said Bernajoux. "I see you've trained in the Shinduro technique."

So that's what it's called. Instead of responding, Ursula kept her full attention on his blade. It glided through the air in a slow serpentine motion, interrupted by an occasional twitch that made her heart jump.

"But have you trained in the style of Calvacabos of Bologna?" he hissed.

She had no idea what he was talking about. But it didn't matter. He was already lunging again. Pain ripped through her thigh as his blade pierced her muscle. She grunted as he ripped the blade out again.

"Did you like that?" asked Bernajoux. "Did you like feeling the tip inside you? Do you want it a bit deeper?"

Bile rose in her throat. *What the fuck?*

Bernajoux darted back, the bloodied tip of his sword dancing before her eyes. *He's toying with me.* Her leg screamed with pain.

Bernajoux attacked again, and she just barely parried it.

"Do you want some more?" he asked. "If only I could take my time with you. Really get to know your body with my blade."

The tip of his sword twitched, and she jumped back. The demon laughed, his tongue flicking between elongated canines.

He pressed in on her, his blade extended. She faltered, stumbling back.

One thing was becoming clearer—her katana was a slashing weapon. It didn't have the reach or precision of his rapier. If she fought on his terms, she'd loose.

The pointed tip of Bernajoux's sword glinted in the pearly light. Still, the sides of the blade were dull.

Adrenaline raced through her body, lighting her muscles on fire. *I need to get out of his reach.* She needed to shadow run. Maybe she could get close enough to slash him with her katana, while avoiding the rapier.

She focused on a spot near him, letting the shadows gather within her. Riding on the wind, she raced forward—right into the tip of the rapier.

It felt like a punch to her stomach, but when she looked down, she saw the blade had pierced clean through her abdomen. Horror ripped her mind apart.

Bernajoux licked his lips. "Does that fill you up nicely? Want a bit more?"

Pain screamed through her gut, stealing her breath. She tried to breathe. *I haven't even managed to attack.* This was a massacre.

She gripped her katana tighter, swinging for Bernajoux. She struck him hard in the side, just below his ribs. He screamed, losing the grip on his sword. He staggered back.

His sword still impaled her stomach, and Bernajoux was muttering in Angelic, trying to staunch the blood flow from his side.

She had to attack while he was still weakened. But first, she needed to get the godforsaken blade out of her gut.

Dropping her katana, she gripped the rapier in two hands, piercing her fingers. Gritting her teeth, she pulled the hilt away from her. Pain splintered through her.

With tears streaming from her eyes, she tugged on it again. With a final, agonized scream, she ripped it free. Just as Bernajoux finished the final words of the healing spell, she flung the sword away. It arced into the air in a whirl of blood and metal.

Too bad he doesn't have a weapon.

"My blade!" Bernajoux screamed.

Hot blood poured from her stomach, but she kept her focus on him.

"Do you like that?" she snarled. "Do you want me to take my time with you?"

Bernajoux's face twisted with rage, and he leapt for her. She jammed her katana up, piercing his throat. The attack speared his brainstem.

Bernajoux the Unvanquished no longer lived up to his name.

His body went limp, spasming as it fell to the ground. She pulled her sword from his neck.

Agony rippled down her body, and she glanced down at the wound in her gut. Staring at the pumping blood, her vision began to darken. The crowd's frantic cheers sounded a million miles away.

A chill seeped into her bones, and it wasn't shadow magic.

She fell back against the cold dirt, staring at the bright blue and green of the Earth. In the next moment, Bael's face appeared, eclipsing the Earth. He lifted her in his arms, and she could smell the scent of sandalwood.

Chapter 45

$\mathcal{B}$ael brushed his fingers over her cheek. "Ursula? I need you to wake up."

She opened her eyes, blinking at the starlight. The Earth, nearly full, hung bright in the sky.

Her throat felt dry, her mind foggy. Around her, the crowd roared.

Hothgar's voice cut the braying crowd like a foghorn.

I'm still here. Lacus Mortis.

She licked her lips, then swallowed. *I need water.* "What happened?"

"You slayed Bernajoux, but he injured you terribly. I healed you, but you missed an entire round."

"Who fought?"

"The Gray Ghost and Chax of Azimeth."

She was pretty sure she already knew the answer, but she asked anyway. "Who won?"

"The Gray Ghost." He frowned. "I'll be fighting next. I don't expect it to last long. Will you be ready to fight after?"

No bloody way. "Of course."

"Good. You fight the Gray Ghost—"

Hothgar's voice cut him off, announcing his name. "I must go." His pale gaze pierced her, and she watched as he rose, pulling on his silver helm. "You'll be fine."

She didn't get a chance to ask him what exactly he knew about the Gray Ghost. As she pushed up onto her elbows, he was already walking toward the center of the arena.

Ursula rose unsteadily to watch the fight. She shot a nervous glance at the man next to her. Despite having already fought a battle, the Gray Ghost's clothes still shone a pale gray, like the skin of a corpse.

A shudder crawled up her spine, and she turned her attention back to the duel. Inth—the knight—stood opposite Bael. He held a new, unbroken pole arm. His armor gleamed in the starry light, good as new. *I guess I wasn't the only one who's been healed.*

Hothgar gripped his gong. "For the next battle, Inth of Alboth versus Bael the Fallen." He slammed the mallet into the gong with a thunderous clang.

Immediately, Inth began to charge up his weapon, twisting the spearhead in a complicated pattern. Bael stood opposite him, his body perfectly still, sword held casually.

Inth's pike sparked with dark magic. He swung it in a sharp arc, blasting magic from the tip. But Bael effortlessly sidestepped, holding his sword loosely at his side.

Inth unleashed another bolt. Again, Bael sidestepped. Didn't break a sweat, nor use shadow magic. Didn't even bother to wear armor. *Cocky bastard.* She was beginning to understand why he'd been so confident before the battle.

Worse, a growing certainty bloomed in her mind. The vision of herself lying against the dirt, Bael's knife pressed against her heart.

It wasn't just a fear. It was a premonition.

Inth's pole arm glowed white-hot, and he took a tentative step toward Bael. Meanwhile, Bael stood still as the statue of Nyxobas

Ursula had learned that the stiller Bael's body, the more deadly his thoughts.

When the knight lunged, thrusting his blade at Bael's chest, Bael leapt into the air. Wisps of shadow magic trailed behind him as he cleared the tip of the pole arm. He soared over Inth's head, gripping his sword with the blade's tip pointing down. With a single, vicious thrust, he plunged it through the top of the knight's helm.

Bael landed gracefully on the sand. As Inth crumpled, Bael wrenched his blade from the knight's skull with a sickening crunch of bone.

The oneiroi ran onto the field of blood to drag the body away, and the crowd booed. Another execution.

As with Zoth, the entire fight had lasted only seconds. Bael turned, stalking back to his spot at the edge of the field of blood. Again, his glacial gaze flicked to her for just a moment, his face devoid of emotion.

Her knees were going weak. This was it—she had to defeat two more demons before she could live. The Gray Ghost—a reanimated corpse.

And Bael.

"Congratulations, Bael, on reaching the final duel," said Hothgar, his voice quavering. Was that fear? If Bael were going to resume his position as the Sword of Nyxobas, Hothgar had every reason to be afraid. Bael's vengeance against those who had wronged him would be swift and ruthless.

"Emerazel's whore will now fight the Gray Ghost on the field of blood. The winner of this round will fight Bael the Fallen."

Ursula's heart pounded like a battle drum, her blood pumping hard as she stepped into the center of the arena.

The Gray Ghost prowled forward, taking his spot across from her.

Hothgar sounded the gong, and her nerves blazed with anticipation.

She gripped her katana, keeping her gaze on her opponent. Her stomach throbbed where she'd been stabbed, but otherwise it seemed to be fully healed.

She'd seen the Gray Ghost fight when he'd first announced his participation in the tournament. She'd seen him slay five demons in the melee, and not one of them had touched him.

And yet, she'd also seen Bael revive him in the mushroom forest. So what the hell had happened there?

The wind toyed with the gray scarf wrapped around the Ghost's face and he stood, still as a corpse. Which, perhaps, he was.

When she'd seen him fight before, every movement had been precise, like he was thinking multiple steps ahead of his adversary. Just like Bael, he'd waited for his opponents to attack first, then countered.

Maybe she could throw him off.

Hothgar's voice boomed over the field of blood. "The fight is supposed to begin." He sounded the gong again.

The Gray Ghost raised his blades. Pearly light sparked off them, but he didn't move.

Ursula lifted her katana, her palms sweating. *Any minute now.*

The icy lunar wind rippled over her skin, and she could hear her blood pounding in her ears.

Maybe I can goad him into attacking.

She pointed her blade at his chest, slowly approaching. When she got within striking distance, he stepped back. She followed him, but he stayed just out of range.

She feinted, and he immediately parried—one of his blades flashing up to deflect hers, metal sparking against metal. Her sword vibrated in her grip.

For a corpse, he was strong. Very strong.

She backed away. *Maybe he will come after me now.* Instead, he simply stood there waiting. She feinted again, and he parried, their blades clashing.

"Why won't you fight me?" said Ursula.

The Gray Ghost simply watched her from behind his scarf. She'd seen how he'd baited Vepar into tiring himself out. Only when his opponent was thoroughly exhausted did he attack— diving for the tendons behind his ankles to immobilize him.

A brilliant thought sparked in her mind—what if she faked fatigue?

She feinted again. When he parried, she immediately followed up with another strike. To conserve strength, she didn't attack with full velocity, but with each strike, she allowed herself to be a little wilder.

The brethren loved it, chanting her name: "Ursula! Ursula! Ursula!"

Slowly, she began to drive the Gray Ghost toward the far wall. When they reached it, she pretended to falter at the end of a particularly wild strike.

She'd made herself an inviting target. Would he take the bait?

He dove at the ground, but she'd anticipated his strike, leaping into the air. She swung her katana low, but the Ghost had rolled out of reach.

He crouched, blades drawn, ready to strike.

She began backing away from the wall. "Let's see what you can do."

The Ghost stalked toward her. His daggers didn't have nearly the reach of her katana, but he had two of them, which meant he could throw one. Also, she might need to dodge if he launched a swift counter-strike.

Abruptly, she lunged forward, slashing at his head. He ducked, then dove for her ankles again. She leapt to the side—but not fast enough. One of his blades slashed into her calf, and the pain shrieked up her leg.

Hot blood dripped down her skin inside her trousers.

The Ghost advanced on her. His posture had changed. He leaned forward now, his knives pointed straight at her. He'd wounded her. Like any good predator, he sensed when a kill was imminent.

And maybe she could make him a little more confident then he needed to be...

Grimacing, she forced herself to yelp with pain, hobbling on her leg. Without a moment of hesitation, he dove into his roll—just as she'd expected.

As soon as he was in range, she slashed down, ramming her blade through his throat. And not a single drop of blood spilled from the wound.

Her hand shook as she leaned down and pulled the scarf from his face, and her stomach turned at what she found beneath the cloth.

The thing that looked up from the sand wasn't human, and Ursula was pretty sure it wasn't a demon, either.

So that was why they called him the Gray Ghost. He had no face, just a smooth expanse of gray skin. No eyes. No nose. He had a mouth—now hanging open—but no teeth.

Her blood ran cold.

"A golem!" Hothgar's voice boomed. "Who has entered a golem into the tournament?"

Ursula yanked her sword from the creature's neck. A sticky, gray substance covered the blade.

She glanced at Bael, her next opponent.

She'd seen him raising one of these creatures in the mushroom forest. So what, exactly, did he know about this? From what she could remember of the demon books in her New York library, golems did as their masters commanded.

As she walked across the field of blood, Hothgar's demon guards circled the golem where it lay on the sand.

"Destroy it," Hothgar shouted.

Ursula turned to watch the action.

Around the golem, the guards chanted in Angelic. A chill rippled over the crater as air thickened with shadow magic. When the demons incanted the final words of the spell, the magic condensed into a sphere no larger than a marble.

The sphere hovered above the golem's body. The gray flesh seemed to lift and bend up toward the marble. A crack reverberated over the crater, the golem's body snapped, condensing. The sphere of magic sucked the golem into its darkness. An instant later, nothing remained of the golem but a few lonely pieces of gray cloth fluttering on the sand.

Chapter 46

*T*he soldiers cleared the field of the golem's ichor.

It was just her and Bael, and she couldn't bring herself to look at him. Right now, the thought of him terrified her.

Pain splintered up her leg. The cut in her calf wouldn't kill her on its own, but it would slow her down considerably. That in and of itself was probably a death sentence. Especially given her opponent.

She stole a glance at him.

He kept his eyes on the horizon. He didn't want to look at her, either.

Hothgar spoke, "Great men—and a golem—have bled their last on the sand today. Before the final duel begins, let us honor the sacrifice of these champions of Nyxobas."

A great cheer rose from the crowd.

Hothgar continued, "I would have never believed it myself, but the final duel will be between Bael, the Lord of Abelda, and Ursula, the hound of Emerazel."

Finally, at least, he was using respectable names.

"This will be a clash of the fallen versus the filthy…" Hothgar continued.

Anger simmered. *Okay. Fuck this guy.*

"...Of night versus fire." His voice boomed over the crater. "Neither worthy of the House of Abelda." He raised his hands to the sky. "But let us hope that it will be epic!"

Ursula glanced up at the Earth, bathing the crater in a blue light.

From beneath Nyxobas's statue, Hothgar declared, "Step forward onto the field of blood."

Ursula looked down at the blood-streaked sand as she walked, her heart a hunted animal. Only when she'd taken her place in the center of the arena did she look up at Bael. He wasn't even bothering with his helmet for this fight, and she could see his grim expression, his lips pressed tight. She tried to catch his eye, but he looked past her like she wasn't there.

Instinctively, she scanned his weapons a final time. The silver sword, still stained with Inth's blood. Right now, he was probably thinking about how much power he was about to regain. He'd claim back his wings, his manor. His immortality. All he had to do was slaughter her.

And given everything she'd seen tonight, he hardly had to break a sweat.

Dark terror clawed at her ribs, and her legs began to shake. She knew what was coming—Bael's dagger in her chest. The slackened jaw, her skin as gray as the golem's. And then, the void.

Don't give up yet, Ursula.

Her teeth chattered, and she gripped the katana tighter, her palms sweating.

"The final duel." Hothgar gripped his mallet.

Ursula's calculations gave way to raw panic, and her mind raced, desperately searching for an escape. But this place wasn't built for an escape, and it wasn't like she could flee unnoticed with this crowd watching.

The katana shook in her hand. *I need to focus. I need calm so I can think straight again.*

She imagined her fingers wrapping around the silver ring in her pocket, feeling its smooth solidity. Just like her white rock. Her breathing slowed, and her gaze flicked to Hothgar.

He slammed his mallet into the gong with a thunderous crash, and the sound vibrated through her bones.

She kept her eyes locked on Bael—that perfect, godlike face. His chiseled chest. He stood unmoving, shadow magic flickering about him.

And if there was one thing that terrified her about Bael, it was his stillness.

His eyes bored into hers. He wasn't going to move until she attacked. She'd already watched him fight.

The other champions had tried to attack him first, and that had backfired on all of them. Brutally. Like the Gray Ghost, she needed to get him to move.

"Are you going to fight?" she yelled.

He didn't stir. Not a single twitch of a muscle.

She tightened her grip on the sword. "It was me, by the way. I broke into your quarters." A risky move. He might give her a painful death now instead of an easy one, but she wanted to throw him off balance.

The sad truth was—even though she knew he'd come here to kill her, that he'd do whatever he could to reclaim his manor—she still couldn't bring herself to drive her sword through his chest. Not unless he was coming for her, his sword drawn.

She still wasn't thinking like a real predator. And how could she? She'd saved his life—but he'd saved hers countless times. He'd healed her wounds, taught her magic. He'd brought her a sword, freshly sharpened.

So how the fuck am I supposed to muster up any bloodlust?

She swallowed hard. *His wife.* Cera had told her what he'd done—he'd murdered his own wife. There simply wasn't a good explanation for that, no matter how much she wanted to like him.

She let the words play in her head like a mantra... *Wife-killer... wife-killer...wife-killer....*

She needed to shatter that cool, impenetrable exterior. If she wanted any hope of saving her own life, she had to light a fire in him, to see the real Bael.

A chill spread through her body, and she looked him dead in the eyes. "Don't give me any of your false chivalry," she said in a cool, even voice. "The women in the Shadow Realm are just property, isn't that right? Nothing more, nothing less. I thought maybe you were different, but now I know the truth."

A muscle twitched in Bael's jaw, and a deathly silence fell over the arena. Maybe the Brethren knew what she was talking about.

"Nice of you to keep Elissa's portrait up there for a while." A gnawing void seemed to open in her chest as she spoke. This wasn't her—but it was a role she had to play if she wanted to live. She had to let the ice take hold of her heart. "Until you stuffed her back into your storage room."

Across from her, Bael's muscles tightened. The shadow magic flickered around him, thickening into a mist. At that moment, Ursula knew she had him. Her pulse raced hard, and her fingers gripped the hilt so hard her knuckles turned white.

"Because what would you be without your guilt?" she said. "Forget Abelda Manor. Regret is your real home, and you'd be nothing without it."

With a terrifying roar, Bael charged, shadow running right for her. Ice rushed through Ursula's veins. But she was ready. At the last possible instant, she ducked, and brought her katana up, spearing him in the gut. Hot blood pumped onto her hands.

Her eyes flashed to his sword hand, searching for a counter attack.

But he hadn't brought his sword. He'd charged without his weapon.

The world seemed to sway below her feet. *What the fuck have I done?* "I'm sorry," she whispered, tilting her head to look up at him.

He stared at her, his eyes wide.

Her hands shaking, she pulled the blade from his gut. "I'm sorry," she whispered again.

He clutched his stomach, blood pouring between his fingers. But he didn't fall. Instead, he stood, staring at her, his eyes darkening to a wrathful black.

Now, she no longer saw Bael looking back at her. Near death, the primal part of his mind had switched on, and the void itself stared back at her.

Chapter 47

The Bael she knew was gone. And now, she'd meet the real predator.

Faster than a heartbeat, one of his hands clamped around her throat. And in the next moment, she fell back, her skull slamming against the ground.

The knock of her head against the sand dizzied her, and she looked up at Bael. He pinned her to the ground, a dagger pressed into her heart.

Despite the damage she'd done to his stomach, he seemed to be at full strength. Obviously, she wasn't a real predator. She'd missed all the organs.

Panic ignited. *This is it. This is what I've known was coming.*

The crowd roared, but Ursula could hardly hear them over her own rushing blood. She wouldn't be able to move an inch without Bael thrusting his dagger into her heart. He had her completely pinned to the ground, under his control.

Her breath came in short, sharp bursts, and she gazed up at him.

The void had left his eyes, and he stared at her instead with his pale gray eyes.

Terror ripped her mind apart.

He said he'd kill me quick.

Longingly, she looked up at the earth, and a deep sadness welled in her chest.

Tears wet her eyes. "I'm sorry about what I said." She had no fucking clue why she was apologizing to a man about to kill her. "About the guilt, and the painting, and that I went into your quarters."

A weariness—a sadness glinted in his eyes. His lips moved. She couldn't hear him over the crowd, but it looked like he breathed the word, *Sorry.* Shadows thickened around him, and his magic whispered over her skin—almost as if he were soothing her before the kill.

This is the end of my life, and no one knows who I am.

With his free hand, he brushed a finger down her cheek.

"Please do it fast." She closed her eyes. She was going to die here, as far from home as it was possible to be, and she still didn't know who she was. She slipped her hand into her pocket, pulling out the ring to feel it one last time between her fingers, rubbing its smooth surface. All she knew was that it reminded her of home, of something solid and constant.

And god, she wanted something constant, tangible. Something she could feel—anything but the void.

She gasped another shaky breath. All around, the crowd screamed for blood.

After a few moments, she forced herself to open her eyes again. But Bael's gaze had landed on the ring.

His ring.

Distantly, she heard Hothgar's voice. "Kill the hound, and take back your wings."

"Just do it," she whispered. "This is agony. Make it quick. Please."

Instead, he pulled the dagger away, snatching the ring from her fingers.

What the hell is going on? He couldn't wait until after he'd killed her to take the ring back?

"Where did you get this?" he growled.

"The ring? I found it in the jewelry box."

Bael grabbed her by the shoulders, pulling her up. She stumbled, nearly falling into him. Her legs shook, and Bael wrapped an arm around her waist to steady her. He stared at her, his piercing eyes burning with ferocity.

Then, he held the ring above his head. "I claim the hound as my wife," he shouted.

Ursula's jaw dropped. *What the fuck?*

Bael yanked the cord from his neck, slipping off the thin silver ring. He grabbed her left hand, holding it up so everyone in the arena could see. Then, he slid the ring onto her finger.

Ursula stared at Bael, realization dawning. Asharoth had told her that a man is forbidden from killing the woman he's claimed. And more than that—no one else may harm her, either.

"No!" Hothgar bellowed. "She is a demon of the infernos. A whore of Emerazel. You cannot claim her!"

"I take what I want," roared Bale. "There is no law forbidding such a wife. A warrior may choose any wife he pleases."

The crowd had fallen completely silent.

Hothgar's black eyes glared at them. "Does the hound consent to the proposal?"

Bael pressed the thick, silver ring into her hand, and he fixed her with a fierce stare.

On the one hand, he killed his last wife. On the other hand, this seems like the best way out of certain death right now. She exhaled, then shouted, "I consent."

Bael cupped the side of her face, seemingly oblivious to the wound in his stomach. He leaned in, his breath warming the shell of her ear. He smelled of sandalwood. "I need to claim you now. Publicly."

She nodded, looking up at him. In the next instant, his fingers tightened around her waist, pulling her closer. Dark tendrils of his magic thrummed over her skin, healing the slash in her leg, snaking up her thighs. It was as if he were doing it on purpose, running his fingers over the most intimate parts of her body.

His body's heat warmed her, and his piercing gaze mesmerized her. He threaded his fingers into her hair, gently pulling back her head. Slowly, he grazed his teeth over her throat, one of his hands lazily stroking her back. Then he kissed her neck softly. Her back arched into him. Heat shot through her belly, and her heartbeat raced.

She slid her arms over his broad shoulders, pressing her body against him. She could feel his heart beating hard under his skin. Bael traced his powerful hands down her back, then slid them under her bottom, lifting her up. She wrapped her legs around his waist. His powerful arms encircled her, his fingertips stroking her thighs. Here, in Bael's arms, she felt safe for the first time in weeks. Years, maybe.

Her pulse raced, and desire burned through her, lighting her on fire. *Kiss me, already.*

As if hearing her thoughts, he pressed his lips against hers. Slowly, his tongue parted her lips, brushing against hers. The kiss grew deeper, sensual. As a wave of pleasure rushed through her body, she lost all sense of time. He tasted of the sea.

The gong clanged again, pulling them out of their kiss, and Bael lowered her to the ground.

All around, the Brethren roared. Bael grabbed Ursula's hand,

and turned to address Hothgar. "I have won the duel, but I will not kill my betrothed. Return my wings."

Hothgar's eyes burned with cold fury. "Kill them, Abrax."

Chapter 48

Panic tore its claws through Ursula's mind.

In a blur of shadows, Abrax leapt onto the sand of the arena. Powerful shadow magic swirled around him—a vortex of night. A black tendril flew over the sand wrapping Bael's chest, and in the next moment, he was on his knees, blood pouring from his wound.

Ursula could hear his ribs crack as Abrax's magic slowly constricted, and she screamed.

Abrax stared at her, a smile curling his lips. "You killed one of my golems, harlot. And your boyfriend destroyed the other. I hope you don't mind if I kill your man."

She glanced around for her sword. How many demons could she fight at once?

Hothgar's eyes were black with rage. "He claimed a hound as his wife. He has desecrated Nyxobas's realm. The god of night could not protect him now."

Ursula could see Bael's muscles straining as he fought against the magical bonds, his face turning blue.

Rage, cold and ancient, burned through her veins. She gathered the last of the shadow magic in her body, concentrating on a spot just next to Abrax. She tore over the sand, slamming into Abrax's side. Knocking him to the ground.

Instantly, his shadow magic lashed at her, wrapping around her chest. Like a giant serpent, it constricted, squeezing the air from her. She could feel her bones flex.

One of her ribs cracked, and she gasped at the pain. Why was Nyxobas never here to oversee his own laws?

Abrax chanted in Angelic, and his magic began to leach into her. She could feel its icy tendrils searching through her veins. The pain was exquisite, like she'd been injected with liquid nitrogen. The magic sucked the warmth from her, wrapping her heart in ice.

Filling with raw panic, she glanced at Bael. He lay on the sand across from her, his eyes open, but unfocused.

There is no loophole, he'd said. *The gods always win.*

Bael had been right.

Slowly, Abrax's magic crept up her neck, stealing her breath. Horror slammed into her as shadow magic slipped into her skull, enveloping her in darkness.

She stood at the edge of the void. Its infinite vastness spread out before her. An endless chasm. A bottomless abyss. If she stepped off the edge, she would fall for eternity. *Only the darkness will save you.*

The lure of the void called to her, a dark lullaby. A siren song. *My mother. My father. My home.*

She took a final step off the edge, and she fell into the abyss. All around her, she sensed Nyxobas's dark power, growing stronger.

"Hello, little one." An ancient voice chilled her to the bone.

"Who are you?" she asked.

"Is it not obvious? I am Lord of the Realm of Shadows, the god of night, king of the void."

A voice rang in her head, clear as a bell, a siren song. *Kill the king. Kill the king.*

"When I look at you, why do I hear the words, 'kill the king?'"

"So you remember."

"Remember what?"

Cold silence greeted her, and dread snaked up her spine. She didn't want to be here. She needed to explain that this was all a mistake. "Abrax and Hothgar have betrayed you." Even as she said the words, they felt meaningless to her—the squabbles of the living seemed inconsequential in the vastness of the void.

"Abrax is foolish and weak," he said.

"He sent me here against my will."

"Then leave."

"How?" she asked.

"The same way you arrived."

"Abrax cast a spell on me."

"Fight back. That's why I brought you here. To see if you are worthy."

"I don't know how to counter his power."

"When you learn to accept the darkness, you will have all the power you could possibly desire."

The icy magic around her grew stronger. Compressing her into a tiny point.

"Don't fight the shadows," he said. "Accept their power."

Shadow magic crawled over her skin, searching for a way into her. She screamed, and inky magic poured down her throat.

Nyxobas was right. The Forgotten Ones were right. And deep down, she knew this was what she wanted. There was no choice but to give in. To accept it. She let the shadows fill her.

"Good, little one. Feel the darkness move within you. The shadows will do your bidding. You just need to ask."

She opened her eyes, blinking at the sudden brightness of the stars in the sky.

Abrax hunched over her. His spell had filled her with shadow magic, and now it hummed in her veins. Power she could use. The bonds that wrapped around her chest melted away.

Abrax jumped back, his pale eyes wide with horror. "Seven hells. What are you?"

"Right now, I'm your angel of death."

Shadows flowed from her, oozing from her pores, pooling on the sand. She bent to pick up her katana.

Abrax charged for her, shadow running at impossible speed. But to her, it looked as though he was moving in slow motion. She sidestepped, just as she had with Bael, then plunged her katana into his chest.

Abrax fell, eyes wide with horror. Ursula pressed down on the hilt of her blade pinning him to the sand.

"I am immortal," he snarled up at her. "You know you cannot kill me."

A strange certainty filled her body, rolled around the inside of her skull. She knew what she had to do. "No, but now I can take your magic."

She leaned down, pressing a hand to his chest. She could feel the shadow magic within him. Cold, ancient, and immensely powerful. Slowly she drew it from his body. Abrax's eyes widened with fear.

"Stop." It was Bael. Blood dripped from his mouth where he crouched on the sand. His skin had paled, and he shook violently. "We need to leave."

"What about your wings?"

"There isn't time to get them." His eyes flicked to something behind her. She glanced behind her at the oneiroi guards now pouring into the arena. Teeth bared, they twitched with the same madness that had possessed Massu. These were Abrax's oneiroi.

Slowly pushing to his feet, Bael whistled, and a dark shaped dove toward them. *Sotz*. The bat flew for them at full speed, but there was only one way to catch him.

She wrapped her arms around Bael's chest. Glancing up at Sotz, she imagined the soft fur on his back, and let the shadow magic coil around her muscles. Clinging tightly to Bael, she jumped into the wind, letting the god of night carry her up to Sotz.

Chapter 49

She and Bael landed on Sotz's back—her body facing Bael's. Bael had a good grip on Sotz with his thighs, and he leaned in, grasping for a solid handhold. Ursula wrapped her legs around Bael's stomach as he tried to steer the bat, breathing in the scent of sandalwood.

"Can you take us to Bael's carriage?" she shouted. Sotz's wings pumped frantically. Barely keeping them aloft, he strained to lift them above the crater's edge.

Ursula twisted, peering down. Below them, the arena filled with the chaos of fleeing demons and rampaging, flesh-starved oneiroi.

At the crater's rim, they landed with a jolt on the dirt next to the carriage.

"Thank you, Sotz." Slowly, she helped Bael off the bat. He could hardly stand on his own, and he leaned on her for support. His weight nearly crushed her.

The door to Bael's carriage slammed open, and Cera poked her head out. "The lord? What happened? I couldn't watch. How are you both alive?"

"We need to get out of here," said Ursula.

In the distance, the Brethren's screams pierced the air.

"They're coming for us," said Ursula.

Cera ran to the other side of Bael, gamely attempting to support his other arm. From her height, there wasn't much point. Together, they helped him into the carriage, and he lay across one of the seats, closing his eyes.

Cera banged on the wall—the signal for the bats to lift off. As soon as they rose into the air, Ursula let out a long, slow breath.

Cera stared at her. "What happened. Why are you both alive?"

"Bael won the duel." Ursula took a deep breath. "But he didn't kill me like he should have."

Cera's eyes widened. "It was you against the lord in the final round?"

"Yes. And he wouldn't fight me. So I tried to make him angry. I tried to make him lose his temper so I could get the upper hand. He charged me, and I thought he was attacking. But he wasn't. He'd dropped his weapon." It all came out in a frantic rush of words. "And I didn't realize, and I stabbed him. But I think I missed anything important on purpose."

Cera simply stared.

"And then... he was on top of me. He held a knife to my chest. But instead of killing me, he claimed me. He proposed."

Cera's jaw dropped. "He did what?"

Bael's voice rumbled from the bench he lay on. "I claimed her. I gave her Elissa's ring."

Cera looked like she was about to faint. "Does that mean..." She stammered.

"There will be no wedding," said Bael.

Cera's hand flew to her mouth. "So you won't need a dress—"

"No," said Ursula and Bael at the same time.

Cera's brow furrowed. "But what happens now? We can't stay in the Shadow Realm if the lords all mean to kill you."

Ursula took a deep breath. "Now, we go to New York."

Cera frowned. "How do we get there? I thought the lord told you. No one can travel to or from the Shadow Realm without the god's permission."

Ursula's ribs hummed with the void's dark magic, and that strange certainty whispered through the hollows of her mind. "I'm not worried about Nyxobas's permission anymore. He will grant it. I know it."

The carriage soared through the dark sky, and she glanced out the window. Earth blazed bright in the sky, a perfect jewel of green and blue.

As the carriage soared through the night sky, Ursula knelt in front of Bael, watching his chest rise and fall. She scanned his menacing tattoos—the thunderbolt, the crescent moon with its lethally sharp points, the four-pointed star.

Swallowing hard, she looked at the deep wound, just above his hipbone. Guilt pressed on her chest, stealing her breath. How could he heal, if he wouldn't use any healing magic on himself? When they got to New York, maybe she'd have to sew him up. Not like she was a surgeon, but she wasn't entirely sure he'd agree to a hospital visit.

His eyes opened and he fixed his pale gaze on her, studying her.

She bit her lip. "Why did you drop your weapon when you charged?"

He didn't answer. He just let his eyes close.

Her body wracked with fatigue, Ursula leaned against his shoulder, listening to his slow breathing as the carriage carried them back to Abelda Manor. His skin was soft as silk, even if his form was pure muscled steel.

At last, they touched down on solid ground, and she lifted her head from Bael's shoulder. He seemed to be completely passed out, and there was no way she and Cera could carry him.

"Can you wake him?" asked Cera.

Ursula brushed her finger across his cheek. "Bael?"

Slowly, his eyelids opened, and he surveyed her with his icy stare. "Is there a reason you keep talking to me when I'm trying to sleep?"

"We're here. At Abelda. I don't think we can carry you."

He nodded, then pushed up onto his elbows with a grunt. Cera flung open the carriage door and hopped out, holding it open for them. Bael leaned against her as she helped him from the carriage and into the lift. The lunar wind stung her skin through her blood-soaked clothes.

Once inside, Bael leaned against the elevator's bars for support, and the lift creaked down past one deserted floor after another. *It must kill Bael to say goodbye to this place. And all he'd needed to do was push the knife in.*

The lift touched down and she pulled Bael's arm over her shoulder, straining to help him walk from the atrium into the portal room. Once inside, Bael leaned back against a wall, catching his breath.

"We're going to have to take off our clothes," Ursula declared.

Before she'd finished her sentence, Cera had already stripped off and jumped in, clinging on to the side of the portal.

Bael didn't move.

"Do you need help?"

"No," he snarled.

"Fine." As her muscles shook with fatigue, she stripped off her clothes. Her bloodstained trousers, the thick leather corset and boots—acutely aware with every movement that Bael's eyes might be on her body.

Goosebumps rose over her skin, and she folded her arms.

When she looked back at Bael over her shoulder, he was

staring at her, but his gaze quickly flicked away.

Her cheeks flushed. "Hurry up."

For a twenty-two thousand-year-old night demon, Bael was shy.

She jumped in, clinging to the portal's side, just like Cera. The icy water chilled her to the bone, and she averted her gaze as Bael stripped off his clothes. She felt his silky, muscled body brush against hers as he plunged into the pool. She let herself drift underwater, enveloped by the cold.

She found Bael's powerful hand and slipped her fingers into his.

Nyxobas. She let the thought rise in her mind like a voice. *Grant us permission to leave. To return home, to Earth.*

She felt his inky magic spool through her body, coiling through her muscles, dragging her deeper into the water. Deep under the surface, she held her breath, carried by the god of night. And at last—she saw light piercing the water.

Golden light—the honeyed tones of an earthly sunset.

With Bael's hand clasping her own, she swam for the surface. At last, her head breached the water, and she sucked in a deep breath, staring at the warm glow over Central Park.

New York City. *Home.*

Thanks for Reading

We hope you enjoyed Nocturnal Magic. Book 3 doesn't come out until the spring of 2017, but in the meantime we think you might enjoy our **Vampire's Mage Series** which takes place in the same magical universe.

Yours,
Nick & Christine

Also by

C. N. CRAWFORD

The Vampire's Mage Series
Book 1: *Magic Hunter*
Book 1.1: *Shadow Mage*
Book 2: *Witch Hunter*

Demons of Fire and Night
Book 1: *Infernal Magic*
Book 2: *Nocturnal Magic*

The Memento Mori Trilogy
Book 1: *The Witching Elm*
Book 2: *A Witch's Feast*
Book 2.1: *The Abysmal Sea*
Book 3: *Witches of the Deep*

Acknowledgments

We thank our editor Jena O'Connor; our cover designer Rebecca Frank; and our proofreader Percival Constantine. We also thank our ARC team and Author's Corner for their inspiration and moral support.

About

C. N. Crawford is not one person but two. We write our novels collaboratively, passing our laptops back and forth to edit each other's words.

Christine (C) grew up in New England and has a lifelong interest in local folklore - with a particular fondness for creepy old cemeteries. Nick (N) spent his childhood reading fantasy and science fiction during Vermont's long winters.

In addition to writing fiction, we love to hear from our readers and can be reached at any of the following links. We always reply to our readers.

19289981R00206

Printed in Great Britain
by Amazon